The Love Potion

My Lady's Potions, Book 1

Katherine Lyons

Text by Katherine Lyons
Cover by Dar Albert

Dragonblade Publishing, Inc. is an imprint of Kathryn Le Veque Novels, Inc.
P.O. Box 23
Moreno Valley, CA 92556
ceo@dragonbladepublishing.com

Produced in the United States of America

First Edition June 2025
Trade Paperback Edition

ARE YOU SIGNED UP FOR DRAGONBLADE'S BLOG?

You'll get the latest news and information on exclusive giveaways, exclusive excerpts, coming releases, sales, free books, cover reveals and more.

Check out our complete list of authors, too!

No spam, no junk. That's a promise!

Sign Up Here

www.dragonbladepublishing.com

Dearest Reader;

Thank you for your support of a small press. At Dragonblade Publishing, we strive to bring you the highest quality Historical Romance from some of the best authors in the business. Without your support, there is no 'us', so we sincerely hope you adore these stories and find some new favorite authors along the way.

Happy Reading!

CEO, Dragonblade Publishing

Additional Dragonblade books by
Author Katherine Lyons

My Lady's Potions Series
The Love Potion (Book 1)
The Truth Serum (Book 2)
The Beauty Serum (Book 3)

Rogues Gambit Series
Rules for a Fake Fiancé (Book 1)
Rules for a Bastard Lord (Book 2)
Rules for a Wicked Wager (Book 3)

Chapter One

"I CAN'T BELIEVE you're doing this." Kynthea spoke softly—urgently—as she and her young cousin entered My Lady's Apothecary Shop.

"What are you talking about?" Zoe said under her breath. "It was your idea."

"It was a joke. To make your father laugh."

"Well, he did, and not in a mean way."

"Because I was being *funny.*"

"Because it was a good idea. Mama said she'd heard of a potion working on an earl!"

Kynthea sighed. Her cousin was being needlessly willful. It was a luxury afforded to people of wealth. Which meant it was not a sin she herself could commit, but as her cousin's companion, she had to stand by while Zoe did whatever she wanted to do. And in this case, that meant making demands inside an exclusive apothecary shop that catered to women.

"I'd like to see the proprietress," Zoe said in a clear voice. Zoe always spoke in a clear voice because she was always certain of her choices. That was not a benefit of wealth, but of rank. As the daughter of an earl, Lady Zoe was rarely ever wrong even when she was clearly in error.

The young girl at the counter nodded, then gestured for Zoe to precede her into a back room. Kynthea trailed along in her cousin's wake as they moved past jars of medicinal herbs, specially blended teas, and rolled bandages ready to be slathered with unguents or wrapped around a poultice. If Kynthea had the time, she would have spent it asking questions about the uses of each and every jar. An impoverished woman needed all the useful information she could find. But there wasn't time, and so she looked with hungry eyes at the shelf while Zoe took the sole seat in an otherwise empty room.

"Zoe, I really don't think—" Kynthea began, but her cousin lifted her hand to silence her. Kynthea gave in because she had no choice. And really, what harm could it do anyway? Zoe had the coin to waste on nonsense.

The harm, of course, was that Kynthea had been hired specifically to keep Zoe from impulsive, impolitic actions. Indeed, Zoe's parents had made that very clear. Zoe was a girl in her first Season, watched and judged at every turn. Kynthea was here specifically to keep the girl from acting in such a way as would set tongues wagging.

A visit to My Lady's Apothecary would cause minor speculation. But what the child wanted to purchase would set tongues wagging, and then Kynthea would be out on the streets without a penny to her name.

Eventually a woman of moderate age came into the room. She wore a standard merchant's dress, neither too fancy, nor too worn. With her came the scents of cinnamon and cloves, both as pleasant as the lady's smile as she bowed.

"Good afternoon, Lady Zoe. My name is Madame Ilie. How may I be of service?"

"Oh, you know me? Excellent. I should like—" Zoe's words were cut off as another woman entered the room. This lady was slightly stooped, dressed in black from head to toe, and leaned heavily on a cane. A little of her weathered face showed through the veil, but mostly, all Kynthea could see was the ponderous way the lady walked. It indicated great care with brittle bones, and if Kynthea had been sitting down, she would have immediately offered the lady her seat. As it was, she leaned forward and pinched Zoe.

"Get up," she whispered.

"What?"

"Stand up. Let the old woman—"

"She's here to serve me," Zoe returned. She wasn't so much annoyed at the interruption as confused. Clearly, she'd never been taught the subtleties between servants.

Kynthea, however, noticed how the old woman stood with a preternatural stillness. She neither deferred nor spoke but stood in what little light filtered in from a window through a dingy curtain. Old servants didn't come in when a younger one was already there. And old women didn't stand in the light and observe unless they had a reason. But all of that was lost on Zoe as the girl smiled at Madame Ille.

"Hello," she said, her voice and manner polite. "Am I correct that you make potions and the like for special clients?" She turned to smile at the old woman as well. "I've got a special request, and I'm willing to pay handsomely if it works."

"I will make a special potion for you," said Madame Ilie. "Whatever you like. But you must pay for it first. Otherwise, I will not have the money to buy the ingredients." She made a gesture with her hands as if to say, what choice do I have?

"I will buy on credit," Zoe said. "You will be paid a hundred times what you ask today if it works."

"A hundred times!" the madame cried. "That is quite the promise. But alas, I cannot buy on credit, and potions cost a lot of money to make."

Kynthea grimaced. "She cannot make it, Zoe. No one can."

"And what is this mysterious potion that you need so urgently?" the woman asked. Kynthea could see the slight smirk on her face. Undoubtably Madame Ilie could guess. What else would a wealthy sixteen-year-old girl want?

"I need a love potion," Zoe declared as if it weren't ridiculous. "Know that I will not settle for the usual waving of hands and rose petals inside burned parchment."

Of course not. She'd already tried those.

"I would like a real potion," Zoe said. "The kind that is expensive because it works." She lifted her chin high. "That is why I will not pay you in advance. It must work first."

"Ah, my lady," Madame Ilie said with a heavy sigh. "A love potion is a very delicate process. It draws two together in a binding spell that only God can break—"

"Yes—"

"And it must be fashioned specifically for the two. Every potion must be different." She shook her head. "It is very difficult. Very expensive."

"I have the money, but I will not be cheated." Zoe leaned forward. "Can you do this?" She turned to the older woman who did not appear to even breathe. "Can you?"

There was a long pause as no one spoke. Then the old woman's veil rippled. That was all, but it was enough, apparently, for Madame Ilie.

"Who do you wish to catch? Do you demand marriage?"

Zoe jerked her head around. "Of course, I want marriage. What kind of person would enchant someone just to have them trail behind them like a puppy? And mind, it does not have to be a long-standing love. Just long enough—"

"For the wedding?"

"Exactly." She arched her brows. "Do you have such a thing? Can you make it?"

"Who is the gentleman?"

Zoe sniffed. "Do you really need to know—"

"It must be made specifically for the woman and the man. I must know his name, his preferences, his past. Otherwise, it will not be effective."

Kynthea had a moment of hope that this would dissuade Zoe from her path. The girl was secretive about her matrimonial choice, though she was open about everything else. But her hope died a second later when her cousin heaved a disgruntled sigh.

"Very well. The gentleman is His Grace, the Duke of Harle."

Kynthea couldn't restrain her gasp. Of course, her cousin

would set her sights on the number one most desired bachelor in England. "Zoe, he's twice your age!"

Undeterred, her cousin put more power into her voice as she listed his lordship's attributes. "He likes cherry tarts and horses. Indeed, he once had the finest stable in England but it's now lost its power because he's not training them correctly. Since I too like horses a great deal, we shall make an excellent match. I have an adequate dowry, a fondness for cherry tarts, and an understanding of exactly what must be done to ensure that his stable remains at the peak of English pride for years to come." She shot Kynthea a self-satisfied smirk. "We shall be an excellent match. All I need is a slight push to get him to realize the inevitability of our union."

"With a love potion?" Kynthea said dryly. "Why not put it to him as bluntly as you have stated now?"

Zoe rolled her eyes. "Because men need to feel as if they have come to a decision themselves." She turned her gaze back to Madame Ilie. "It's an easy thing. We're already well matched. So will you make the potion or not?"

The woman pursed her lips as she seemed to consider. "You know nothing more of this man?"

"I know a great deal more about him," Zoe returned. "His looks are as excellent as my own, his money as well. He became the duke at the age of eleven when his father raced a horse that wasn't ready. The horse stumbled, the duke was thrown, and… Well, his son became the new duke. What else do you need to know?"

"That is his public face, my lady. I need to understand something more personal." Zoe was about to object, but the lady held up her hand. "I can fashion a potion. It will look like water but have a scent. You must wear it like perfume when you next meet him."

"And that will make him fall in love with me?" Zoe asked, her voice high with excitement.

Madame Ilie hedged. "It will begin the process. But you must then get the potion on his skin as well. As I said, it is to match you two together."

Zoe nodded as if that made sense. "It should not be too hard—"

"Not hard?" Kynthea rasped. "Gentlemen are covered from head to toe. Their shirt points and cravats cover their necks. They wear gloves on their hands and hats upon their heads. Do you mean to splash this in his face?"

Zoe frowned. "I suppose if it is necessary. I know! I will trip and accidentally splash it on his face."

"You think that will make a good impression?" Kynthea pressed. "Zoe, this is madness." And if her parents found out, Kynthea would be sacked for sure. Imagine purposely throwing a love potion in a duke's face!

Zoe dismissed the concern with a wave of her hand. "I'll have someone else do it."

"But—"

"So will you make it?" Zoe asked Madame Ilie. "Will it work?"

The woman pressed her hands together. "It will *start* the process, my lady. But in order to work, I must know more about the man himself. The inner man."

"And how am I to find that out?"

The woman smiled. "I have a list of questions. Get him to answer them and I can remake the formula to better suit you both."

Kynthea sighed, now understanding the trick. "And she will have to pay you each time, yes? For every formulation of the potion." A pretty way to make money from rich, gullible girls.

"No, no," Zoe said. "It makes sense. Love is something between two people. It cannot just happen instantly from two random people. It has to grow. So the potion must be specific to each person. But I thought I'd need a lock of his hair or something."

How could a girl know the facts and yet still not see how ridiculous this whole thing was?

Madame Ilie brightened. "Do you have a lock of his hair?"

"Not yet. But I could get it."

"No, you cannot," Kynthea cried. "Imagine cutting a Duke's hair!"

"That would be difficult, indeed," Madame Ilie said before Zoe could respond. "Besides, it is better to get the answers to my questions. Every answer will make the potion more effective."

Zoe nodded. "Very well. Give me the list and the potion—"

"For two shillings, my lady. It must be paid in advance."

Kynthea gasped. Two shillings was an extraordinary amount for something that was probably nothing more than rose water and a few herbs. Zoe, on the other hand, didn't even blink.

"Very well. But I shall expect it to work. There must be at least the beginning of interest from him or I shall know this is all a sham."

"There will be a reaction, my lady. I swear it."

How could there not be one, when rose water was splashed on the man's face? But Kynthea held her tongue. Zoe was determined. Meanwhile, Madame Ilie curtseyed and opened the door to a back room. There was a slender girl grinding up something with mortar and pestle. She looked up, her face as young as Zoe's, but the strain of hard work clearly showed in her clenched jaw and hardened muscles.

"The basic love potion for Lady Zoe," said Madame Ilie.

The girl nodded and immediately set aside her work, presumably to gather the potion. Meanwhile, Madame Ilie turned to the old woman who still stood without moving in the narrow beam of sunlight.

No question was asked. Not a word spoken. But the older woman's veil shifted and a single gloved finger gestured vaguely in Kynthea's direction. Or perhaps the woman merely had a cramp in her hand. It was hard to tell. Nevertheless, Madame Ilie turned to Kynthea.

"And what of you, miss? Do you have needs or pains?"

A great many of both. But she sincerely doubted that anything from here could help her. "We need a salve for the countess's hands," she said. "Her joints bother her constantly." That was the supposed reason they'd come here. "And something for Annette's monthly pains." Annette was Zoe's maid and suffered terribly during her courses.

"We have medicines for that," Madame Ilie said.

"Yes, yes," said Zoe, her impatience showing. "But what about you, Kynthea? Don't you want a love potion, too? You'll be attending many of the parties with me this season. Wouldn't it be splendid if you found love as well?"

"Splendid" was something dreamed up by girls. "What use have I for love?" she said. With her luck, she'd become enamored of someone as impoverished as she. The two of them would marry then end up pining after one another while being tossed into debtor's prison.

"So practical," Zoe scoffed. "Money, then. A charm to attract lots of money. I'll pay for it."

Money was spent no matter how careful one was. What she needed was income—a regular, steady source of money. "Health," she said firmly.

"But you're completely healthy."

"If I stay that way, then I can continue to help your parents long after you have married the duke." Then she'd survive as their poor relation until they died and (with luck) would receive an amount in their will. They were her last hope after illness took her parents. Sometimes she wished she'd died with them, but then she'd miss the joys of having a cousin whom she adored like a sister. A much younger and very impulsive sister.

Heavens, the very thought depressed her, but such was her lot in life. So many people had it much worse.

Ever perceptive in her own way, Zoe rolled her eyes and waved negligently in Madame Ilie's direction. "Give her a money charm *and* a health posset or whatever." Then she looked back at Kynthea. "Never say I don't listen to you."

Kynthea laughed. How could she not? Zoe had a kind heart,

and she did listen when she wanted to. Perhaps after a few more years, she'd come to understand that the world worked differently for her than for nearly everyone else. But until that day came, Kynthea would enjoy the girl's unique personality and occasional bursts of generosity. Because after Zoe's marriage, Kynthea's life would become very bleak indeed.

Chapter Two

"LADIES HEARTS ARE aflutter. The Duke of Harle needs a wife."

Erasmus Oliver Arthur Stace—Ras to his friends—shot his best friend Nate a hard look. "You will *not* print that."

"Of course, I will. Unless you give me something better to say."

"I do not *need* a wife!"

"But I need something to put in my column tomorrow. And since we are indeed headed for Almack's, and everyone will be whispering about your attendance, I most certainly must put it in the paper."

Ras glared at his best friend. He firmed his chin, arched a brow, and imitated his late father's most intimidating ducal look. Nate grinned back in the way only an irrepressible scamp could. If only the man had been born first, then he would have had a wealthy earldom to back his charm. But as a third son, Lord Nate was a hanger-on who wrote a gossip column to keep off the duns. No one but Ras and the publisher knew the identity of the famous Mr. Pickleherring, which meant that Ras was in the enviable position of influencing the *ton's* primary topic of conversation.

"You will not write about me," he repeated, his voice heavy.

"Then you will give me something better to say."

Ras grimaced. "This is beneath you," he grumbled.

"On the contrary, it is beneath you. I, on the other hand, must pay my tailor. So out with it. What juicy morsel do you know that I do not?"

Ras was not a gossip. Indeed, he took special pains to not hear even the slightest tidbit. But knowledge comes to any man who listened more than he spoke, and in this case, he found the information reprehensible. "You swear you will not mention me at all?"

"Ras," his friend drawled. "You know I have to mention you a little. Maybe I could say something about your waistcoat. About how it's dreadfully dull or some such thing."

His waistcoat was dove gray and perfectly matched the pearl swan on his cane, not to mention on his family crest. "You may say that my attire matched the purity and excellence associated with my name."

Nate snorted. "To be sure. I'll certainly say that." His tone indicated he would not.

"You'll write something entirely different."

Nate laughed as he mimed scribbling, then reading something completely inappropriate. His expression was funny enough that Ras's grumble came out more as a snort.

"Come, come," Nate pressed. "Speak up. There isn't much time before we land at Almack's and become bored to death."

Nate would be bored to death. Ras, on the other hand, would be pestered from every direction by hopeful misses and their greedy mamas.

"It has to do with Viscount Valpa."

"Oh! The double V villain. What has he done now?"

"Played much too deep last night." Ras only knew this because he'd retreated to the bowels of his club in search of solitude only to overhear the violent end of the game through the thin wall. "I believe he will bear the marks of his latest mistake on his face."

"How deep did he play?" Nate pressed. "Deep enough to dissuade a certain heiress from her engagement to the bounder?"

Valpa wasn't exactly a bounder in the traditional sense of being dishonest. He simply couldn't control his gambling habit.

But Nate and Ras shared a vehement disgust of fortune hunters which was very odd since, truth be told, Nate was one. As a third son, his only hope of a comfortable life was to catch an heiress, and yet the man was vicious in condemning any man who married purely for money. Nate was a romantic, which meant he was steeped in self-loathing which usually expressed itself in his column.

"Ras! How deep?"

"As of last night, he owes nearly two thousand pounds to a man I'm certain is a cheat."

"Two thousand! What a bloody idiot!"

On many levels. "I trust that is enough to fill your column without—"

"Yes, yes. Your name is safe, but not your fashion sense."

Given that Nate wore a Prussian blue waistcoat that could be seen in the dark at a hundred paces, Ras would take the "insult." Especially since his friend was still deep in shock.

"Two thousand pounds. Imagine what I could do with that much money. Imagine what any of us—well, not you. You already have it. But still. Two thousand pounds! What a bloody idiot."

Ras couldn't disagree, but as a man who famously harbored no strong feelings about anything—no ruinous habits, no mad passions, not even an intemperate item of clothing—he was not qualified to judge those who did. So he said nothing, merely waited out his friend's expression of horror until they arrived at Almack's.

It was early in the Season which meant not quite every hopeful debutante was here, but those who were present were ten times more eager to catch his attention. Every young miss wanted to make a brilliant match this season, and who was more brilliant than a wealthy duke? Ras thought he'd gotten used to everyone looking when he entered a room, but it seemed every female salivated at the sight of him. He nearly bolted then and there, but his mother had anticipated his reluctance. She was waiting by the door and grabbed his arm hard enough that he felt every point of her talons through his coat.

"It's about time you got here," she hissed through a clenched smile. "The dancing is about to begin. People were beginning to suggest I had *lied* in saying you'd attend."

"You threatened to burn every paper on my desk if I did not."

"And I would have. You cannot hide behind those infernal things. You need a wife."

What he needed was a drink, but he didn't say that. He knew that his mother thought their enormous wealth just appeared like magic in their accounts. She had no understanding of the work in handling an estate as large as theirs. Neither did she respect the political matters that held his attention. Instead, she focused on his bachelor status to an obsessive degree.

"You are thirty-four years old last month. It is well past time you did your duty—"

"Mother, you are becoming tedious. I am well aware of my duties, and so I am here. Introduce me to your favorites now for I won't tolerate this much longer."

"Erasmus, you are beyond tedious—" She cut off her words at his dark look. It was actually fun to see her flow through the emotions required to shift her focus to pleasantries. Her brows narrowed in fury, her nostrils flared with aggravation, but then she pressed her lips together hard. It was her way of swallowing down everything that annoyed her. Then she blinked twice. Never once or three times. Always twice. Her lips curved upward into a tight smile, her nostrils flared again as she inhaled, then she lifted her chin. The transformation was complete when her cheeks lifted enough to display teeth in her smile. Her next words would be high with pretend delight as her expression warmed in all the appropriate ways.

"My son, may I introduce you to the daughter of my old school friend. Her name is..."

Good lord, there were dozens of them, all daughters of his mother's friends.

Nevertheless, Ras did his duty. He bowed over the girls' hands. He inquired as to their delight in London, their excitement about the coming Season, and their interest in anything beyond the usual balls, theater, and horses. The last came merely because everyone knew he enjoyed his morning rides, so suddenly every lady was horse mad. He then asked for a dance, was granted whatever he wanted, and then moved on to the next female.

He'd thought that arriving late would limit the number of dances he'd be forced to endure. If he was busy dancing the first set, his mother couldn't introduce him to more women, could she? Unfortunately, his mother and the patronesses of Almack's had an answer to that. They delayed the orchestra until he'd been presented to countless women who all merged together in his mind.

All, that is, except one.

The lady who doused him in the face with a glass of perfumed water.

He'd been bowing over a woman's hand. She registered as fresh-faced (young) and an earl's daughter with the Greek name Zoe, though she looked as blond and fair as any English rose. He wouldn't have seen it if he hadn't been looking down after kissing her hand. Even so, the gesture was quick and well hidden. But he did see it, and so the ruse was exposed.

Zoe tripped a woman coming for them. A quick thrust of her slippered foot at the right moment, and the other lady—who carried a glass of something—stumbled just as she was joining the group.

He reacted as quickly as he could. He reached out to catch the falling woman, grabbing her elbow long before he could see her face. But that meant he had no hand to block the splash of her full glass of water. It flooded his eyes, dripped from his hair, and tasted...herbal? Not then the bland Almack's lemonade but something like cold tea. Either way, it was entirely unpleasant as it dripped into his shirt points.

"Oh my God!" the woman gasped.

"Oh no!" Lady Zoe cried. "Kynthea, how could you be so clumsy?"

"I…I'm so sorry. I do apologize, Your Grace." The lady—Miss Kynthea somebody—was quick to offer her handkerchief. Indeed, so were any number of ladies nearby as they all hastily pulled out slips of fabric for his use. He disdained them all, choosing to use his own inadequate square of linen. Lord, even his eyebrows dripped.

"It's all right," he said as he mopped up as best he could. He smiled at Miss Kynthea to let her know that he held no ill will toward her. Lady Zoe, on the other hand, was about to get a firm tongue-lashing—

"My goodness, Lady Zoe," interrupted Nate as he swept forward. "Are you quite well? Did any of that disaster fall upon you?" Nate was solicitous as he offered his handkerchief. Obviously, the man had not seen who the true perpetrator of the crime was.

"Lady Zoe should be careful where she puts her foot," said Ras coldly. "I saw—"

"It was all my fault," Miss Kynthea interrupted, her cheeks bright red. "I was nervous to meet you and…well, you must get people making a cake of themselves around you all the time. Please forgive me." She sunk into a deep curtsey. She could not have prostrated herself more if he were the king himself.

"It was not your fault, miss," he began, but Lady Zoe interrupted.

"It was an accident, Kynthea. We all know that. And his lordship is rather intimidating. Stand up, stand up. All is forgiven." She looked up at him, her eyes a startling shade of cornflower blue. "All is forgiven, yes? She meant no harm."

Ras was unmoved. The woman was a beauty, but it apparently hid a calculating heart. Unfortunately, he could not make an issue of it now. There'd already been too much of a scene. So he leaned down and pulled the still-prostrate Miss Kynthea up. She rose gracefully, for all that she was a bit of a long meg. It didn't bother him, of course, because he was also unusually tall. In fact, he liked the way she stood at a close level to him. Maybe four inches shorter? A good distance for him such that he did not have to crick his neck to look her in the eye.

"I take no offense at all," he said. "Miss…?"

"Miss Kynthea Petrelli, Your Grace. I am Lady Zoe's cousin and companion, and I must say, she has been very excited to meet you."

His brows narrowed, beginning to form an ugly picture of the two women. The English beauty was the titled, rich girl, no doubt spoiled and used to taking out her peeves on her poorer relation. She obviously had no idea that she was much too young for him. Worse, she thought she could elevate herself by making Miss Petrelli look foolish.

"Actually, Your Grace," Lady Zoe rushed to say, "I have some questions I'd love to ask you about your horses. I've learned that—"

"May I have the pleasure of a dance, Miss Petrelli?" he interrupted.

Which forced Nate, the poor bastard, to request the same of the shrew.

"And I should be in alt if I could have the same of you, Lady Zoe," Nate said with every appearance of eagerness.

"Me? Well, of course," said Miss Petrelli, as she offered up her card.

"I should be happy as well," said Lady Zoe, her eyes glossing straight over Nate to wait for Ras to turn her direction.

He did not. Indeed, he did everything but turn his back on her in the cut direct. And then—thank God—the orchestra finally began the music. He took his leave with a short bow and a reassuring smile.

"I shall look forward to returning for our dance, Miss Petrelli—"

"And I shall count the minutes until we can speak again, Lady Zoe," continued Nate.

"Your Grace," said Miss Petrelli as she curtseyed again. This time it was a very proper, very elegant dip of her chin.

"My lord," said Lady Zoe to Nate. Then she stretched her hand out to Ras. "Your Grace, if I could but ask a quick question…"

At last. It was with great satisfaction that Ras was able to give the woman the cut direct. Unfortunately, it was Miss Petrelli's voice that followed him, making him wonder if his action would cost her more than it would punish the shrew.

"Oh dear," she said. "Don't worry, Zoe. I'll fix it."

Chapter Three

KYNTHEA WAS NOT in the best frame of mind when the high and mighty Duke of Harle came to claim her hand for her dance. Her largest complaint was embarrassment. The plan had been for her to bring the potion to Zoe in a glass who would then contrive to get the duke to *drink* it. The girl's reasoning went like this: the elixir would naturally touch his lips which was akin to skin.

There had been no discussion of Kynthea falling flat on her face while dousing the duke.

Zoe had been all apologies afterwards, swearing she would make it up to Kynthea later, most especially after she wed the duke. Kynthea had managed to exact a promise that the girl would never, ever humiliate her again like that.

Zoe immediately agreed. She was at heart a kind person, but her empathy was usually reserved for horses. It sometimes took stern words for her to see that people had feelings, too. How would a horse feel if it was forced to take a tumble onto hard packed ground?

Once phrased that way, Zoe understood. And Kynthea knew that the lesson would stick. So the two cousins were once again in accord.

The duke, however, was still in Kynthea's black book. Certainly, the man had cause to be miffed. He'd been thoroughly doused with that love potion, after all. No one wanted to spend an evening with damp shirt points, but that hardly necessitated him giving Zoe the cut direct.

Did he not understand how his approval—or disapproval in this case—could ruin a girl in her first come-out? And what cause did he have to cut Zoe when Kynthea had been the one to drench him? The girl had been close to tears all evening, and no amount of attention had restored her confidence. That made her other dance partners gloomy as well, and Kynthea had spent most of the evening commiserating with ignored partners and cajoling Zoe into a better frame of mind.

It hadn't worked. And now His Grace was crossing the room to claim her for his dance when she just wanted to slap him.

"Don't forget to ask him the questions," Zoe hissed in her ear. "Madame Ilie said it would make the potion more effective."

Yes, she remembered the list of impertinent questions. She would never be able to casually work any of them into a conversation. When was the last time you cried and why? Or what was the hardest decision you ever had to make? Her mother would turn over in her grave if she thought Kynthea had asked such things of a duke! Her mother had been raised as the daughter of an earl, just like Zoe. And though she married a vicar out of love (thereby significantly dropping her social status), she'd insisted her children know all the fine points of polite society.

"Aren't you done with this love potion nonsense?" she whispered furiously back to Zoe. "Hasn't it already been enough of a disaster?"

"It's my only hope now!" Zoe wailed much too loudly.

Kynthea didn't answer. There wasn't time as His Grace arrived in front of her. His dashing friend, Lord Nathaniel, was a mere half-step behind, and the two gentlemen bowed before them.

"Miss Petrelli."

"Lady Zoe."

"Your Grace."

"My lord."

"I believe this is our dance," said Lord Nathaniel as he extended his hand in a comically elegant display. It came complete with several wrist flourishes, and it made Zoe laugh in delight. Kynthea, too, because he was so very charming.

"You are entirely too droll," Zoe said to the man.

"And you are entirely too beautiful. Nevertheless, we two imperfect souls must dance. Shall we?"

Zoe pinked sweetly then nodded. She shot one last glance at Kynthea before she allowed herself to be swept onto the dance floor. And as she left, Kynthea felt her shoulders relax. Finally, a man who could keep the girl from ruining herself with a depressed mood.

"Shall we find our place?" asked His Grace.

Oh yes. With her charge taken care of for the moment, Kynthea now felt free to say her peace to the arrogant duke.

"If you don't mind, Your Grace, I should much prefer a turn about the room. There is something I should like to say to you, and it is easier when not dancing."

"As you wish," he said as he offered her his arm.

She took his arm carefully. He was a tall man with chiseled features that included a strong nose and a lifted chin. His shoulders were broad which was pleasing, and she couldn't help but note the strength in his arm where her fingers lay. Even through the covering of shirt and coat, she could feel the shift in his muscles as he directed her through the room. There was weight to this man in body and in presence, as was befitting a duke. How sad that there was no kindness in him to soften all that intimidating wealth and power.

"Are you enjoying the evening—"

"You need to make up to Zoe, Your Grace. It was cruel to cut her so baldly. She is a girl in her first come-out. All the gossips were watching, and now you've severely damaged her reputation. It's cruel of you, and I pray—nay, I demand—that you set things right." Oh my. She hadn't meant to get so fervent in her words, but she'd been storing them up all evening. The damage he'd done to Zoe was real, and as such, it was incumbent upon him to fix it.

Unfortunately, he was not nearly as moved as she was. He turned to look at her, a clear scowl on his handsome features. "If Lady Zoe wants my approval, then she should not trip women out of spite."

Thank God he spoke in an undertone, one that could be heard by her and no one else. "You saw that?"

"I did. And I cannot understand how you of all people can be here demanding I indulge her behavior."

Kynthea sighed. "You don't understand. She was doing me a kindness."

"A kindness? Good God, woman, are your wits addled?"

"No, Your Grace." There was steel in her tone. The situation was complicated, and he had no right to judge her so quickly. Or Zoe. And so she would tell him, except for the dozens of prying eyes that watched them promenade about the room and the half dozen sets of ears straining to hear their every word. Worse, there were women in every direction trying to get the duke's attention. They winked, they fluttered their fans, they even pretended to stumble in his direction as a way to catch his gaze for a mere second. It was ridiculous, and she could not so much as whisper the words "love potion" without risking everyone in earshot repeating the phrase ad nauseum.

But that was Almack's on the first Thursday of the Season. Wall to wall debutantes and their hopeful mamas, especially when everyone knew that the most eligible bachelor would be there looking for a bride.

"We cannot speak freely here," she whispered.

"I cannot imagine what you think—"

"Oh my, Your Grace," she said in a high, reedy voice. "it's so hot in here." She waved her fan in front of her face. "Do you think, perhaps, that we could step outside for a moment?"

He looked down at her. "You are a terrible actress."

He was critiquing her performance? What an ass! "You would prefer I faint into your arms?"

His expression hardened. "You will not get a declaration from me, Miss Petrelli, no matter how compromising a position you create."

She gaped at him. Good God, did he think she was trying to trap him into marriage? Of all the idiotic, arrogant ideas! "I am an impoverished relation of Lady Zoe," she snapped, not bothering to lower her tone. "Her dowry includes property worth a thousand pounds per annum. All I have to recommend me is my average looks and witless charm. I assure you, Your Grace, no one expects you to propose even if I were to throw myself naked into your arms. I am merely overheated and wish to step outside." She took a deep breath. "Now do you accompany me or not?"

Well, that outburst certainly wiped the smug look off his face. And left him dumbfounded because after a moment's startled look, he lifted his arm to her.

She took it. How could she not after she'd made such a scene? And now her cheeks were burning with embarrassment. What a fine companion she was turning out to be. When news of this debacle reached Zoe's parents, she'd be sacked for sure. But in the meantime, all she could do was gather what dignity she had left and accompany His Grace out the door.

Almack's was on the second floor, so they had to go all the way down and out the front door before the cooler air hit her overheated body. Sadly, one glance at the upstairs windows showed an excessive number of people leaning out to eavesdrop on their conversation. She wasn't surprised by their presence, just dismayed at the blatant lack of decorum in the women. Especially since they claimed to be the leading ladies of society.

His Grace saw the crowd as well. She saw his grimace before he hid it beneath a bland expression. He didn't attempt a conversation. She wouldn't either, if she were in his position. After all, she'd been the one who'd chastised him upstairs.

She took a deep breath and attempted to explain. "We haven't much time," she said quietly, "so I'll get straight to the point. Lady Zoe commissioned a love potion to attract your attention."

The man blinked twice before frowning. "I beg your pardon—"

"You heard me correctly. She's sixteen years old and a romantic. She's been told all her life that she must make a brilliant match this season. Six weeks to catch an exalted husband. You have no idea what kind of pressure that puts on a girl."

"A love potion, you say?"

"Yes. She's actually quite clever and would make a good match—"

"A sixteen-year-old girl?" He sounded horrified.

"You and I know that you won't marry her. But you shouldn't ruin her just because she threw a little water in your face."

They had been standing facing one another at the base of the steps leading into Almack's. Now, he crossed his arms and leaned back against the column outside the door. "*She* didn't throw it. She tripped you such that you would spill it, and then she blamed you for your clumsiness."

Ah. The duke had a sense of fair play. That was good. "The potion had to go on your skin, you see. I was going to pretend to sneeze and splash you with my fingers, but she rightly pointed out that that was repulsive."

"I should say so," he commented dryly.

"It wasn't going to be a real sneeze!" she returned hotly. "Just, you know, a flick of my fingers." She demonstrated for his benefit. He seemed unmoved. "It's some herbs in rose water. You wouldn't have sustained any damage."

"Why not refuse to participate in the entire charade?"

Kynthea lifted her hands in disgust. "Because she's sixteen and under enormous pressure to settle the rest of her life in six short weeks!" She glared at the duke, but he obviously had no compassion for the strain society's rules put on girls. "The second plan was to convince you to drink it—"

"A love potion."

"Yes! But she realized you wouldn't be so obliging."

"She was correct."

"And so she tripped me," Kynthea huffed. "She was desperate, and..." She blew out a breath. "And she and I have discussed it. I have forgiven her. And now you must publicly apologize to her."

"Me?" he scoffed. "Because she's trying to poison me?"

"Because she needed an outlet for her fears and as ridiculous as it seems, a love potion was a harmless way to distract her."

"Harmless if you forget the damage to your reputation. You are neither clumsy nor on the shelf. Do you forget that you, as well, need to find a husband?"

Of course she hadn't. But she was the daughter of a vicar. She knew from helping her father that marriage to a cruel man was much worse than life as a spinster. And even the most well-matched couples grew bitter when there wasn't any love between them.

"My prospects are already doomed. I have nothing to recommend me on the marriage mart and well you know it." No title, no income, and no expectation that anyone in the peerage would look beyond that.

Not that she didn't hope, of course. There was always hope. And his next words reinforced that.

"I know nothing of the sort. As for Lady Zoe, she will find a match because she is young, beautiful, and well dowered. You have the same six weeks as her companion to attract a husband, and she declared to one and all that you are clumsy and slightly daft."

"She said it was an accident—"

"She said it was all your fault."

Kynthea winced. Yes, she had. "But I know she didn't mean it."

"Perhaps. But everyone else won't. And if I've destroyed Lady Zoe's chances this season, then what did she just do to yours?"

He had a point. If she'd ever harbored the secret dream of marrying well, then she'd started off on a very bad foot this night. So she said what she always said when trying to console herself for a life turned hard. "There is no sense in hoping for something that will never happen. I have no prospects, and therefore will make the best life I can now."

"And how will you do that?"

"By helping my charge with her ambitions." She took a step forward. "If I do well here, then perhaps I will find other positions as I chaperone other young ladies."

"Not if you throw water on dukes."

"Exactly!" she said with a great deal more enthusiasm than she felt. "That's why it was better to have tripped than sneezed."

He shook his head. "Do you actually believe your own nonsense?"

"Absolutely," she said, a sense of total defeat coming over her. "It makes it easier to convince everyone else."

"Not me."

Yes, she could see that. She sighed. They needed to head back inside. The tongues were already going to wag. "My lord, I am not angry with Zoe for tripping me. What gives you the right to punish her so harshly?"

His mouth thinned and his chin came up. It was the look of a man who had become a duke at age eleven. He was not used to being questioned or having his face drenched with herb water. She could not fault him for that, but neither could she allow him to end Zoe's chances this Season.

Finally, he spoke. "She violates my sense of fair-play. Tripping people and love potions, indeed. She does not have the character to make anyone a good wife."

"She is sixteen!"

"And on the marriage mart."

He was right. Of course, he was right! But sixteen-year-old girls were routinely married, and neither she nor he could change that. She huffed out a breath. "So don't marry her, Your Grace.

But don't ruin her chances with someone else. It's not *fair* to damn her future based on a childish game."

She could tell her emphasis on the word "fair" was having its effect. He was a duke, and therefore his opinion carried enormous weight in the *haut ton*. A debutante was the weakest among all the *ton*. It wasn't fair for him to wield his power without careful thought. Thankfully, the man heard her. Or perhaps he wearied of the scene they were making in front of... Oh heavens. The windows of Almack's revealed at least a dozen faces pressed up against the glass.

"What would you have me do?" he asked wearily.

Success. She felt her shoulders sink in relief. "Invite her to ride with you in the morning. It will be an enjoyable outing, I promise you. She is an accomplished rider and, in truth, it's your stables that attracts you to her."

"Did you just say that she prefers my horses to me?"

Well, yes, she had. "Haven't you said you'd prefer to ride than attend a society event?"

"Not the point."

She chuckled. He really did have a dry way of speaking. Why it tickled her sense of fancy, she had no idea, but he did make her smile. "Given that marriage is a business enterprise, you could do worse than having her expertise. She's an excellent equestrienne, but more important, she understands their husbandry like no one else. It is thanks to her that their family's stable has managed well these last ten years."

"Ten years!" he scoffed. "That would have her managing things when she was six."

Kynthea grinned. "You should ask her about that. It's quite the tale of her squaring off with their stablemaster."

He stared at her hard, clearly wondering if she were joking. She wasn't. And in time, his expression softened. "Miss Petrelli," he said with a voice that carried. "Would you do me the honor of riding with me in the morning?"

Oh, excellent—wait, what? "No, no," she whispered in surprise. "You're supposed to ask Zoe!"

His brows rose. "Was I? My apologies." He didn't seem the least bit apologetic. "Are you able to sit a horse?"

"Of course, I am. It was Zoe's primary requirement in a companion."

"Then I should like you to enjoy the sweetest mare in my stable. She is docile when needed, but has a mischievous quirk to her spirit I find endearing."

She stared at the man. He spoke with such a flat tone that one might miss the humor beneath the words. "Did you just compare me to a horse?"

"Did I? Hmm, no I don't believe so. I said that I believe you will enjoy my peculiar horse."

He was teasing her. At least she thought he was teasing her, and the idea was so absurd that she giggled. Imagine, a duke teasing her, a nobody miss companion. But she was not one to let such an opportunity pass. "You know that where I go, Zoe must follow."

"If she can find a companion to join us, then I shall provide mounts for them as well."

An excellent idea. "What about Lord Nathaniel?" He was the only gentleman who had managed to make Zoe laugh.

The man snorted. "Awake before noon? I doubt it."

Oh dear. Well, there were any number of men who would stir themselves out of bed if it meant more time with an heiress. "I do hope she finds an accomplished one. She's very particular about her riding companions."

He extended his arm out to her. "She sounds like a remarkably difficult charge."

She sighed. That was not the impression she meant to convey. "She's the privileged daughter of an earl. I challenge you to find one who is not."

"No, thank you. I am perfectly content doing without."

She chuckled. "I do not believe your mother would agree." And here she scored a true hit. Indeed, everyone knew how keen his mother was to see him married and busily filling his nursery. And just to underscore her point, who was waiting at the top of the stairs? His mother…looking like she wanted to murder them both.

She squeezed his arm to commiserate. "I apologize for taking up so much of your time."

"And there you go apologizing for something that was not your fault. I chose the exact length of our conversation. My mother's annoyance will not fall upon you."

She doubted that was true, but she didn't argue. It wasn't until they were three short of the top step that she caught sight of Zoe's anxious expression. The girl was waiting a step behind the dowager duchess with hope and terror written in clear lines upon her young face. Kynthea suddenly remembered her promise.

"Damnation, I forgot!" Kynthea cried.

The duke paused and looked down in concern. "What is it?"

"There isn't time now." She was an idiot for forgetting.

"What?"

"Nothing. Simply tomorrow, please indulge us if Zoe asks you strange questions."

He sighed. "Part of the love potion, I imagine."

"Yes."

"And shall I be subjected to another deluge of herb water?"

"Most likely. She's quite determined."

He sighed. "Very well. But don't shower me with it. Put it on a handkerchief. I shall wipe my face with it."

"Thank you." She peeked up at him. "You are being most generous to endure it."

"Yes," he drawled. "I am."

Well, that was rude. His answer implied an excessive sense of his own importance, as if a slight wetting in the face and an impertinent question were too much to bear. But when she drew breath to respond, he winked at her.

She nearly missed it. They were starting to climb the steps again, and her attention had been on making a graceful entrance.

But she had looked at his face and saw the wink, clear as day. It startled her enough that her response was forgotten as she gaped at him.

He was teasing her? More than that, was he poking fun at his own vanity? She couldn't credit it. And yet, the way his lips quirked at her shock made the truth absolutely clear. Beneath that stuffy exterior, the duke had a wicked sense of humor. And he didn't mind ridiculing himself.

"Your Grace—" she began, but he cut her off.

"Miss Petrelli, I look forward to our morning ride. I shall come for you at seven." His words were loud enough for everyone to hear. And if they didn't, the sight of him bowing before her as he kissed her hand surely painted a picture. Especially when her cheeks burned crimson at his attention.

Damnation, she had been trying to get him time with Zoe, not create a stir around herself. But there was nothing to do now except curtsey as was proper and pray that Zoe understood the truth of the situation. Either way, tomorrow morning promised to be an interesting opportunity, if only Kynthea had the wit to manage it right. And more importantly, if Zoe managed to act like a lady twice her age. As for the duke…

Well, what did she hope for the duke?

Goodness, she didn't want her thoughts to wander in that direction. Because, truth be told, she already had too many exciting thoughts about the man. By God, the memory of his wink set her belly aflutter. And that smile of his? Parts of her were tightening in a way she'd never felt before.

What was wrong with her? And damn it all, she had to throw the man at Zoe. Sometimes the life of a companion was horribly unfair.

Chapter Four

RAS WAS WRONG about Nate. Apparently the man was desperate enough to find an heiress that he maneuvered to join the morning ride. He showed up bleary-eyed at the stable, but he was there, his curly hair in rakish disarray.

"Good lord, man, did you sleep at all last night?"

His friend shrugged. "A gossipmonger's work is never done. Especially when one wants to put it in print. Many people deny the words, but I—"

"Use a pseudonym so that no one knows who pens Mr. Pickleherring's salacious tales."

Nate grinned. "It pays the tailor bill, and that is all I care about."

He cared about a great deal more since he did verify his gossip. Ras knew the real reason Nate haunted the gambling dens and society ballrooms was so he could expose the liars and the cheats. If someone had warned Nate's father about the conman who sold shares in a bogus investment years ago, Nate wouldn't be reduced to penning a gossip column to pay his tailor now.

But that was yesterday's tale. Today's activity included a morning ride with the most intriguingly odd woman he'd ever met. She spoke with absolute rationality about the business of marriage and in the same breath discussed love potions. The discontinuity of that made him smile and, more important, she seemed to understand when he was making a joke. His sense of humor was lost on most people, so he appreciated that she looked a little deeper. That was so rare that he immediately wanted to know her better.

What he hadn't expected was that he'd spend the night reliving every second of their conversation together. For all that she tried to appear a conservative chaperone—with modest brown hair, a simple gown, and restrained gestures—it took very little for him to see that she had strong thoughts and wasn't averse to challenging his opinion. No one had taken him to task in years, and he was startled to discover that he found the experience arousing. Unpleasant, to be sure, and yet so interesting as to make her the most attractive woman in the room.

What a perverse creature he was, and yet the pleasure he had derived last night from remembering every moment with her, even the uncomfortable ones, had led to erotic imaginings that still had him randy at seven in the morning.

He glanced at Nate, who was not as bleary-eyed as he looked. "What's got you so happy? You're practically dancing in the saddle."

They were on their way to pick up the ladies, with the grooms and other horses following at a steady pace. Thankfully, the streets were not very crowded.

"I am my normal happy," he responded levelly. "I enjoy my morning rides."

"No, you're not," Nate returned as he scratched at his jaw. "You're practically grinning."

He was not. But he might be smiling which, admittedly, was rare. Fortunately, they arrived at their destination and headed for the door. Lady Zoe was the daughter of the Earl of Satheath and so resided in an appropriately grand residence with a butler who opened the door well before he and Nate made it up the steps. They were escorted inside with all the normal pomp, only to find Lady Zoe nearly vibrating with excitement.

"I see you brought Swirl and Rumble," she said when they entered. "Excellent choices, though I do hope you will allow me to ride Rumble."

Ras paused in the middle of his bow, only to straighten up with a frown. "Swirl and Rumble?"

Lady Zoe had been perched at the edge of a settee, looking out the window. She now seemed to drag her gaze off the horses to him. "Yes, the two mares, Swirl and Rumble. Swirl because of the whirls she has on her cheeks and Rumble because of the noises she makes when you groom her."

"The mares are named Epona and Nevarra."

"They're…oh." She pressed her hand to her mouth as her cheeks heated. "I am merely repeating what the grooms called them."

Ras straightened until he was peering down his nose at her. "And how do you know what the grooms call my horses?"

"Um, well, as to that…" The girl fidgeted with her riding gloves. "I happened to be near your stables a few weeks ago. I love horses, you see, and couldn't resist."

Nate chuckled from where he stood beside the tea tray. He hadn't waited to be served but had helped himself to a strong cup. "You cheeky minx. You have been secretly visiting Ras' horses."

"It wasn't a secret!" she cried. "I, um, I…"

"Good morning, my lord, Your Grace." Miss Petrelli entered behind them, moving quickly as she brushed an errant strand of hair out of her face. "My apologies for being late. The countess required some extra attention with her morning chocolate. Ah, Lord Nathaniel. I am so glad you didn't wait on ceremony with that tea. It would be cold otherwise." She shot a hard look at Zoe who had apparently forgotten she was supposed to serve.

"Not at all," Nate said with his customary enthusiasm. "We were just discussing how Lady Zoe is already familiar with Ras' horses."

"Well, of course she is," the woman said smoothly. "It's been tedious, you know, being in London well before the Season began. Lady Zoe and I have made several excursions outside of the city, and we discovered your stables completely by—"

"Design?" Nate interrupted. "It would be the smart thing to

do, after all, if one intended to catch the duke's attention."

Ras glowered at his friend. "That is not the best way to catch my attention."

"Of course, it isn't," Miss Petrelli said, pouring another cup of tea. "And it wasn't by design. Or at least not completely. Sugar, Your Grace? Cream?" she asked as she held out a cup of tea for him.

Courtesy required that he take it though he was not accustomed to waiting this long before his morning exercise. "Lemon alone, thank you."

"An excellent choice," she said as if he were deliberating an affair of state. "Zoe—"

"None for me, thank you," the girl quipped, clearly eager to be outside with his cattle. "But I shall take a couple strawberries dipped in sugar." She glanced at Ras. "It makes Rumble, um, rumble quite loud. If you would like to hear it."

Strawberries hadn't been in season long enough for her to know that. Unless, of course, she had been very recently in his stables. "Just how well do you know my horses?"

"Zoe has been a regular visitor, my lord. She had the stablemaster's permission. Mr. Barnes knows her as Miss Daisy Duncan."

"He only calls me Daisy. He thinks I'm a local girl who has a passion for horses. He's never let me ride any of them, but I've helped with their training and grooming. There's always something to be done at a stable."

"At *my* stable," he pressed.

"How else am I to get to know *your* horses?" Zoe returned.

Nate chuckled. "She has you there, Ras. Come on, don't make a fuss. She was perfectly well supervised, and it's not even improper."

"To work a man's stable without permission?" Good lord, what if his mother found out? What if anyone in society found out? They'd insist he'd compromised her somehow and he'd have to marry her. The very idea that the daughter of an earl had been running around his stable like a common laborer would do such damage to her reputation that she might not recover. And it would do no favors to his own. "You cannot tell anyone about this!" He shot a glare at Lady Zoe, but his words were for Nate. Or rather for Mr. Pickleherring.

"Yes," Miss Petrelli interposed. "We have kept the excursions secret. And they've ended now that the Season has started. But in happy news, Zoe can finally ride Rumble as she's always wanted to." The lady stood up and gestured for them to precede her outside. It was the action of a seasoned hostess. She kept the party moving, smoothed over any unpleasant realizations, and functioned as if everything were exactly proper, even when her own charge had been running about the countryside as Miss Daisy Duncan and doing the work of a stable boy.

He was still absorbing the shock of Lady Zoe's impropriety when the girl leaped up to rush outside. She barely kept herself from running. Nate followed her, a grin on his face, but Ras held back to speak with Miss Petrelli.

"You're her chaperone. Do you have any idea how you have risked her reputation?"

"Have you never known a girl with high spirits, Your Grace? One who chafes at being indoors, who is used to daily exercise, and is simultaneously terrified of the coming Season where her life will be determined by so many factors she cannot control?"

"Other girls do not impersonate stable hands."

"Are you so sure?"

"Not my stable hands!"

"Again, Your Grace, are you sure? Would you have known it if Zoe hadn't just confessed it all?"

No, of course he wouldn't. He barely spoke with his stablemaster given that there were so many more important things clamoring for his attention. He enjoyed riding, of course, and hunting had been a favorite pastime when he was younger. But right now, he couldn't remember the last conversation he'd had with Mr. Barnes. "You can be sure I'll speak with Mr. Barnes forthwith. Good God, what if something had happened to her?"

"She was perfectly safe, Your Grace. Your stablemaster is a good man with a kind heart. And Zoe is well able to take care of herself around horses."

"But—"

"But nothing. You are being prickly for no reason at all."

Was he? "You have no idea how vicious society can be," he said softly. "Have you ever had a Season, Miss Petrelli?"

"You know I have not."

"Have you ever resided in London before? Been in society with any of the *haut ton?*"

She scowled at him, her voice growing hard. "You know I have not. My parents died two years ago when I came to live with Zoe's family. The Earl and Countess are aging, and I was grateful to help them."

"And to act as Zoe's chaperone."

"Yes."

"Then believe me when I say, you have no concept of how dangerous her games have been. Last night you accused me of ruining her chances—"

"Because you cut her for no reason."

No reason? He strangled the urge to argue that point and plunged ahead with his main one. "What you have allowed with love potions and pretending to be a stablehand? That is madness."

She didn't like the way he was speaking to her. Her jaw grew tight, and her expression turned hard. But she didn't argue, and he saw a flash of uncertainty in her eyes. In the end, she tilted her head in the smallest acknowledgement. "It doesn't matter. The Season has started now. There is no more time for visits to your stable."

"You can be sure of it."

The lady winced at his hard tone. "But don't be surprised if she wants to visit your real stables. She learned a great deal about the horses at your family seat. She knows that these are just the ones brought to London for the Season. She has been desperate—"

"Her desires are not my concern," he said coldly. "Only that her reputation does not entangle in any way with my own." Why wouldn't she understand? "I do not want to marry her, Miss Petrelli. She is a child. But given that she is an eligible woman of the appropriate rank, we could both be forced into a disastrous arrangement. I do not want that for either of us."

He spoke the words forcefully, wishing he could impress upon her exactly how manipulative society could be. And how punitive, if one stepped outside of the prescribed bounds. The *haut ton* would see nothing wrong with him marrying a child half his age provided that she was from a titled family. Which Lady Zoe was. He, on the other hand, wanted something more from his bride than a sixteen-year-old girl who thought nothing of impersonating a stable hand and blithely confessed it as if it were nothing more than a trip to a candymaker.

Fortunately, Miss Petrelli had more sense. Her gaze lowered and she nodded. "I understand your point, Your Grace."

"Good."

"You are more experienced in the ways of society, and I would be stupid not to listen. But I am much more versed in the management of spirited girls and of Zoe in particular. There is not a cruel bone in her body. She has energy and intelligence. It is hard for a girl such as her to be stuffed into the rigid lines set around every debutante."

"It is your job as her chaperone to see that she is. Or I fear you will watch her get crushed when she is finally caught." Indeed, she *had* been caught because this was exactly the kind of gossip that Mr. Pickleherring might share. He shuddered to think what he would have to trade to Nate in order for the man to hide this particular tidbit.

"You really think it is as serious as all that?" Miss Petrelli asked.

"I do. And she will not like what happens when society finds out what she has been up to. They love nothing more than a villainous tart, and it is damned easy to create one, no matter the truth."

Chapter Five

KYNTHEA AND THE duke headed outside to mount their horses. Zoe, naturally, looked resplendent in her blue riding habit, but more important, she looked like the incredible equestrian she was as she quickly seemed to become one with Rumble. Kynthea, however, knew she looked average in her riding habit, average in her horsemanship, and completely mundane in her demeanor.

Because she was steeped in doubt.

Had she truly risked Zoe's reputation? She knew it was risqué for a lady like Zoe to work as a stable hand, but the girl truly was horse mad. And she'd been going crazy cooped up. She'd needed a diversion, and this had been relatively harmless. Or so Kynthea had believed.

But she hadn't considered what a malicious gossip could do with the information. Nor had she believed that someone might use the indiscretion to force a duke into marriage. The idea was ridiculous, and yet, His Grace clearly believed it.

"Don't look so down," Lord Nathaniel murmured as he maneuvered his horse close to her. "Ras can be a stickler for propriety, and you caught him off guard. I'm fairly shocked myself that she'd managed to work as a stable hand and he was none the wiser."

"But is the duke correct?" she pressed. "Could the information be truly damaging?"

"Oh yes, without a doubt." Then he flashed her a cheeky

grin. "But have no fear. She won't be exposed by me or Ras, and if you two keep mum, then all's well."

All would be well if Zoe could keep quiet, and that was not something the girl was good at. Her emotions tended to overflow, and her mouth kept going long before her brain interfered. "I'll speak with her," she said, praying that would be enough.

"The Season will keep her busy. And besides, many men like girls with some spunk." His gaze travelled to where Zoe clearly wanted to go faster. She was leading their party, oblivious to the fact that she was pulling ahead and would soon lose sight of them in the maze of London streets. Kynthea was about to call the girl back when a groom rode up beside the girl and gently forced her to slow down.

Clearly the duke had thought of the problem well before Kynthea, but rather than go himself, he sent a groom. Indeed, the man took up the rear of their party as if he wanted to put as much distance as possible between himself and her young charge.

She was just turning back to invite him to ride closer when he spoke, his voice carrying clearly despite the distance.

"What possessed her parents to have her come out so young?"

Well, that was a matter of some delicacy. "The Earl would like to see her settled. Her siblings are much older, married, and well into growing their nurseries. Zoe herself was an unexpected surprise long after they thought they were done with children."

"That explains why she is young, not why they are pushing her to wed so soon."

Trust the man to see that she'd sidestepped the question.

"Oh dear," Lord Nathaniel moaned. "Her dowry isn't what they say—"

"It *is* exactly as they have claimed. Land worth a thousand pounds per annum." A fortune. And if absolutely necessary, a life for Zoe if she never wed.

"It's not the dowry," said the duke, his voice low. "It's the earl, isn't it? I've heard his health is precarious."

Very.

"And the Countess?" Lord Nathaniel pressed. "She hasn't been seen much in society these last two years."

Not at all.

And when both gentlemen noticed that she said nothing, they came to the obvious conclusion.

"Neither is well," said the duke, "and therefore they wish to see her married before they pass."

Kynthea looked down at her hands rather than answer. The truth was that both of Zoe's parents were sickly. The earl had a persistent cough, and the countess had joints so swollen, she could barely walk. They'd both said how Kynthea was a godsend when she'd come to live with them. She eased their pains and acted as companion to their youngest child. But when last winter's cold had settled into the earl's bones such that he was freezing all the time, he declared it time to see his youngest child married. He would not wait even one year for his daughters-in-law to complete their confinements. And so it fell to Kynthea to manage Zoe's come-out, to chaperone and guide the girl when she herself had never set foot in London until two years ago. And she'd never been part of high society at all.

Fortunately, they arrived in Rotten Row before she was forced to give more detail than was appropriate. Having just been chastised for being indiscreet, she would not speak out of turn now. But she didn't need to. She could tell by the gentlemen's expressions that they understood the situation. And hopefully, they understood how watching her parents prepare for death placed an added strain on Zoe.

They settled into the queue, and Zoe was clearly excited to gallop away on Rumble. Lord Nathaniel took his place behind her, and Zoe flashed him a happy smile. Kynthea, on the other hand, was all too aware of the dashing equestrians around them. She would not show well in comparison.

"How did your parents die?" His Grace asked from her elbow.

She started at the question. It was not that she'd forgotten he was there—far from it. In fact, she seemed hyper aware of his presence and any shift in his expression. It was the question that startled her, as well as his thoughtful tone.

"I apologize," he said immediately upon seeing her expression. "I do not mean to pry."

"No, it's all right. It was a sickness that grabbed hold of their lungs and never released." It didn't help that they had little money for coal to heat the house or good food to help them recover.

"You never caught it?"

She shook her head. She'd often wondered about the vagaries of illnesses. "I was ill for a short time but recovered quickly. My parents died within weeks of one another."

"And your siblings? What of them?"

"I have only an older brother. He was at sea at the time. He is a captain now in the Royal Navy, and I am quite proud of him."

"And well you should be," he said. "My father passed suddenly from an accident. He was racing and the horse stumbled, throwing him. We think the fall killed him instantly. At least that's better than being trampled by the following horses."

She shuddered as much from the image as the deadpan way he spoke of it. She'd heard that he'd been eleven years old when he inherited the dukedom. What a shock to a young boy on so many levels.

"It must have been terribly hard," she said.

"It was," he agreed. "But sometimes I look at parents who age slowly, dying by inches, and I think at least my father went fast."

Kynthea nodded. "That is a thought we share, Your Grace. I lost my parents in little more than a month, and it felt like a blow to the chest. The pain of it was horrendous." As were the difficult discussions with creditors and even a very cruel moneylender. When they were done with her, she had nothing beyond two gowns and a coach ticket to Zoe's home. She was lucky her aunt and uncle took her in or she would have been in dire straits indeed. "But I see Zoe's heart break every time she tells her parents of her plans. They talk every day, you know, especially her and her father. She puts on a brave face, but seeing them so frail cuts her deeply."

"And you too, no doubt," he said. "What will you do after they pass?"

"If I am lucky, Zoe will hire me as her companion or governess to her children."

"And if you are not?"

She didn't want to think about it. She'd been saving her coins with the vehemence of a miser. "Perhaps I will find a husband this season as well," she said lightly. She doubted it though. And not because she doubted her worth. She would be a good wife to any man she married, but it was hard to stand out next to Zoe's stunning beauty. And given her lack of dowry, the best she could reasonably hope for was a quiet life in Zoe's shadow.

The very thought depressed her. She'd grown up blissfully ignorant of the financial pressures on her family. They lived in the vicarage and had food and clothing. That was a fortune compared to others in the parish. She hadn't known that her father maintained their lifestyle thanks to a moneylender. And now her poverty stole any hope of what she most wanted: a husband who loved her and children of her own. She could bring nothing to a marriage contract, and therefore was doomed to the life of a poor relation companion or governess.

And yet, she clung to her dream anyway. "I hope that there is some man who will see my worth beyond my prospects."

"Assuredly there are," returned the duke. "But not, I think, in Zoe's circle. You must look among the merchants."

There was no cause for him to say it like she was dropping into the sewers. "There are fine men among the lower orders," she said, her tone sharp.

He glanced down at her, his expression open with surprise. "Of course, there are. Many better than the *ton*." He grimaced. "But you will never meet them while dancing attendance on Zoe.

If you want something different than being a paid companion, you should meet those men while your looks are still striking."

Good God, did he think she was fading with every breath? "Thank you for your advice, Your Grace." Her tone implied the exact opposite. "I am not exactly in my dotage, you know. But I shall strive to remain hale enough throughout my time in London so as to attract some of the—"

"I've insulted you. I did not mean to. My gravest apologies."

She sighed, seeing that he was truly sorry. But the idea that she could not have reasoned such things out for herself was ridiculous. She did not need him to explain her options to her. Nor did she enjoy his commiseration, as if marrying a merchant was a choice akin to death. It might be societal death for him, but she had never had such lofty goals.

Or rather, she hadn't since the day she learned the state of her finances. Once upon a time, she had dreamed of marrying a prince. But didn't all girls? And then they grew up and faced a life of work in their wealthy cousin's shadow.

Good God, she was tired of feeling this wretched. "I believe I should enjoy a brisk canter, Your Grace."

"A canter?" he asked, clearly grateful for the change in topic. "Why not a gallop?"

Why not, indeed? "A gallop, then." With a jaunty wave, she kicked her mount and set off at a bruising pace. Naturally, he kept pace, but she didn't care. The wind was in her face, the world rushed past in an exhilarating rush, and she felt younger than she had since her parents' passing. She lost herself in it much as Zoe did, and she laughed in true delight. His Grace certainly did have fine horses.

They rode for nearly an hour, Zoe leading the way. Her cheeks were in high color, her eyes sparkling, and when Kynthea finally caught up to the party, she could hear that her charge had launched into the list of questions for the love potion.

"Think about it, Your Grace," Zoe was saying. "What would you do if you had to spend a million pounds in a week?"

The man was confused by such a bizarre question. She wasn't sure why. She had loved 'What if?' games when she was younger. What if she were a man? What if she possessed all the gold in the world? What if she had to choose between the man of her dreams and becoming a queen? They were silly hypotheticals meant to pass the time. But apparently, no one had ever played such a game with His Grace.

"But I don't have—"

"That's not the point," Zoe huffed. "See, if I had a million pounds to spend right now, I would buy several very good Irish sport horses perfect for breeding. And I would sell them to you one by one at great profit once you see how important they are."

"And why would I need an Irish sport horse?"

Oh my. He'd stepped right into the trap, and Zoe grinned as she pushed her answer. "Thoroughbreds are all well and good," she said, fondly stroking her mare's neck. "But their bones are too thin. They're built for racing and nothing else. Your Grace, you've been hunting with your thoroughbreds, and that's not good for them. Breed in a little Irish and they'll be strong enough to do what you want."

"And you think I want to hunt?"

"You have been, haven't you? Didn't you put down two horses already this year because of broken bones?"

His Grace's eyes narrowed. No one in their party needed to ask how Zoe knew that. Obviously, she'd learned it when working as his stable hand. And far from being apologetic about her indiscretion, she was blatantly using the information she'd gleaned to challenge His Grace on the composition of his stable.

"From everything I've heard, your father had a talent for racehorses, but you're more of a hunting man. Personally, I prefer the racetrack." She giggled. "Well, I prefer racing, but ladies can't be jockeys, though I think that's a silly rule. Anyway, your stables have declined somewhat. Good showings overall, but I gather it was your grandfather's passion, shared in part by your father. But it's definitely not yours. Which means you should stop pretending to be a racing stable and get the horses you truly want." She dimpled as she smiled. "Get Irish sport horses. They're the best for what you want. And that's what I'd do with a million pounds."

"That you had to spend in a week," prompted Lord Nathaniel.

"Right! In a week. What about you, Your Grace?"

The man still looked dumbfounded. Kynthea was making a study of his expressions, and she guessed that he wasn't shocked by Zoe's audacity, but startled by her knowledge of his cattle. Which made Kynthea laugh.

"She can get a great deal more specific about what she thinks you should do. Breeding stock is the least of it. She has very detailed opinions about their food, training, and even sleeping quarters. She's quite knowledgeable and—"

"And I have a stablemaster who has performed excellently without her advice."

"Well," Zoe inserted. "I wouldn't quite say excellently. There are the two horses you had to put down, but even more, you haven't won a race in years." She softened her gaze and moderated her voice. "Mr. Barnes is an excellent man, but he's old-fashioned and narrowminded. He will never bring your stable back into prominence without help."

"You mean, without your help," the duke said, his tone icy.

Undaunted, Zoe shrugged. "Mine or someone equally clever." She leaned forward. "But beware, Your Grace, if I choose to help a different stable over yours. You may find your horses lost in the dust behind mine."

"What ho!" Lord Nathaniel cried. "She's throwing down the gauntlet to you, Ras."

"Yes," the duke drawled, his attention caught elsewhere. "Yes, I deduced that." He barely glanced at Zoe. "I shall keep your idea in mind, Lady Zoe."

"Don't take too long," she quipped. "I am very clever and therefore will be in demand."

That wasn't the least bit true, but Kynthea thought Zoe could be forgiven her arrogance. It was true that all the local gentlemen in Cornwall sought her opinion. With good reason. But that wouldn't carry much weight with His Grace.

"Perhaps—" Kynthea began, but the duke held up his hand to silence her. His gaze was narrowed as he looked about them with critical eyes. It was only then that she noticed that they were the object of much attention. Or perhaps not *they* but *her*. Several people sneered when she looked at them, and one woman hissed the word "hussy" before turning her back.

Kynthea turned back to the others in confusion, but they too had noticed the pointed attention and seemed equally at a loss. Only the duke acted. He dismounted from his horse and quickly crossed to a cluster of people gathered around a newspaper.

"What is it?" he asked in a frosty accent.

"Oh, Your Grace," cried one woman. "It's nothing—"

"You've been deceived, is all," said an older gentleman. "Happens sometimes with evil women." At which point he glared at Kynthea.

"Give me that," growled the duke as he yanked the newspaper out of a woman's hands.

Far from being upset, she pointed at a part of the paper. "That's what you want to see, Your Grace."

He started to read, and then his face took on a scowl that had generations of ducal fury compressed into every line. He gripped the paper into a fist and stomped over to Lord Nathaniel. "Mr. Pickleherring!" he snapped.

"What?" Lord Nathaniel frowned as he took the paper. Zoe sidled her horse closer and read over his shoulder. Kynthea, however, was not in a position to look. She was trapped on her horse and in the middle of several glaring pairs of eyes.

"Oh dear," she heard Zoe moan and felt her heart sink. Had the girl been exposed? Was she ruined because Kynthea hadn't been more strict?

"Your Grace," she said softly. "What is it?"

"Lies," he snapped. And he accompanied the word with a heavy glare at all the onlookers. But he couldn't intimidate everyone, especially as there was quite a crowd this morning, both riders and those who wished to socialize with the equestrians. In the end, he gestured to his grooms. "We're heading to my London home," he said in no uncertain terms. "I have a breakfast prepared for all of us." He scowled at a pair of tittering girls. "It will be more pleasant there."

Then he made a show of leaping onto his horse and setting it beside hers. His back was rigid with fury, and his gaze hopped from one on-looker to another. It didn't work to intimidate any of them. If anything, it made them whisper all the louder once they passed.

And then the absolute worst thing happened. Someone threw an apple core straight at her. At her! Her horse shied, but she was able to control it. Unfortunately, His Grace could not control his temper as well.

"Who threw that?" he demanded. "Who did it?"

No one answered, but a few bucks grinned from their positions languishing against a tree.

"Pierce. Reid." He spat their names. "Typical."

"Not so typical of you, Harle. Taking up with a trollop."

The word hit her broadside. They couldn't. They didn't! But apparently everyone here thought Zoe a demi-rep. But that couldn't be. The bucks had thrown the apple core at her. But why? What had she done?

Meanwhile, Lord Nathaniel maneuvered closer. "Ras, I did not write that. I didn't—"

"Not here," the duke growled.

"Perhaps we could ride a little faster," Zoe said from very close behind. And this time, it wasn't because of a love of cantering. Her voice was tight and, when Kynthea chanced to see her face, her expression was miserable.

"What did it say?" Kynthea asked. "What—"

"We'll discuss it over breakfast," the duke said, as he deftly maneuvered their party through the growing London traffic.

Kynthea saw the wisdom in that. Indeed, it was taking a great deal of her concentration to control her horse on the crowded streets, especially at the speed the duke set. So she bit back her fears and held onto her patience. Whatever disaster had befallen them, there was nothing she could do about it now. But it was excruciatingly hard to wait when everyone else knew what had happened and she didn't.

The duke dismounted as soon as they arrived at his home. He was at her side a mere second after his feet touched the street. And when she meant to leap down herself, he murmured to her under his breath.

"It'll pass, Miss Petrelli. You needn't worry. I swear it."

That didn't bode well at all. She let him hold her ribs tight as she dismounted, his hands large and reassuring. He should have let her go immediately, but he lingered as if trying to protect her. She appreciated the gesture, but she needed to know what had happened.

The duke guided them up his front steps and into his home, all while keeping Kynthea by his side. Her brother used to do that, she realized. He'd stand tall beside her when the crowds on the dock pressed too close.

"Thank you," she whispered, though she doubted he understood why.

She waited while the butler took their things. Then she waited while the housekeeper escorted them into a room with a hot tea tray already there. And finally, she waited for the servants to leave after the duke said a hard, "Thank you. That will be all."

She stood with her hand outstretched to Lord Nathaniel. "The paper if you please."

The man hesitated, but she pulled it out of his hands. "Maybe we can get the paper to issue a retraction," he said.

Zoe snorted. "Of a gossip column? Damned that busybody Mr. Pickleherring. I hope he dies by his own poisoned pen."

Kynthea should have admonished the girl for her language,

but she had just managed to open the paper. She didn't have the mental space to do more than read. The first paragraphs were about a gentleman she didn't know who had vastly overestimated his ability at faro and lost a great deal of money. It went on rather long and she began to skim rather than learn more about the card sharps that frequented such places in search of victims. It was only at the end of the column that her world began to crumble.

> *But the real excitement last night was at Almack's where a certain lady's companion threw herself at a very eligible duke. Miss Petrilli was heard to demand that the gentlemen escort her outside and then used the words "throw myself stark naked into your arms." Everyone was scandalized that such a brazen hussy could be allowed into those hallowed halls. Indeed, that's a mistake that is sure to be corrected forthwith as no good hostess should allow such a woman into their homes, much less near their children.*

"Well," Kynthea said, her belly clenched with pain. "Now I understand," she said softly as she calmly set the paper on a nearby table. Damn it, why wouldn't her hands stop shaking? "It would seem society has found this Season's first villainess."

Her.

Chapter Six

DAMNATION! HOW COULD he be such an idiot? After a lifetime of keeping himself scrupulously in control, he'd allowed an innocent lady to become embroiled in a scandal. If there was one thing his parents had impressed upon him, it was that—as the son of a duke—scandals would slide off him, but they would land with ten times the force upon those around him. He could go blithely about his life, but there would be scores of ruined lives following in his wake.

He'd sworn on his father's deathbed that he would be an honorable man, and for the most part, he'd achieved it. Until today. Until he'd let his guard down around a beautiful, feisty companion.

Ras paced the small confines of his morning parlor while Miss Petrelli sank onto the settee in shock. Her charge hovered nearby, clearly miserable. The child had no idea what to do. However, she could not look any more wretched than Nate, who had to have been the perpetrator of this particular crime. Yet it seemed to come as a surprise to him too…

"Damn Mr. Pickleherring!" exclaimed Lady Zoe. "How could he print such lies?"

"That's the problem," Miss Petrelli said weakly. "It's not a lie, is it? I did say those words. I did create a scene."

"But not to seduce me!" Ras snapped. "If anything, your intent was to give me a thorough disgust of you." It hadn't worked. He'd been more intrigued than ever. Her words might have been overwrought, but her logic had impressed him. And he was not used to anyone, much less a female, taking him to task as she had. With logic instead of emotion.

"I merely wanted to explain," she said.

"It's not your fault," he said as he sunk down to look at her wan face. "It's that blasted Mr. Pickleherring." He looked up at Nate. "What if he printed a retraction? Said he got it all wrong."

The man shook his head. "First off, it won't work. It will only add fuel to the gossip."

True. "Then we need a newer story, a bigger one."

Lady Zoe brightened. "Then everyone will talk about that one, yes? And this will be all forgotten."

"No one forgets that fast," Miss Petrelli said. "I shall still be barred from parties. I won't be able to act as your companion." Her eyes abruptly widened. "Your parents will have to sack me. For your own good, Zoe, they'll have to get rid of me." She pressed her hands to her cheeks. "Where will I go?"

"It won't come to that!" Ras snapped. Though God alone knew how he was going to prevent it. Lady Zoe was fierce in her denial as well.

"You will not be tossed out in the cold! I won't have anyone else but you." She abruptly brightened. "We'll go home now and stop them from reading the paper. They won't ever know."

Miss Petrelli looked up, her expression a combination of tragic and amused. "Your father reads the paper first thing."

"But he's probably still asleep—"

"And," interrupted Nate, "your parents will likely be flooded with visitors today all wanting to hear the story of Miss Petrelli's disgrace and how she was summarily removed from your household." He looked at Ras. "I don't understand how this happened. I truly don't."

Ras believed him. His friend would not have betrayed him this way and Nate's horror was genuine. But it didn't matter how it happened. Only that it had.

"She didn't do anything wrong!" Lady Zoe wailed.

"That's the problem with gossip columns," Ras growled out. Mostly because he didn't want to say it was his fault for being an eligible duke. As his mother was wont to say, scandal would dog him until he settled his nursery and became a boring adult. And that scandal would hurt people—other people—so he'd best settle the matter immediately.

And look, the first casualty of the Season sat on his settee.

Meanwhile, Nate was gripping the winged edge of a chair with white knuckles. "That's damned easy for you to say," he snapped. "You've more money than the Crown. But that column could be the writer's only source of income. The one thing keeping the blighter from starvation."

Lady Zoe frowned. "Well, that can't be true, could it? There are all sorts of other ways to make money, isn't there?"

Young and naïve. Both Nate and Ras knew the column was indeed the only thing keeping Nate from the duns. Indeed, they'd both celebrated when Nate had gotten the steady money from the job. Plus, he wasn't trained in any other occupation. He was a writer, and the column allowed him to keep up the appearance of his title while he searched for an heiress and his father tried to find a way to make their estate profitable. All it cost Nate was some clever turns of phrases about people he socialized with every day.

"How could that have gotten in there?" Ras asked. He knew nothing of the inner workings of a newspaper.

Nate shrugged, his expression miserable. "No one knows who Mr. Pickleherring is. And there's something else. I've heard that there are a dozen people between the writer and the printer. Any one of them could add a paragraph or two without the original writer's knowledge."

Miss Petrelli sighed. "It was the first Almack's assembly of the Season, attended by the most exciting bachelor in England. Of course, our interaction would be remarked upon. Of course, it would end up in the paper. I have created my own demise." She dropped her head into her hands, and her slender shoulders tightened against the pain.

He wanted to accuse her of overreacting, but he could not. Gossip like this was disastrous to a woman looking for employment. No one would hire her now. And without a position, she would be cast to the streets.

"Do you not have a relation who can help you?"

Lady Zoe stomped her foot. "I am her only relation, and I say that we will not cast her out. I won't allow it."

Nate smiled as he turned to the girl. "And what will you say to all the busybodies who tell your parents that they have brought a viper into their home?"

"A viper!"

"That's the nicest thing they will say."

The girl lifted her chin. "I will say that they are wrong. That Kynthea has done nothing wrong."

"They will call you a child who knows nothing of the real world. They will say you are an innocent who must be protected from grasping women." He touched her hand. "Will your mother stand firm against such attacks? Especially when your invitations disappear, and you have no opportunity to meet any eligible gentlemen."

Miss Petrelli lifted her head. "She won't keep me on, Zoe. She can't. Your future is at stake."

"No!" the girl cried, but no one heeded her. She was only voicing the same misery that they all felt.

And into this silence came an even greater disaster. The door knocker sounded like a gong announcing the devil. Everyone looked up, but none with more concern than Ras. Then, sure enough, his fears were confirmed. It wasn't Satan at his door, but the devil's handmaiden in the guise of his mother. She burst through the threshold and demanded to see him.

Ras had the childish urge to refuse to see her, but knew that would only delay the inevitable. So he opened the parlor door and spoke in weary accents. "In here, mother."

She began scolding him before she crossed the foyer. "You

had to create a scandal at Almack's, of all places. I warned you this would happen. Indeed, didn't I say last night that Mr. Pickleherring would get wind of it? It was the talk of the night. But you disagreed. You thought that an altercation at Almack's was too commonplace an occurrence for the blighter to notice."

"Mother—"

"And good God, what is she still doing here? Lady Zoe, for your own protection, you must release this creature immediately."

"Mother!"

At his cold explosion, the dowager duchess turned to him with ponderous consequence. Her movements were slow, her brow was raised, and she looked as if he appeared before her like a dirty toddler in his nappies.

Ras would have none of it. "This is not Miss Petrelli's fault."

"And what does that have to do with anything?" she shot back. She held up a broadsheet in her hand. Apparently Mr. Pickleherring was so popular that *The Times* had sought extra revenue by printing just his column on a broadsheet for everyone who didn't want to buy the full paper. "She's ruined herself. Or you've ruined her. You forget that I witnessed your abrupt departure from the assembly myself."

"Miss Petrelli was feeling overheated. She needed air, and I merely escorted her."

"Well, yes. Everyone knows how overheated she was. It involved nakedness."

"Mother! She is sitting right there! She is a guest in my home who is blameless for the current situation."

"Blameless!" the woman sniffed. "She chose to make a scene with a duke. It is one thing to have free manners in the country, but this is the *haut ton.*" She looked down on Miss Petrelli. "It is unfortunate that you were not better trained on how to go on. But if you swim in these waters, then you must learn how to act or be eaten alive. And you, I'm afraid, have been devoured by a very large shark indeed. Mr. Pickleherring has destroyed you, and now you must go back to wherever you came from. Hopefully there is some country squire or some such who is too stupid to know or too desperate to care about your ruined reputation. Either way, your time in society is done."

She spoke that last sentence like a judge pronouncing "Transportation!" at the end of a trial.

Meanwhile, Nate spoke up. His tone was hopeful though Ras knew he was clutching at straws. "What if Mr. Pickleherring were to write that he'd made a mistake? That Miss Petrelli was blameless?"

The duchess rolled her eyes. "There were witnesses," she said darkly. "All the ladies of the *haut ton*."

"I have the answer," said a small voice. It was Lady Zoe, who started speaking in a meek voice that grew stronger with every word. By the end, she spoke as if she were delivering a pronouncement from heaven. "It will set everything to right. It will be a bigger story and it will restore Kynthea's reputation, allowing her to stay with me as my companion. It's perfect."

Everyone waited for her to explain. They held their breath waiting for this child to give her solution, but for some reason, she hesitated. Indeed, her gaze lay heavy on him, and Ras felt dread creep up his spine.

"Speak up, girl!" his mother snapped. "What is your idea?"

"Propose to me," she said, looking straight at him. "If we are engaged, then all is forgiven. Kynthea was obviously not throwing herself at you, and it wouldn't matter anyway because she will still be my companion. The bosom friend of a future duchess. No one would dare say a word against her."

Ras swallowed. He understood the logic. Indeed, the noose tightening around his neck told him so quite specifically. But he waited for his mother to declare that solution as impossible, ridiculous, and completely preposterous.

Except it wasn't. Hadn't his mother specifically introduced the girl to him last night? She'd considered Lady Zoe an eligible candidate to be the next duchess. Her young age was completely irrelevant. The girl had pedigree and dowry. And if he demurred, she would point out that the child was also beautiful and would likely be a good breeder.

The very idea made him nauseous.

Meanwhile, Miss Petrelli whispered a single word. "No."

"Yes!" Zoe retorted as she rounded on her cousin. "It's not how I expected the love potion to work, but there it is. I'd be an asset to the dukedom. I can fix his stables if nothing else. You'd be at my side, completely redeemed. His Grace would get my considerable dowry, and everyone would talk about it with admiration. Indeed, it would be the engagement of the Season, and all done after one party!"

It was clear the girl believed her words. Worse, he could see his mother considering it. The financial alliance would do his estates no harm, and indeed, on a practical nature, everything made sense.

"Absolutely not," he said. "I will not marry a child."

"I'm not a child!" the girl returned hotly.

"You bought a love potion to trap me and had your cousin throw it in my face. That, Lady Zoe, is the act of a child."

The girl bit her lip, obviously embarrassed. Nate gasped, clearly startled. But the wildest reaction came from his mother. She pursed her lips and nodded.

"Clever girl," she said.

"What?" Ras gasped.

His mother shrugged. "I've heard worse stories. And it worked, didn't it? You're considering her hand right now."

"I am not because it will not happen." He said the words as loudly and firmly as he could manage. And when no one appeared moved, he made his decision. "What will happen is that I shall return Lady Zoe and Miss Petrelli to their home where I shall have a frank discussion with her parents. I will explain that Miss Petrelli is the height of propriety—"

His mother released a snort of derision.

"And I shall consider it a personal insult if they sack her."

Nate shook his head. "That might work to keep her off the streets, but it won't help Lady Zoe find a husband. If her family stands behind Miss Petrelli, the hostesses will cut her from the guest lists."

"Then I'll throw a ball," Ras declared. "A big one and make it known that anyone who cuts either of them will not be invited."

Silence reigned as everyone mulled over the possibility.

"That might work," said the duchess.

"Mr. Pickleherring could release the news along with his retraction," Nate offered.

Lady Zoe pursed her lips. "It would make me the most interesting debutante of the Season. Everyone would want to talk to me if only to find out how I'd attracted the attention of a duke." She looked up at the duke. "Your ball would have to come after mine." Her come-out ball was scheduled for the next week. The only reason she'd been allowed to attend Almack's was because she'd gotten the vouchers. And because she hadn't wanted to wait.

Meanwhile, Nate snorted. "Ras, your ball would have to be the last of the Season. Otherwise everyone would attend it, then cut her afterward."

Ras shrugged. He didn't really want to throw one anyway. "Last is fine with me." He looked around the room. Everyone had agreed except the one person he was most concerned about. "Miss Petrelli?" he asked. "What say you? Are you prepared to become the most celebrated lady this Season?"

She looked up, her brown eyes wide and beautiful for all that they held the hint of tears. "Celebrated? Or notorious?"

His mother sniffed. "As if that matters!"

"Of course, it matters," the lady shot back as she gained her feet. Good. She was showing some spirit. "No companion or governess can be notorious! Assuming this works, how will I survive after the Season?"

"Well as to that, my dear, you have the same difficulty as every other debutante. Catch your husband now while you're still interesting to the beau monde. Afterwards, you'll be no more relevant than yesterday's fish."

And so it was that Miss Petrelli became the focus of all his matrimonial designs. Not his own, of course. His intent was to find her a suitable husband this Season so that he wouldn't be forced to offer for Lady Zoe. If keeping himself out of the parson's mousetrap was his goal, then he would have to see that Miss Petrelli found her one true love. Or at least a gentleman who would honor her as she deserved.

"Goodness," Nate quipped as they headed out to speak with Lady Zoe's parents. "Who knew this Season would be so dashed intriguing? And it has only just begun!"

Chapter Seven

ZOE TRIED NOT to fiddle with her purse as she waited in the front room of the apothecary shop. A lady wasn't supposed to show nerves, but she was bubbling with anxiety. Her father was getting worse, his cough loud enough to be heard in her bedroom. The London air was bad for him, and she feared he wouldn't be strong enough to dance with her at her come-out ball. That wasn't her real fear, but the thought of him dying was so scary, she flinched away from the idea even in her thoughts. Instead, she focused on this Season, her come-out ball, and the need to get the duke to propose.

Which was why she was at My Lady's Apothecary this afternoon.

Someone of note was in the back room, so she had to wait for her private discussion with Madame Ilie. She stood in the corner fussing with her gloves while the dark haired shopgirl offered her tea. She demurred. Her stomach was too upset. Her maid, however, appeared grateful for the cup and was now happily settled in the corner drinking, as if her mistress weren't in a knot of anxiety.

Kynthea would know how to settle her stomach, Zoe thought ruefully. But Kynthea was right now suffering every sly word and nasty innuendo the *haut ton* could fling at her. No less than two dozen people had come calling this afternoon, all under the guise of deep concern for her mother's health and Zoe's welfare.

They were gossipmongers, every one of them, trying to stir up trouble for their own amusement. And Zoe told them so, in no uncertain terms. Which helped not at all.

Naturally, Kynthea had more poise. She listened, she apologized for her outrageous behavior, and she served tea. It helped that the duke sat right next to her, appearing the picture of propriety in his austere black coat and snowy linen shirt. He was a handsome man, she had to admit, in a stiffly correct sort of way. Not a hair nor a cravat fold out of place. Zoe could appreciate the effect of it even if she couldn't emulate it. She liked him and thought they could be friends, if she weren't trying desperately to get him to fall in love with her.

Fortunately, he had convinced her father not to sack Kynthea, but it was a touchy matter. Neither parent was pleased that the woman they'd brought into their home had become an object of gossip. And even Zoe could see how this whole thing was weighing on her father. He had coughed several times during his private discussion with the duke in their library. She'd been trying to eavesdrop upon the conversation but could only hear her father's hacking cough. And her mother had shredded a handkerchief while they both waited for the decision.

This whole matter had to get resolved quickly—for everyone's sake—which is why she had come back for more love potion. She wasn't doing any good sitting in fury in the drawing room with all those biddies. So she had left to do the only thing that might make things right.

She needed more love potion to make the duke marry her. She would manage his stables, she'd hire Kynthea as her companion, and her parents could rest easy. All would be well.

That was her plan. Unfortunately, she hadn't been able to get the duke to divulge any answers for the questions Madame Ilie had given her. She'd tried with the easiest of them all. What would he spend a million pounds on? Didn't everyone wonder what they would do if everything suddenly became easy? But he was either so old or so rich that the question meant nothing to him.

Then a miracle happened. It was as if God Himself had arranged it just to help her. Lord Nathaniel stepped out of the apothecary's private room.

"My lord!" she cried, belatedly realizing he looked very serious indeed and perhaps didn't want to be disturbed.

He started, looked around him with an expression of panic, then finally focused upon her. "Lady Zoe? Whatever are you doing here?"

"I'm getting a powder for my mother. Her joints swell, especially in the mornings, and they have a tea here that helps." It wasn't a lie, just not the full truth. "Why are you here?"

"What? Oh, I was picking up a headache powder for a friend of mine. She is too ill to come herself."

A headache powder wasn't usually put in a bottle, and Zoe was sharp-eyed enough to see him casually slip one into a pocket. She wanted to find out—indeed, part of her was burning with curiosity—but she had more important things to ask, especially as he was starting to tip his hat to her order to leave.

"Well, Lady Zoe, I must get on—" he began, but she interrupted him.

"Please, my lord, I would be most grateful if you could help me. I fear I am in great distress."

"Yes. Miss Petrelli's situation is dire, but I think Ras has the right solution. At least for the moment."

She huffed. "A momentary solution is not a permanent one, my lord, which is why I need your help. You've known the duke for a long time, haven't you?"

Lord Nathaniel rocked back on his heel as he looked at her. He kept his expression genial, but she felt the reserve in him. "Yes. We met at school and have been fast friends ever since."

"Good." She pulled the folded list of love questions out of her reticule and held them out to him. "Do you know how he would answer any of these questions? They're important, and I couldn't work any of them into the conversation the other day. Not so he would answer, that is."

"Ras is rather private," he murmured as he began to read. Then his brows rose in surprise. "I can see why you'd have trouble working these into a conversation." He frowned down at the sheet of foolscap and read two of the questions aloud. "What is the most foolish thing you've ever done in your life? What did you think of me when we first met that you don't believe now?" He looked up at her. "He'll never answer questions like that."

Which was exactly her point! "That's why I need you to answer them for him. You know him best."

"Lady Zoe, what is this for?"

She bit her lip, desperately trying to come up with a convenient lie.

"Does it have to do with the love potion?"

She winced. "You heard that."

"It was hard to miss." He folded up the paper and handed it back to her. "You must know that he will never marry you."

She sniffed. "He would, if he fell desperately in love with me!"

"And why do you want him anyway? He's old and proper, like a good duke ought to be."

"And don't old men like young wives?"

The man winced. "Not Ras. Not like that." He folded his arms as he regarded her. "I do not understand your determination to wed at all, much less him. You are a young woman. You could have several more Seasons until you're considered on the shelf. We are one day into your first Season, and yet here you are, determined to wed the one man who will never choose a young wife."

It was no business of his why she did what she did. She'd been very logical in her thought process. "Can you not think of how he'd answer even one of these? Perhaps he told you what he thought of me when we first met."

"He thought what we all did. That you are very young."

"I'm not that young!" she huffed.

"Lady Zoe—"

"The London air does not agree with my father. He coughed seventeen times this morning in just an hour. Horrible, hacking coughs that are terrible to hear."

Lord Nathaniel frowned. "I am very sorry to hear that."

"Mama wears gloves all the time because her knuckles are so swollen. She thinks her hands ugly. She is better in Cornwall where I have a special liniment for horses that works well on her hands. Plus, the water is much cleaner where we live."

"I shouldn't doubt that. I fear that London has a deleterious effect on everyone's health."

"Exactly. I will not put them through another Season. It will kill my father!" There. She'd said it, and damned that her eyes were tearing up at the thought of losing her parent. She knew it was coming, of course. Everyone saw how her father was fading a little more each day. But the London air had accelerated the process to a distressing degree.

His lordship took her hand and squeezed gently. "Perhaps then, it would be better to leave London altogether. Skip this Season and return next year after all this bruhaha is over. Or does a year seem like too long to wait?"

"It's not me who insisted on this course, but my mother. She's afraid she won't be able to properly launch me when my brother inherits."

"Is he as bad as all that?"

"What? No. He's wonderful, but he despises London and has this mad idea about shipbuilding. His business requires all his time and energy, and he won't take the time out for my Season. I'll be stuck in Cornwall with him for the rest of my life!" That last part came out more as a wail than true conversation, and she immediately tried to moderate her tone. But it was so hard.

Meanwhile, Lord Nate nodded wisely. "So there's the crux of it then."

No, that wasn't the crux of it. Why didn't anyone understand? Her father wanted her wed this year and would not leave until that was accomplished. "My lord, isn't there anything that makes you happy beyond reason? Something that absorbs your every waking moment and even haunts your dreams? I'm talking about a passion, my lord, that consumes you."

He looked startled by the question, his gaze darting around the small shop. There was no one there except the shopgirl and Zoe's maid. Both were whispering together over their tea, so no one else could hear. But it did make her wonder what drove this man.

"I have one, yes, that I hope to make come true one day. But we were speaking of you—"

"My passion is for horse racing. I know every stable in England. I study the racing sheets the way most girls discuss fashion plates. I have spent my entire life around horses and have more knowledge than even the duke's stablemaster. Horse racing, my lord. That is my passion."

"And so you are marrying Ras for his stable?"

"Yes! And because he is old, so he will be too tired to keep up with me. Most men can't, you know. Not even my brother."

"Ah."

"And because old men die sooner. The things I could do with control of his estate! I would make his stable the envy of the world!"

He stared at her with a new kind of respect in his eyes. "I can see you have thought this through."

"I have thought of little else since my father first spoke of seeing me settled five years ago. He said that as soon as I was old enough, I should look for a husband."

"But five years ago? You were eleven!"

"Exactly. I know the disposition of every racing horse in England and the marital status of every owner. The duke is my best option." And lest he feel left out, she smiled as warmly as possible at him. "Your family had good stock once upon a time. Then your father sold it all to the duke, at a very good price, too. They're the basis of my attraction to his horses. They don't necessarily have the best bones for the job, but your horses were smart."

He blinked at her. "That happened when you were a small child. My father sold them to Ras's father because we couldn't keep up with the expense."

She nodded. She knew. Running a stable was enormously costly and Lord Nate's grandfather had been a gambler and a spendthrift. At least, that was the rumor. If one needed to economize, horses would be the first thing to sell.

"During that time," she explained, "the former duke ran a spectacular stable. But the current duke has no interest in it. I should like to restore it to its former glory." She grinned, and her heart lifted for a moment as she imagined what she would do. "So you see," she finally said, "why it must be the duke and why it must be now."

"I do see," he said, his tone grave.

"So you will help me?" She pressed the sheet of foolscap into his hand. "How would the duke answer these questions?"

He nodded as he took her elbow. "Let us go inside Madame Ilie's private chamber. We will bring her in and discuss the details of your love potion."

"We will?" she asked, her heart leaping with joy. "Thank you!"

"It won't work," he began, but she cut him off.

"It will work, my lord. Why else would you be here just when I most needed the help?"

Chapter Eight

RAS WAS WAITING in a café, his tea cold and his temper hot. He sat in a strategic location so he could see when Nate left the newspaper office. Then he watched with narrowed eyes as the man took his time crossing the street before oh-so-casually wandering into the café.

"Well?" Ras said by way of greeting, even as he gestured for a plate of tea sandwiches.

"Nothing useful. The publisher swears that he printed exactly what I wrote."

"And you believe him?"

Nate shrugged as he sat down. "I think he is so busy he doesn't remember."

"So he didn't add it himself?"

"Definitely not."

Ras felt his teeth clench. "If you didn't write it—"

"I didn't."

"Then someone tampered with the missive before it got to him." Ras glared down at his tepid tea. "Did you get a look at the handwriting? Do you know—"

"No and no. I made sure at the beginning that the man would burn everything as soon as he had it set for print. The less evidence that ties it to me, the better."

And that was why Nate had used intermediaries to deliver his writings to the paper. A primary requirement of being a secret gossip columnist was to remain secret. But that did nothing to solve the current mystery of who had attacked Kynthea in print.

"Who delivered that missive?"

Nate rolled his eyes. "We've been over this. I use street boys who cannot read, much less write."

"But if you pay them, someone else could have paid them more to deliver a different message."

"To what end?" Nate smiled as the waitress delivered a small tray of sandwiches, quickly grabbing some as he spoke. "Forgive me, Ras, but Miss Petrelli is hardly worth such effort. She's a nobody companion from the country. Who would benefit from destroying her?"

Ras looked away. The world might see Kynthea as a nobody, but she was rapidly taking over his every waking second. It made no sense, but he couldn't deny that he thought of her night and day. She'd even become Kynthea in his thoughts, instead of the very proper Miss Petrelli.

"Why do you care so much?" Nate pressed as he finished a cucumber sandwich in one bite. "You've shown your support. I'll write another column that absolves her. It should all blow over soon."

Good question. Ras had tried to rationalize his interest. After all, in the four days in which he had sat with her to show his support, he'd been impressed by her calm reserve. She had poise in a very difficult situation. It was no easy thing to sit there and listen to sly innuendoes as people tried to goad her into revealing a lack of character. Or suggest to her aunt that she should be dismissed.

His presence had kept the worst of it at bay, but he had heard plenty at his club. And he was sure that even more had reached her aunt and uncle's ears.

And yet, simple poise did not explain his desperate need to be near her. He hadn't felt this strongly for anyone before, not even during his adolescence. In truth, it shook him. But that didn't stop him from spending every afternoon in her parlor in a show of solidarity.

"I fear for her," he finally said. "She is holding up remarkably well, but I see her shrink every day that this goes on. And her aunt and uncle are hardly immune to the innuendo. If the *ton* is not distracted soon, she will be dismissed. And then what will happen to her?"

"Nothing good," Nate agreed. "How did you convince her aunt and uncle to keep her on?"

"I told them it would be a personal favor to me."

"And how did you explain that interest?"

With a lie. "I said that it was clear that Lady Zoe has a strong love for her cousin. And since all the rumors are absolutely false, there was no reason to hurt both women by cutting their connection."

Nate was quiet a long moment while he studied Ras to an uncomfortable degree. "You know they will see that as a statement of interest. In Lady Zoe."

He knew, and it couldn't be helped. "I won't have a good woman destroyed simply because I walked outside with her for a moment." He rubbed a hand over his face. "She took me out there to give me a dressing down! She was defending Lady Zoe, for God's sake. Now I wished she'd slapped me or something. Anything to show people that she was not setting her cap for me."

"You're taking this quite seriously, Ras."

"Of course I am!"

"Of course, nothing. There's been gossip about you since the day you were born. About you and the people you associate with. Some of it was to their benefit, but just as often, to their detriment. This is the first time I've seen you this exercised over it."

The truth of that statement hit a little too close to home. Why exactly was this bit of gossip harder to bear than any other? "It's the first time I've destroyed a woman."

Nate frowned, clearly thinking back. "What about that maid who claimed you'd fathered her child?"

"An *innocent* woman," he corrected. "Miss Petrelli has nothing. She's the blameless daughter of a vicar who might have made a good life for herself had her parents lived. And because of me, her future looks very bleak indeed."

"So it's guilt?" Nate asked, his tone laced with doubt.

"Of course it's guilt." He said the words, even put force behind it, but in his heart he knew that wasn't the full truth. There was something about Kynthea that drew him. Something compelling that he could not dismiss. And until he figured out just what she had that fascinated him, he would not abandon her to drown in society's treacherous waters. He couldn't.

"You know you cannot marry her," Nate said, his voice very low. "At best, you could make her your mistress."

"I will not!" He said the words to himself more than Nate. Lust had surged through his body at the idea of having her in his bed. Indeed, he'd fantasized about it every night since first meeting her. He'd pictured her mouth in places it should not be, imagined her naked body moving across his, and wondered what sounds she'd make when he entered her. "She's a proper woman. I would not insult her that way."

But he wanted to. Indeed, he worried what he'd do if he ever got her alone.

"Ras! She's a nobody with a father who gambled."

"How do you know that?"

Nate shot him a hard look, and Ras felt his cheeks heat. His friend had surprising resources sometimes. He knew things well before anyone else. He would sometimes appear with bruises or, once, a bloody gash for which he had no good explanation. The man was often underfoot, and then mysteriously absent for days at a time. No explanation, no apologies. But when he reappeared, he would have coin enough to pay his bills.

And though Ras had given him money as often as Nate's pride would allow, it had been a long time since his friend had accepted any help. Longer still since Nate had shared how he made his money. Every time Ras asked, Nate pushed it off as success at the gaming tables or some other such nonsense. The man rarely gambled, and he was a lot smarter than the face he presented to the world.

But rather than pursue that line of questioning, Ras focused on Kynthea. He was uncomfortably obsessed with finding out more about her. "What else do you know about Miss Petrelli? Is she hiding something disastrous?"

"As far as I can tell, she is exactly as she appears. An impoverished relative to Lady Zoe's family. Her father was the one who created the situation. Every vicar has his vices, I suppose."

"Not *every* vicar."

Nate shrugged. "Near enough. And as vices go, gambling isn't the worst by far."

"It just severely damaged her future."

"Yes."

"And I came along and finished the job."

"*You* didn't do anything of the sort," Nate countered. "I cannot understand what happened. Who would add such a thing to my column?"

"Your publisher had no idea?"

Nate sighed. "None. Though he did say that sales that day were quite high. And that he wished I would add salacious tidbits like that more often."

Ras could tell the idea sat uncomfortably with his friend. He was not a cruel person at heart, and gossip was almost always cruel.

"Nate—"

"He even suggested that he'd hire someone else to do the job if I could not."

Ras frowned. "Nate," he began carefully, "how badly do you need this work?"

His friend flashed him a warning look. He did not like discussing money, even with his closest friend, but his answer was honest enough. "It's not the pay, though that's very useful." He grabbed the last sandwich and popped it in his mouth. "I like directing the attention of the *haut ton* where it ought to go."

In short, Nate liked exposing blackguards and thieves. But most times, those people were hard to expose. At least in a way that could credibly be printed without revealing the source. And society did love tearing down innocents even more than it liked cutting a blackguard from their ranks.

"You walk a fine line," Ras said.

"Always."

"But if you need—" Ras said.

Nate cut him off. "My name is not Broderick."

That was an old code word between them. Broderick had been the king of all sycophants when they were in school. An older boy who'd been charming, athletic, and a good friend to anyone who paid for his trinkets. Broderick was also a liar and a thief, and had taken advantage of the younger, naïve Ras.

It was Nate who had shown him the truth of the older boy. Nate who had brought Ras secretly to listen when Broderick was drunk and bragging about how he had "a duke dangling by the nose." And Nate who had stood by him when Ras went to the headmaster to expose Broderick as a thief.

The ordeal had cemented their friendship. It was also the one wedge between them. Nate would not live off of Ras's charity, no matter how tight his purse became. And Ras knew better than to challenge his friend's pride. But damn it, the man had more pride than the third son of an impoverished earl ought to have.

"Not Broderick," Ras grumbled. "You're Nate the Ass, who has too much pride to ask for help."

Nate flashed a quick smile. "Don't worry about me. I'll find out who is tampering with my columns. And in the meantime, I'll turn in my work in person."

"That's a risk, isn't it? To be seen going in and out of the paper so often?" Ras knew that was why his friend had always sent in his writing through the street boys. It was too easy for someone in the *ton* to see him frequenting the paper and guess his identity.

Nate shrugged. "It's worth the risk," he said, his tone flat.

Then he looked up with a flash of mischief in his eyes. "And you're going to tell certain gossips that I'm trying to get a series of poems published."

"Poems? Do you write poetry?"

His friend nodded. "Terrible ones. But I've got a few funny ones that I think will serve."

"Are they better than the ones you penned for Lady Rebecca?" Years ago, his friend had nurtured a deep tendre for a lady who would never be his bride. It was a true Romeo and Juliet story because the two families had been feuding for years. Fortunately, the only casualty of their infatuation had been a few mangled poems.

"I've improved as a writer since then."

"Good to know."

With the last of the sandwiches consumed and the tea long since cold, Nate sat back in his chair. His gaze was focused inward as he undoubtedly started planning something. What, Ras had no idea.

"Ras," his friend finally said. "Do you plan to go to Baron Francke's evening of masculine entertainment?"

"Good God no! Whyever would I want to watch drunkards fondle tarts while they play cards?"

"Because you could bring me," Nate said. "I have not been invited."

Nate hadn't been invited because most people knew he didn't have the ready cash to drop at such an event.

Ras grimaced and mentally added the boorish and often expensive evening to his calendar. "What do you plan to accomplish while watching me play?" Because Nate wouldn't gamble at an event like that. He would wander around listening to whomever was too deep in his cups—or in a tart—to mind his words.

His friend grinned. "Can you think of a better place to get salacious gossip to print? Not everyone frequents the bawdy houses for entertainment. Some just like to drink, play cards, and—"

"And brag about their lives while someone else pays for their drink." The Baron was known for serving a generous amount of alcohol at his evenings. "You know, we're likely to get pickpocketed as we leave. I heard that the street boys wait right outside the Baron's home just for the opportunity."

"So win at the table. Then you can lose your winnings without ever noticing the loss."

Ras shot him a grumbling look which Nate laughed off. They both knew that Ras would do as asked. He and Nate had been the best of friends since they shared a room at Eton. Nate had helped him through his father's death, and Ras had similarly helped Nate through the realization of his grandfather's debts and the loss of Lady Rebecca's love. They had supported each other throughout the years and an evening of cards was a small price to pay for their friendship.

That didn't mean that Ras couldn't exact a price of his own.

"You can repay me by finding out everything there is to know about Miss Petrelli."

Nate's expression tightened. "To what end? You cannot marry her."

Ras snorted as he stood up. It was time to get ready to escort his mother to the next ball. "I'm a duke," he said. "I can marry whomever I want."

"Think, man!" Nate matched his friend's movements. "You are a royal duke in the line of succession."

"Distantly."

"It doesn't matter. Any girl you marry must have Prinny's approval, and he will never give it to a girl like her. She must have better ancestry if she could someday be queen."

Ras scoffed as he pulled on his coat. "If I inherit the Crown, then England has much more to worry about than my wife."

"That is not how it's done, and you know it."

He did know it. He just didn't want to acknowledge it. He had no designs on the Crown, though he took his political position in the House of Lords seriously. He found that being distantly in the line of succession a complete burden. And it especially irked him that he could not choose his own bride without royal approval.

There were many things he happily left to Prinny. Ras's choice of bride was not one of them. Unfortunately, the law said otherwise.

Chapter Nine

KYNTHEA'S HAND SHOOK as she fastened a single pearl necklace around her neck. It was a replacement for one her mother once owned, given to her by her aunt last Christmas. Her mother's necklace had been sold along with everything else to pay her father's debts. And now, against all odds and thanks to the kindness of her uncle, she was about to attend her first ball.

It was Zoe's come-out ball. Kynthea was a lowly guest who would also keep an eye on the servants, but that didn't lessen her excitement. She'd practiced all the dances at the same time Zoe had. She'd learned how to plan a ball from Zoe's mother who was a genius hostess. The woman had organized every detail of tonight's entertainment, and Kynthea had absorbed it all while the woman had tried to teach Zoe the task. The girl had barely listened, but Kynthea had been fascinated by the process. After all, she'd been the one to organize her parents' household including their few parties. This was the same thing but on a much grander scale, and she enjoyed learning how such a grand event was implemented.

Indeed, it was so much fun that if she somehow managed to redeem her reputation, she would add it to her skills as a lady's companion. There had to be other ladies in the *ton* who wanted to throw parties but were uninterested in the details.

In any event, tonight was the big event. It had already started with dinner for the family and a few intimates, including the duke and his younger sister Sara who was not yet out. Her aunt thought it would be better if Kynthea ate in her room rather than upset any of the guests with her awkward reputation.

That slight stung. She was family. Her mother and Zoe's father were brother and sister. But she understood that Zoe's parents were being especially careful and Kynthea didn't want to rock the boat. Her situation was too precarious to be upset. So she'd swallowed the hurt and then let herself grow excited by the ball which she would attend.

It started in an hour. She'd already seen to the decorations, refreshments, and orchestra, acting on the countess' behalf since the lady was dining with her guests. And now she was putting on the finishing touches to her appearance before her first society ball.

With her necklace on, its single pearl resting delicately at the base of her throat, she surveyed her appearance. Her gown was simple as it was one of the countess's cast-offs. She would have taken one of Zoe's gowns, but the girl was nearly a foot shorter and possessed of a full bosom. So she'd removed all the ruffles and broken lace from her aunt's gown, then stitched on a simple ribbon to cover places where the silk had holes. Happily, the dark russet silk hid where her handiwork was less than perfect.

It had been six days since her disastrous evening at Almack's. In that time, she'd been the subject of the entire *ton* as they debated whether she was a brazen hussy or an ignorant country miss. The duke, everyone seemed to agree, was simply a lustful dupe to her licentious nature. Nevertheless, he had remained staunch in his support, and she was so grateful, she could barely look at the man without feeling weak in the knees. Especially since her own aunt and uncle weren't nearly so generous.

There was no reason for the duke to rise to her defense, but he had and that made him a hero in her mind. And now, despite all the bad talk about her, she was to attend her first society ball as if she were an equal to the glittering, glamorous *ton*.

She fussed with her hair that she'd set in the simplest style. Without any headdress or ornaments, she'd managed to twist a couple flowers into her curls. Which meant everything about her said simple and poor, but she was lucky just to be invited, so she stopped fussing and headed down to the ball.

As she passed the dining room, she heard the duke speak and everyone else laughed in response. His voice probably wasn't any louder or richer than any other man's, yet she heard it like the ring of a low bell. Not as brash as a gong, but the echoing call to attention as all eyes and ears turned to him.

She was no different. She paused by the door, straining to hear his words, wishing that he was looking at her when he spoke. She remembered every kind word he'd said to her, relived those precious seconds when he'd looked straight at her. Two days ago, he'd told a shrewish clergyman's wife that Kynthea was "a lovely woman who defended her charge like a virtuous mother hen."

He was being kind, restoring her reputation so that he need not marry Zoe. And yet, she held those words to her heart like a teenager experiencing love for the first time. She stroked them in her thoughts and imagined he looked her straight in the eyes as he said even more beautiful words. Something about devotion, maybe. Or lust. And in her most private thoughts, she pretended he loved her.

Indeed, there had been several moments in the last week when she'd caught him looking at her with hunger in his eyes. It was possible she imagined it, but she felt it. And she yearned, as she never had before, for a man who could never be hers. Their social status was too disparate for a match.

And yet, she dreamed of him every night. What harm did it do for her to imagine a duke saying he loved her? None, except that it made her heart beat faster when she heard his voice. It made her toes curl when she thought of when he might next look upon her. It made her heart break when she reminded herself that a duke would never look twice at an impoverished miss at the mercy of her uncle's charity.

She swallowed down her childish game of pretend and forced

herself to move on. Perhaps, if she were very lucky, there would be an earnest merchant's son who noticed her tonight. Perhaps an older widower in need of a mother for his children would look kindly upon her. Or best of all, an older woman in need of a companion would chat with her tonight and find her perfectly acceptable.

These were her thoughts when she stepped into the ballroom to make sure that everything was in order.

Forty-five minutes later, all was indeed settled for the first guests. Kynthea stepped out from the kitchen into the back alley for a breath of fresh air. Or at least, as much as one could have in London. As she walked to an oak tree, she lifted her head to the sky, trying to remember what size the moon would be above the clouds.

"There you are!" he said from behind her. No need to identify who "he" was. His voice trembled down her spine to settle low in her belly. Damn her for weaving dreams about him in the middle of the night. It made her heart beat in her throat as she turned to see him. He would have been handsome in whatever he wore, given his broad shoulders and pleasing face. But tonight, he was dressed in perfectly tailored black that flowed smoothly down his back and revealed muscular legs that needed no padding. She'd seen that when she'd spied on everyone collecting in the parlor before dinner. Now she saw the perfect white of his cravat shining bright in the fading light. But his smile upon seeing her was the brightest of all.

"Your Grace," she said, doing her best to keep her voice steady. She dropped into a curtsey before him. "What brings you outside? I was taking a moment before the festivities began."

"Should I lie and say I'm doing the same thing?" he asked as he made it to her side. "I was looking for you, you goose."

She frowned at him. He was being exceptionally genial for the normally reserved man. "You seem to be in a good mood, Your Grace."

"Do I?" he asked. "I suppose I am hopeful that the end is in sight. I have stood by you for days now. That quelled a good deal of the gossip. The invitations to my ball will go out next week, and Mr. Pickleherring has moved on to other targets."

She'd seen. He'd written about some baron with unsavory appetites who could not keep staff because he was so awful. No one cared. Lustful aristocracy was so common as to be boring. The column had added that perhaps the writer had spoken too soon about the character of one Miss Petrelli. By all appearances, he wrote, she was an upstanding lady.

Everyone assumed that the duke had forced the paper to print that as a kind of retraction, which meant that nobody believed a word of it. She'd lost count of the number of times she'd heard the phrase 'Where there's smoke, there's fire'. As if her character carried some sort of devil's flame set to burn everyone else.

At least she'd kept her job. "I must thank you for speaking out on my behalf."

"It's the least I could do. Though I thought it unfair that you could not join the family at dinner."

She snorted, then abruptly covered her face at the unladylike noise. "Unfair? Your Grace, with my current reputation, I am lucky to be allowed to attend the ball at all."

"Ridiculous. You're part of their family, and dinner before a come-out ball is for family."

That might be how it worked for a duke, but life for a penniless relation was very different. She swallowed and turned her head toward the oak tree. It was far better to press her hand against the rough bark than allow herself to reach for his arm or hand. She'd been kissed before in her youth. A baker's son had read her poetry and stolen kisses from her before her mother discovered their tendre. Back then, the family had some claim to status and her mother had hoped that her sister-in-law—Zoe's mother—would sponsor her come-out. They had economized in preparation for Kynthea's debut, but then it had all gone wrong. Her parents had become sick, and the depth of their financial woes had been exposed.

And now, here she was all alone with the duke beneath a towering oak. A perfect setting for an illicit kiss, but she knew it would never happen. And it hurt to put away such thoughts, especially with him so close.

"How may I help you, Your Grace?" she asked. "Do you require—"

"Good God, what happened to the sharp-tongued woman who took me to task for destroying Lady Zoe's reputation? I swear you were here a few days ago, but lately, you have done nothing but scrape and bow before me."

Kynthea reared back at his sharp tone. "I'm sorry?"

"I'm sorry, too! Miss Petrelli, pray tell me what has happened to your spunk?"

Her spunk? Was he joking? "I have had my likeness ridiculed on broadsheets! If I did not scrape and bow, what do you think would become of me?"

He winced as he stepped closer to her. They were well into the shadows of the tree now and exactly where a proper chaperone would never be alone with a gentleman. And yet, she was so besotted that even arguing with the man, she would not leave.

She sighed, trying to steel herself to be proper. "I should go inside."

"Not yet," he said as he tilted his head to the sky. He couldn't see anything but the budding branches of the tree, but there was enough light for her to see the masculine shape of his neck, the strength of his profile, and the exact shape of his mouth. She took way too much interest in his mouth. "I enjoy your company," he finally said. "You have a subtle wit that most people don't catch. You're icily polite to those who deserve to be spanked. And I like your smile. Your eyes crinkle at the edges even if your mouth barely moves. I know you have found something absurdly delightful, and I want to know what it is."

She stared at him, her body flushed with heat. How did one answer when a duke made such a study of her?

"You don't even smile," she blurted. "But I see it, too. Your brows raise and you catch my eye to see if I found something funny too."

"And you do. Every time," he murmured. "You do." He shook his head. "Not even Nate has the same sense of humor as I do. We've come to understand each other over the years, but at the beginning we had to explain our jokes to each other."

"That's always awkward."

"You have no idea," he answered, and the words echoed with loneliness.

She felt the pull then, stronger than ever. His eyes were dark here in the shadows, but they mesmerized her nonetheless. What would she do for the chance to be in his arms? What would she give up to be a duke's lover?

She was afraid of that answer, and so she looked away. Best to focus on his words instead of the way he made her feel.

"You sound weary," she said. "Didn't you enjoy dinner?"

He fell back against the tree trunk, heedless of how the dirt might mar his clothing. "It was nice to take Sara on an outing. She did well, I think. She seemed happy when she headed home."

Sara was his younger sister and since she was not yet out, she could not stay for the ball. She was also a safe topic. No one could think lustful thoughts when speaking of a man's sister…right? "Tell me about her. From what I saw, she seems a very poised young woman."

"Sara? I suppose so. She's been taught since birth how to behave in public. But that's not how she is with me."

"No? What's she like then?"

He closed his eyes as he seemed to think on his answer. "She has a laugh that sounds like bells to me. I have not heard it often of late, but when she lets it free, I know she is truly happy."

"What does she like?"

"She is the opposite of Lady Zoe in that horses hold little interest for her. She likes to mix things."

"Things?"

"Potions. Chemicals. Alchemy. What happens when one mixes one powder that I do not understand with another liquid that I've never heard of."

"What does happen?"

He chuckled. "Usually nothing, though I wouldn't advise drinking her concoctions. Sometimes they bubble, sometimes they change colors, and sometimes...they explode."

"What!" She laughed, sure he was joking.

"Only four times that I can recall. No, five. And several more that she never tells us about. Mother gave her an entire barn to do things in and we do not ask."

She couldn't imagine a child given such leniency. "Why does she do this?"

"Because she's a bluestocking. Because she's hiding from my mother who wants her to be feminine. And because no one has the will to say no to her. She took my father's death very hard." He glanced back at the house. "She's the same age as Lady Zoe. Mother hopes my wife will bring some guidance to Sara."

"That will never happen if Lady Zoe becomes your wife. Zoe's more likely to join her in this barn of experimentation in the hopes of finding a new poultice for an aging horse."

He turned to regard her, his face in enough shadow that she could not read his expression. "I have no intention of marrying Zoe."

That was not what Zoe's parents were thinking. They'd encouraged the duke to remain close in the hopes that an offer would come by the end of the Season. After all, the two would make a nice match in title and fortune. And many society couples had a large age difference.

Kynthea didn't want to ask the obvious question. She knew the answer would be like a stab to her heart. And that was exactly why she asked. It would do no good for her to get stars in her eyes where he was concerned. "Do you have any ladies in mind? You've been to several balls this week alone."

He groaned. "Don't remind me. Most nights I escort my

mother to every ball, musicale, or whatever other function where young misses might gather. She has debutantes lined up just to curtsey at me and flutter their fans."

"Have none stood out?"

"None." His gaze seemed heavy upon her, and she shifted awkwardly where she stood touching the tree trunk.

"Surely someone has caught your attention, if only for a moment. That is enough to further your acquaintance."

He smiled, his white teeth cutting through the shadows. "Only one lady has impressed me with her calm, her grace, and even her wit during a difficult time."

She winced. She *knew* he had met someone. He was an eligible duke. Every lady in the land would act their best before him. "Is she your age? Does she know?"

"Yes and no. But I'm about to tell her."

She turned to face him, forcing herself to smile. "Then someone is about to be very happy."

He grinned. "I hope so." Then he cupped her cheek and kissed her.

She should have seen it coming. She should have known what he was about. Why else would a man follow a woman into the shadows beneath an oak tree except to take liberties? And damn her traitorous heart, she wanted him to. She'd dreamed of just this thing. When everyone said nasty things about her, he'd been the one to stop their gossip. He'd been the one to defend her honor.

And now he was moving his lips across hers, plunging his tongue between her teeth, and supporting her head as he did what he willed with her mouth. Her breath caught, but her body responded as if she had been kissed like this a thousand times before. She hadn't. Indeed, no one had ever enveloped her so completely and yet been gentle against her mouth.

Their tongues dueled. Slow at first, but then with growing urgency. Soon she was clutching him, pressing against him, wanting to feel every moment of his attention. She threw herself into the madness of it all. Until he wrenched himself back.

Her heart was pounding, and her breath was short. She gulped air for a moment, and then much too quickly realized what she had done. She had welcomed his advances. More than that, she had thrown herself against him just as the biddies had accused. A brazen hussy. That was what they'd said, and now…

She pressed a hand to her wet mouth and fell back against the tree. What had she done? Why had he defended her this last week just to make improper advances now? And why, why, why had she allowed it?

"Miss Petrelli?" he said, his voice low. "Kynthea—"

She held up her hand to stop him from talking. She needed to think, to regain control of her body and mind. Had anyone seen? Did she look like a woman who had just been ravished? She certainly felt like one. Or at least, she felt like she wanted to be.

"Kynthea, what are you thinking?"

"What game are you playing?" she rasped. "Why would you defend me all week just to do this?"

He touched her cheek, but she flinched back. "I thought it was obvious. You are the woman who has caught my eye. You are—"

"Stop!" she hissed. "Stop!"

God, how this hurt! She'd been dreaming of him loving her. She'd spent her nights pretending that they were intimate within the bounds of marriage. To have his attention now, knowing that he only wanted a mistress, destroyed not only her dreams, but the idea that there were honorable men in the world. And not just a good man, but a duke. One who had restored her faith in the aristocracy and England.

What he had just said shredded that ideal. To know that he was just another licentious lord hurt far deeper than the discovery that her hero was a man after all. To know that she had been a willing participant hurt even more. She thought she had more self-control than that.

"What was your plan, Your Grace?" she asked. "Do you take

me against the oak tree? Do we meet up tonight after the ball is over?" Her throat constricted. Good God, she wanted to. Part of her was praying he'd ask her to come to him tonight. What delights could he bring her?

"That was not my plan." His voice was cold. His body stiffened and pulled back from her. "Kynthea, I did not intend any of that."

"Really?" she taunted. Her words came out sharp because she hurt. Her hero thought of her as a lightskirt. "Did you trip and fall upon my lips?"

She hadn't thought he could stand up straighter, but he reared back far enough to look down at her. "You accepted my kiss. You grabbed my shoulders and—"

"I know!" she cried out. Then she pressed her hands to her mouth. She had to lower her voice. What if someone overheard? "Of course, I wanted it. You are a duke!" She would not confess that up until that moment, he had been her hero.

"I did not take advantage," he said stiffly.

"You are a duke!" she all but screamed. "You get everything you want, even me." Those last two words cut her. She wanted to give herself to him. Her body still burned for him. "But I must think of what happens afterwards."

"It was just a kiss," he said. Then he looked around. "No one need know."

He *did* think her a lightskirt. So long as no one knew, then it was all right for him to take her virginity to pass the time before Zoe's ball. "I would know, Your Grace. And what would I think of myself in the morning?"

That it had been worth it, whispered a sinful part of her. That same part that ached to be back in his arms. That part that knew her breasts were heavy and her nipples tight. The part that reminded her how boring, how lonely the life of a paid companion could be. This might be her one chance to know a man's passion. And of all the men in the world to love, she'd found a duke. When she was old, she would still be able to whisper to herself that she had known the passion of a duke.

"I was overcome. I wasn't thinking." He looked at her. "It was just a kiss." He didn't say it as a man sneering at a woman's silliness. He said it as someone thinking to himself that what was nothing to him, might be a great deal to her.

"I am nothing compared to you," she said. "A kiss under a tree is like an apple at breakfast to you. One is no more special than another. And yet, to me, you are… You could be…" She closed her eyes. She had to say the truth out loud and pray that the sinful part of her nature heard it clearly. "You will not be my everything, Your Grace. I will not allow it. You will not marry me. You will not ever remember me. Therefore, I refuse to give you more of myself than you surrender to me."

She opened her eyes. She lifted her chin and dared him to force her to give him more. Inside, she was pleading. *Please, please say you adore me. Say you want me as much as I want you.*

But her rational mind knew he would not. What passed for adoration in a man was very different than what it was for a woman.

She saw him swallow. He took a firm step backwards, tugged on his waistcoat to straighten it, then executed the most formal and deep bows before her. She felt no mockery in his movement. Indeed, if she had to guess, he seemed earnest in this gesture of respect.

And when he straightened, he looked her in the eye.

"You impress me, Miss Petrelli. And I have acted very badly. I apologize."

This was exactly what she wanted. He apologized. He admitted he was at fault and showed her the respect he might give to the Queen. She dipped her chin and curtseyed back. All very proper. All exactly as it ought.

And yet, inside she sobbed. She didn't want his formality. She wanted them both to be overcome by their needs. She wanted to throw herself into the madness of his arms. Other women did it. She could rattle off the names of mistresses to kings and powerful noblemen. But she couldn't take that step. She was still a vicar's daughter, and some things were anathema to her.

She straightened up from her curtsey and ran her hands over her gown. "Does it show?" she asked as she touched her hair. "What we did?"

His gaze was critical as it cut across her hair and body. "You look as pristine as marble."

Was that good?

He sighed. "I mean that as a compliment, Miss Petrelli. I have visited the statues of Athena and Aphrodite. Marble goddesses that looked so real, I believed they could step down from their pedestals to greet me."

"And yet they are cold and remote."

"Beauty to be honored, Miss Petrelli. Not abused." He glanced behind him. "I will go in now. Follow in a bit when you feel more composed."

That would be never. Or at least not for a long while. "Thank you, Your Grace."

He cast her a wry look. "It is the least I can do."

So many men would do much, much less. She curtsied again which made his expression turn to a self-mocking grimace. "Good evening, Miss Petrelli."

Then he walked away.

Chapter Ten

RAS FELT THE cold seize his lungs. It was completely imagined—he knew that. He was not ill. He certainly wasn't dying of the same disease that took his father. But the sensation persisted nonetheless. It happened whenever he failed the one task he'd promised his father. It wasn't the last thing his father had said to him—that had been more about love and taking care of his mother. But the one abiding instruction his father had given him was to be a good man. His words hadn't included the word "duke" but the implication had been there. A good man didn't harm anyone else, and it was damned easy as a duke to ignorantly hurt other people.

As he'd just done.

He hadn't gone out to the tree planning to kiss Miss Petrelli. He'd merely missed her at dinner and wanted to see her. All throughout the meal, he'd wanted to catch her eye. What did she think about the current cost of cotton? Would she be shocked that money was discussed at table? Would she be patient when Sara stumbled over something she wanted to say? Did she think it was funny when Zoe likened the fish soup to a mixture she'd devised to add into an ailing horse's feed?

He wanted to know what she thought about these things, so after dinner, he'd gone to find her. He couldn't stop reliving the moments of the last week when she'd been especially clever. When a lady had impugned Miss Petrelli's manner of dress, Kynthea had gently reminded her that the queen herself had favored a similar style. The woman who quoted verses from the *Bible* about modesty and been told not to judge lest she be judged. And the ones who had offered advice on the pretense of helping had been asked about their own children who were not paragons of virtue.

The responses hadn't helped matters at all. Every woman had been insulted or upset by the retort, but he had seen the mind beneath Miss Petrelli's responses. She abhorred hypocrisy, just as he did. She held her tongue as people heaped coals of derision upon her, but she could not contain herself when someone castigated her from an equally tarnished pulpit.

And there were a lot of tarnished people in the *ton*.

He admired the hell out of that.

And because he admired her, what had he done? Acted like the rawest teenage boy drawn to her out of instinct and lust. He'd been as charming as he knew how to be, and he'd kissed her. Why? Because that was what teenage boys did, without thought to the consequences beyond the prodding of their cocks.

And that was something his father had always abhorred. Long before Ras had been old enough to understand, he had been taught to condemn men with unbridled emotions. Men who pursued their appetites without restraint or intelligence. Those men left a wake of destruction behind them. Fortunes gambled away, corpulent bodies stuffed overfull while children starved nearby, and pregnant women infected with the pox. And he had acted the same toward a woman he admired.

Ras was ashamed of himself.

But he could not afford to hide away when he was excoriating himself. He was a duke and had an image to uphold, not to mention a mother to escort. So he went into Lady Zoe's come-out ball with his shoulders thrown back and his chin tilted slightly toward the ceiling. And he waited, as all good sons did, for his mother to arrive such that she could introduce him to another set of eligible misses who were no more interesting than wallpaper. Sure, each one had a fresh design, but in the end, they were all thin on wits and propped up by something else.

He still asked them to dance.

Lady Zoe was his first partner. As the highest-ranking gentleman here, he was given the honor of the first dance after her father. The girl was stunningly beautiful in a gold gown. He didn't understand the specifics of fashion, but her eyes were bright, her smile wide, and she vibrated with the kind of happiness a girl in her come-out should have. Especially if she was dancing with a duke.

He enjoyed seeing her like this, but when they finished the opening steps of the dance, she whispered urgently in his ear.

"I have to speak with you!"

He winced. He feared she would take him to task for what he'd done to Miss Petrelli. And damn it, if Lady Zoe knew, then everyone else would likely know of his perfidy soon after. Worse, he knew that the blame for what he'd done would somehow land completely on the lady and not him.

"I assure you, Lady Zoe, I intend to make amends." Though how he intended to do that, he hadn't yet figured it out.

"Damnation," the girl cursed. "So it's gotten worse?"

The steps of the dance separated them long enough for him to realize that were likely speaking of very different things.

"I don't understand," he said when they returned to one another.

"Whirl!" she growled back. "She's gotten worse?"

Whirl? His horse? It took him a moment for him to wrench his thoughts away from Miss Petrelli to his cattle.

"Well?" the girl said when the dance brought them back together. "Has Whirl improved or not?"

"I have no idea," he said honestly. He hadn't even known the horse was ill.

Lady Zoe grimaced. "I noticed a problem with her gait last week. I've been sending messages to your stablemaster, but he hasn't returned a single one."

It would be highly inappropriate for Mr. Barnes to do such a thing. Interestingly, Lady Zoe seemed to know that but didn't care.

"I know I'm not supposed to get involved, but not everyone would see such a thing. And if you don't care about the creature herself, think of your investment in her." She canted her eyes up to him in what most would call a flirtatious look. "It would be a shame to lose the money you've already put into her training and care."

Lady Zoe was flirting with him so that he would care for his horse. Now that was a new experience.

"What would you suggest?" he finally asked.

"Make your man answer me. And if she is worse…" She pulled unusually hard on his arm when they were supposed to draw together. The motion brought her close enough to hiss into his ear. "Come see me tonight. I have the recipe for a poultice."

If this were an attempt to trap him into marriage, it was an unusual approach. Either way, he couldn't allow it. He shook his head. "I cannot, my lady," he said as they once again separated.

"You must," she whispered when he came back again. "It's my own recipe. It works very well."

He was sure it did, but he would not be caught climbing into her window at night. Though, naturally, his baser nature had a suggestion. And so the words were out of his mouth when he next got a chance.

"Can Miss Petrelli bring it to me?"

She pursed her lips and nodded. "Leave after the supper buffet. I'll send her to you during the last orchestra set. If anyone asks, she's on an errand for me. Which she will be."

He grinned. "Where?"

"There's an oak tree—"

"I know it."

The girl shook her head. "Walk down a block from there, near the alley. There's a hidden corner where the servants make babies."

He nearly stumbled at her words. Surely she hadn't just said that. But apparently she had because the girl shrugged.

"That's what I'm told, at least."

This was getting ridiculous. Fortunately, the dance was ending. "Lady Zoe," he said as he bowed over her hand. "May I invite you and your lovely companion to ride with me the day after tomorrow? We'll go to my estate just outside London. You can have your pick of my horses there and we can share a lovely supper before returning home in time for the evening's entertainments. There would be still time for you to indulge in any number of amusements, if you wish."

"What a capital idea," she returned loudly. "I should love that above all things."

He thought the situation handled then, but she still managed to whisper into his ear. "Wait in your carriage after the supper buffet. I'll send Kynthea to you with the recipe." And when he drew back to frown at her, she cast him a furious look. "Whirl's health is important!"

There was no chance to object, and indeed, he could see from the girl's fierce expression that she would insist. So he held his tongue and went in search of his next partner. And so went the evening until the first waltz.

He had remained scrupulously correct in his behavior all evening. But even as he bowed and pranced with each new partner, he had been excruciatingly aware of Miss Petrelli. He kept silent track of her partners, who were all younger sons or rakes. He saw when she directed the servants on the countess's behalf. He noticed, too, when she brought wraps for the dowagers or intervened on a shy wallflower's behalf. There was a great deal of silent direction that a hostess must manage during an event such as this. A man of his status was usually ignorant of these things, but he had been around when his mother began teaching Sara the task. So he was aware of the value Miss Petrelli brought to this household, and again, he was impressed.

Which is why he had bribed his friend Milo to write Ras' name down for the first waltz with Miss Petrelli. The cost had been an ugly rock that he'd picked up during his grand tour, but Milo had a fondness for geology and had long coveted the thing.

So it was that Ras presented himself to the lady in question two minutes before the first waltz began. She was speaking quietly to a dowager seated among the chaperones and was understandably startled when he presented himself.

"I believe this is my dance, Miss Petrelli," he said.

She looked up at him, her expression clouded. "I don't believe so, Your Grace."

"Perhaps you should check your dance card."

She frowned as she looked at the card upon her wrist. It was moderately filled with names. Enough to hide his own one scrawled upon the current dance line.

"Why would you do that?" she asked.

He dropped down to one knee before her. She was seated, so this brought him eye level with her. But it was also an extraordinary posture for a duke to take. He watched her gaze widen. Even more, he heard the collective gasp of all the matronly chaperones watching with unabashed curiosity.

When he spoke, he was cognizant that his every word would be dissected and relayed over and over. "You have been treated badly lately, Miss Petrelli. Pray let me restore your reputation to the best of my ability. Let me have this dance. Everyone here will bear witness that you attempted to turn me down."

He caught the eye of several of the women there. One by one, they nodded their agreement, including the most vicious gossipmonger among the chaperones. If he could prevent them from casting aspersions on Miss Petrelli, then the battle was half won.

"Your Grace—" she began, still intending to defer.

"I insist," he said as he caught her hand.

The dowager seated next to Miss Petrelli poked her in the ribs. "Oh, go on. You're too young and pretty to turn down a dance, no matter what anyone says about it."

"Well said," he agreed. Then he rose up, drawing Miss Petrelli's arm up with him. She came to her feet gracefully. He was coming to realize that her body movements were generally smooth, and he wondered if her grace was natural or learned. "Were you given comportment lessons as a child?" he asked as he led her to the dance floor.

"What?"

"My sister Sara had them. She hated them, and yet somehow recently learned to walk as you do. I wondered if that was the reason."

"Book on her head, shoulders back, mincing steps? That sort of thing?"

"Yes, I believe so."

"Yes, I am sure so." She shrugged and he found the motion endearing even though it disrupted the glide of her step. "I may not have been raised with a title, Your Grace, but my parents were part of the gentry. My mother earned money by teaching the local girls some polish. As her daughter, it was incumbent upon me to master every miniscule detail of her curriculum."

He caught the wry note in her voice. "You did not enjoy it?"

"No girl enjoys it. You try dancing with a book upon your head while your partner purposely pinches you or steps on your toes."

He snorted at the image of a child being subjected to that. "You are joking, of course."

"I am not," she said stiffly. "Do you think a lady is supposed to lose the pattern of a dance just because her partner has trod upon her foot? And what is she to do if his hand slips to an inappropriate location?"

He frowned. "What is she supposed to do?"

Her lips curled in a purely wicked manner. "My father taught us ways to deliver pain to young men. Subtle ways that even innocent girls might execute."

He believed her, given the sheer delight she had in her smile. "I would think he would tell you to get him or your brother to—"

"Defend my virtue? You forget, Your Grace, that the girls we taught were often without adequate protection. Such was the nature of our lives. Why even—"

"The most proper of girls can be caught alone and unawares?"

He spoke seriously as he referred to their time outside. He could tell she understood by the dark flush to her cheeks.

"I owe you the sincerest of apologies, Miss Petrelli."

"You already apologized."

"And yet, I still feel deep remorse."

She nodded as he gathered her to him for the first steps of the waltz. He thought for a moment that she might say something to him. She opened her mouth, but no words came out. In time, she pressed her lips back together without speaking.

Very well. He would have to work harder for her forgiveness. "I ask for the duration of this dance that you pretend that you believe me. I shall find another way to make it up to you later."

"You mean in your carriage tonight?" Her words were barely audible, but he heard the cynicism in her tone.

"Lady Zoe's idea."

"Yes, so she said."

"I will not touch you. I swear."

"Of course not. I will not be there."

"Most proper of you."

She lifted her chin, her brow arched as if in challenge. He took up her gauntlet. It made no sense. There had been no challenge issued in word or deed, and yet he saw her raised brow and felt a clarion call within him.

He would prove to her that he was an honorable man. Better yet, he would see that she enjoyed herself in his company, that she learned to trust him to protect her from harm. And that he, as her champion, was worthy of her greatest respect.

He had no idea where this medieval idea came from. It was not typical of his adult mind. And yet, he could no more deny it than he could refuse to take her on his arm in the most delightful waltz of her life.

"Why are you acting this way?" she said. "What do you want?"

He had no clear answer and no time to form a careful one. So he simply said the first thing that sprang to mind.

"I have wronged you, Miss Petrelli. I have damaged your ability to marry. Therefore, in order to make amends, I resolve to find you a good husband. One worthy of your regard."

That was what he said, and once spoken, he felt the intention solidify into a vow. He would find her a worthy man.

Though just the thought of that burned....

Chapter Eleven

KYNTHEA GAPED AT the man and would have slugged him in the shoulder if they hadn't been in public. Worse, she knew he thought he was being helpful, chivalrous even. In his mind, he'd wronged her and so he would find her a husband as if it were as easy as making a mark in a tally sheet.

Only a duke could so blithely believe in his own ability to solve a matrimonial problem. But she was the daughter of a vicar. She knew that some marriages did not work no matter how good the pair appeared together. And other matches that rightly should fail, thrived for no earthly reason whatsoever.

She should have been outraged. Indeed, she was outraged! But how could she be angry at a man who was earnestly trying to help her? It didn't matter that her heart wanted him, not whatever dubious replacement he could find. The duke was being kind. Misguided though his efforts might be, she couldn't fault his intentions.

She could, however, tell him exactly what she thought of his plans.

"I don't need you to find me a husband," she said tartly. "Any more than you needed to bribe Mr. Spencer to write your name on my dance card."

He arched his brow at her as they made it to the dance floor. "You knew all along?"

Of course she had. And she'd spent much of the evening wondering if she would dance with the duke or not. Would she pretend to be surprised or not? And why had he paid someone else to put his name down on her card?

The questions spun in her head with no answers until the moment came and—damn it—she'd been distracted talking to Dowager Countess Pearce.

The moment she'd looked up, she'd gotten lost in his eyes. He had lovely eyes of a steady, warm green. She smelled his scent, saw his broad shoulders, and then looked into his face as contrition seemed to wash through his expression. He was genuinely sorry, or so he seemed. And when he dropped down to one knee beside her, she could not refuse him anything.

"Did you really think I couldn't read the names on my own card? He told me that he'd get an uncut diamond if I allowed it."

The duke gaped at her. "Bloody hell," he murmured. "Is that what that rock is?" He said the words with a kind of distraction as he pulled her into his arms. For all that his mind seemed to be on his bargain with Mr. Spencer, his hands were assured as he set her in place. She knew how to waltz. Indeed, she'd practiced it with Zoe and knew how to play the part of the man or the woman. But in this, the duke was clearly the masculine dance partner. His hand was large upon her hip, and it acted as a heat source that seemed to burn through her body. His other hand dwarfed hers but still felt gentle where they were clasped together.

She set her left hand upon his shoulder, felt the strength in his body, and tried not to react when her gaze finally met his. She did not want to feel like she looked into the face of a god. He was a man, no more, no less. But he was also a duke with a great deal of political and financial power, and he was gazing at her as if she were important to him. He did not look away, he did not divide his attention, and when she met his gaze, his lips curved into a smile that matched the warmth of his eyes.

Not a god, and yet she felt as if she were held by one nonetheless.

"You are too much for me, Your Grace," she whispered. Then she bit her lip because she had not intended to say that aloud.

His brows rose in surprise. "Funny," he drawled. "I was about to say the same thing to you."

"What?"

"You are a beautiful woman, Miss Petrelli."

Her brows rose. And because she was feeling overwhelmed by him, her question came out too sharply. "Why?"

He smiled as if such a question was a normal reaction when it definitely was not. "Because you have spoken honestly to me every time we have met. And honesty is a most potent aphrodisiac. At least, it is for me."

She didn't know what to say to that. She had never considered that people would lie to him simply because he was a powerful man.

"I'm too forgetful to lie," she said. "I can never remember what I've said to whom."

"You have experience with this?"

She shrugged. "Doesn't every child? I learned early that I couldn't keep my stories straight and adults compared notes anyway."

He grinned. "You had good parents then who paid attention."

"They did." And she missed them terribly.

The music began. Indeed, it had started a few moments earlier and he had guided her in her timid, careful steps. That was her choice. She was not one who liked to go crashing about the dance floor. But in this, he steadily overcame her resistance.

With every beat, he encouraged her to take a larger step, to relax into his hold a bit more, to trust that he could support her as they traveled about the room. They were moving no faster than every other couple in the room, and yet she felt breathless as the dance continued. His gaze was upon hers, his lips curved into a smile that dared her to enjoy this time together.

Her reserve slipped away. She might be a poor relation, but this was her moment to dance with a duke. How many girls dreamed of such a thing? Here she was doing it. And, it turned out, he was a good dancer.

She smiled back.

His eyes widened in horror. His gait hitched for the briefest of moments but then smoothed out.

She frowned. Had she done something wrong? For all that they continued to twirl about the ballroom, his expression seemed strained, and both his hands tightened.

She wanted to ask what had happened, but she hadn't the breath. And his expression didn't seem to encourage conversation. It was too intense and a little bit sick. His steps were not as smooth as before and—

Oh no!

She stepped down on a piece of fabric. She knew immediately what it was. Her slippers were so thin, she could feel the shape of it immediately.

Most gentlemen wore a thin piece of fabric over the laces of their shoes. It was called a spat, and it was attached to the shoe by simple buttons. Sometimes, especially when one was dancing vigorously, the buttons came undone. The fabric then flapped about and sometimes it got caught underfoot. Not very dangerous in the normal course of a dance, but they were waltzing in very close quarters.

She'd had no idea what was wrong until she stepped on his undone spat. She felt the fabric, knew then that he wouldn't be able to move as he needed, and immediately saw all the other couples whirling about the dance floor.

Oh hell. That was all the time she had to think as she tried to push off the fabric. But she didn't have the right balance, and her foot slipped out from under her. She overbalanced backward. He couldn't possibly hold her. Which meant she was about to land flat on her backside and go skidding across the ballroom floor.

On her one dance with a duke.

Her hand slipped off his shoulder. She might have gripped him if she'd had the chance, but she didn't. Besides, there was no sense in bringing him down with her. Except he didn't let go of her.

He must have felt her slip. His hand tightened around hers as he wrapped his arm about her waist. She threw her free hand out, planning to stop the full descent to the floor, but the moment of impact never came.

He picked her up and spun her around.

She was so startled, she gasped. But that quickly turned into a laugh as her feet flew out behind her. It felt just like being spun in her father's arms when she was a child, only it was so much better. The duke was a man with strong arms, and he grinned at her as he held her aloft, slowly spinning to a stop while the couples around them abruptly scrambled out of the way. She had no idea how he kept her feet from hitting any of them, but no one was harmed, least of all herself.

And when she at last touched down to the earth, his eyes seemed to twinkle as he chuckled. "I haven't done that since my sister was young."

"I'm sure I'm a great deal heavier—"

"You were perfect."

She could have happily stood there just gazing into his eyes for the rest of her life. But all too soon, she became aware of the stares all around her. The musicians had stopped playing, the dancers formed an angry circle around them, and most everyone was glaring at her.

She felt her cheeks heat to burning. After all, she was a simple companion with a dubious reputation. And she'd just gone flying about in a duke's arms. The biddies were going to crucify her for this.

"My fault," the duke said by way of apology. "Entirely my mistake."

With a dramatic air, he stuck his one foot straight up in the air. There, flapping about, was the dangling spat. He grabbed it with one hand and ripped it off, tossing it aside as if it were so much trash. Kynthea saw a footman scramble to grab it off the floor where it landed.

"I've always hated those infernal things," he said. All around them, other gentlemen nodded their agreement which lightened the mood considerably. The women, however, were not so easily convinced. Which meant that Kynthea needed to beat a hasty retreat.

She started to back away, an apology on her lips. "I'm so so—"

"Gentlemen," the duke interrupted as he gestured to the musicians. "Once again, if you please," he said. Then he turned back to her and made as if to begin the waltz again.

"I should go," she whispered. She'd risked a glance at her aunt. The lady looked purple with fury.

"Don't be silly," the duke said, loud enough for everyone to hear. "You have promised me a waltz and I intend to collect it. If you don't mind risking yourself again, that is. I am wearing one more spat, you know."

Oh my. He was being delightful, and after all the strain of the last week, she needed the flash of levity. Besides, how could she resist a duke who smiled so sweetly at her?

She arched a brow and feigned looking down at his foot. "Is it securely buttoned down?"

"Good point," he said. Then he abruptly dropped down and unbuttoned the second spat, neatly tossing it to the footman who had recovered the other one. Then he glanced at the nearest young man to him. "Go on," he said as he straightened up. "You know you hate them too."

He'd picked the right gentleman. "Too right, I do," the man said as he too knelt down and pulled off his own spats. And he wasn't the only one. As the duke turned his gaze to the other gentlemen, most of them grinned and happily removed their own spats.

After all, no one wanted to refuse a duke.

She'd begun to think that she'd gotten away without complete disaster when she heard the whispers. As the speakers no doubt intended.

"She's getting them all to disrobe!"

"Hussy."

It was only a couple of the more vicious women, but their words carried. And worse, her uncle was *not* one of the gentlemen who'd pulled off his spats. He was older and generally very proper in his notions. Whatever anyone else thought, he and her aunt would make the final decision on her behavior. And from the looks on their faces, they were not pleased.

In short, she was done for. Her position would be terminated by morning and there was nothing she could do about it.

"Don't think about them," the duke whispered in her ear. "Come, come. The music is starting."

She sighed as she looked back at him. "I suppose I will," she said. She could not stop what was coming for her and so she might as well enjoy the moments she had left. She was dancing with a duke. When she was old and gray, she wanted to look back on this moment with pleasure.

"There it is," he said, smiling in approval.

"What?"

"Spunk." He said the word as if it were a good thing when she knew most everyone would not say so. In any event, he gave her no time to refuse. The music had started up again. "Do you trust me?" he asked as he began to move her about the room.

She laughed. How could she not? "I'd trust you with my life," she said. It was an extreme statement. He'd only saved her from a fall. And yet, she didn't doubt the statement. He'd also stood by her when she'd destroyed her own reputation at Almack's. If he'd tarnished his hero status beneath the oak tree, he was now back to Herculean proportions in her mind.

He grinned at her statement and pulled her tighter than was appropriate. "Then let yourself relax into my arms," he said. "Let us really dance."

She knew what he meant, at least intellectually. The waltz was considered scandalous because it could be a fast, exhilarating experience that overwhelmed a lady's delicate sensibilities. Or so she had been told. And now he was daring her to trust him enough to try it.

How could she refuse? Especially since this was likely to be the very last time she danced at a society ball.

"Yes," she whispered. And then she tried to keep up.

He held her in strong arms, guiding her with assurance. She let herself flow with his body as he whirled them around the room. He danced, but she felt as if she flew.

Spinning. Swirling. Intoxicating.

It was so wonderful that she wanted to laugh again. Only she hadn't the breath. Instead, she enjoyed every second.

Thrilling.

And when the dance ended, he slowed, then steadied and stopped. She came to a standstill before him and wished with all her heart that she had the nerve to kiss him again. Right here. Right now. If only to thank him for an experience she would never forget.

"So beautiful," he murmured.

"So overwhelming," she returned.

He slowly lowered their arms, using the motion to lean closer. "Zoe has a recipe—" he began.

She knew. "I'll bring it."

"Carriage?" he mouthed.

"After supper."

Done. If she were to be tossed out in the morning, why not take every moment of happiness she could tonight?

Chapter Twelve

RAS STRIPPED OUT of his coat with a happy sigh. It was dark inside his carriage, but his eyes quickly adjusted. Never had he had a more enjoyable evening. His mother had been appalled, of course. She had strict opinions on a duke's proper behavior. They did not include stripping off any attire in the middle of a ball, even something as innocuous as his spats.

He didn't care. He couldn't stop reliving the moment when Kynthea had laughed in his arms. The joy that had suffused her expression had filled his heart to overflowing. That she'd laughed at his antics lit him up, like when clouds parted on a dismal day.

He knew she'd pay for the disruption to her cousin's ball. The lady always paid for social breaches, and yet...God, he'd had such fun. She'd been delighted, and when she'd finally relaxed in his arms, they'd both had a marvelous time.

Dancing should be fun, but it usually wasn't for him. When he was younger, he was too afraid to make a wrong move. Eventually, the steps became second nature, but all too often the lady would use the dance to pull him into conversation or draw him closer than was proper.

They weren't trying to trap him into marriage, per se. But the experience was not about dancing. It was always about trying to capture his interest in the very short moments they had together. That put too much pressure on everything, and he usually withdrew mentally rather than engage in such situations.

Kynthea was not trying to trap him into anything. Indeed,

she'd made that very clear beneath the oak tree. And so he had been able to just dance with her for the pleasure of the dance. And when disaster had struck, she hadn't been shocked or appalled or disparaging, as his mother was wont to be. Instead, she'd laughed. She'd set him at ease when he was the one who was trying to ease the situation for her.

It was liberating. And it made him want her even more.

He relaxed as the carriage rumbled down the street and around the corner. He'd given Miss Petrelli directions and soon...

Yes!

The carriage stopped, the coach door opened, and a figure in a dark cloak leaped inside. He extended a hand to help, but there was no need. Miss Petrelli had command of her balance. A second later, the horses started up again, but she jerked her head up in alarm.

"Where are we going?" she demanded in a whisper. "My absence will be noted!"

"We're travelling in circles," he soothed. "We'll be less conspicuous that way."

She settled onto the squabs across from him. Her eyes were wide, and her hands clenched something. She clearly was not used to secret assignations in carriages.

"I-I just came to give you this." She held out a paper. He caught her full hand in his to steady her trembling. "It's Zoe's recipe for your horse. She said to warm it, then rub it into the knee joint with..." She gestured vaguely with her free hand. "Zoe said to use a circular motion, but not a big circle. More of a figure eight but not exactly because you have to go around the whole joint." She sighed. "Zoe was very particular, but I was...I can't remember exactly... Damnation, she's going to be annoyed with me."

"It's all right. I'm sure my stable master will know."

"That's just the point. Zoe doesn't think your stablemaster cares about the older mares. She said he'll slap it on and think nothing of it. But it won't work unless the joint is rubbed in a particular way." She pushed the recipe forward. "Zoe's very worried about Whirl."

"She seems very concerned about my horse."

"Yes, well, Zoe isn't just horse mad. She loves the creatures more than some people love their children. She's studied their anatomy, their medicines, the way one breed moves as opposed to another. Her knowledge is breathtaking. If she had been born a man, she would have her direction. Since she is a woman, she must find it second hand through her husband."

He took the recipe and carefully folded it into a pocket. "I don't think Lady Zoe is ready for a husband."

Miss Petrelli folded her hands in her lap. "That is not up to me, I'm afraid. Her father is anxious to get Zoe settled before his ailments get the better of him."

Yes, Ras had spent a great deal of time with Zoe's parents during dinner. He had seen the frailty in both of them. Her father had barely made it through the opening dance. A bad illness this winter could be the end of him, and if he were Zoe's parent, he'd want to see the girl settled as well. But marriage seemed too extreme a solution.

Meanwhile, Miss Petrelli looked at her hands. "You recall the lady I was speaking with before our dance?"

The dowager countess Whelan? "Yes."

"According to her, everyone expects you to make an offer to Zoe. I know Zoe's parents do, and your mother has given her approval as well. The *ton* has decided that you two—"

"I do not make my decisions according to society's whims."

She nodded. "But your very attention to her may dissuade other eligible suitors—gentlemen more appropriate to her age."

He was aware of the situation. He knew that every minute he spent in the Satheath household—and he had spent a great deal of time there in the last week—cemented his possible marriage with Lady Zoe. Even a duke could not resist all societal forces. Just this morning, he had received a message from Prinny indicating that the Crown approved of his match with Lady Zoe. The missive said that St. James' cathedral would be at his disposal when it was time for the nuptials. That was as close to a royal decree as one could get.

It seemed everyone wanted him wed, and they had decided Zoe was the woman best suited to be his bride. Everyone, that is, but him.

"It's true," he said, "I have spent a great deal of time in your drawing room of late. But it wasn't so I could court Lady Zoe."

"You were trying to redeem my reputation," she said. "That was most gracious of you and speaks to the kindness in your heart. But I think after tonight's waltz disaster, there is little hope for my place in society."

"You tripped over my spat."

"No one will care. I created a scene, and I will be the talk of the *ton* instead of Zoe. It was her come-out after all. No one respectable will hire me as a companion now." She spoke in the quiet tone of defeat, and he realized anew just how fragile her place in society was.

"You will not be destitute," he vowed. He had plenty of resources. If nothing else, he could give her enough to survive. Everyone would think her his mistress, but he was not averse to that situation. Though, at present, he had another thought in mind entirely.

"Miss Petrelli," he said gently. "Kynthea, you must know that I am interested in you. My kiss this afternoon was proof of that."

Her shoulders abruptly stiffened, and her gaze hopped uneasily about the carriage. "Perhaps I should leave. There is no need to wait until we return to the house. I am very used to walking."

As if he would allow her to walk alone in London. They might be in the nicest area of town, but he would never allow her to be that vulnerable.

"What if I courted you instead of Lady Zoe? What if—"

Her scornful laugh cut his words short. "Do you truly think I am that stupid?"

He didn't know how to answer that. He'd expected her to

blush prettily at the thought. He expected she would overflow with the honor of the question. That is, indeed, what any girl would do when a duke suggested he wanted to court them. And in his silence, she continued.

"You are a duke. I am nothing. And this is no better than what happened beneath the oak tree." She looked like she wanted to say more, but her words choked off as if she fought tears.

"This is completely different," he said, choosing his words carefully.

"Why? Because we are in a carriage instead of out in the open?"

No, because he had been thinking deeply about the insult he'd offered her beneath the oak. Because he had never been one to dither over his decisions. Perhaps he had been impulsive before, but in the last few hours, a question had formed in his mind.

Could he marry her?

It was too easy to say that a duke could marry anyone he wanted. He had responsibilities to his title and his lineage. His children must be raised with a sense of duty that so many of his peers ignored. His wife would need to be a proper duchess as she helped him with official responsibilities, cared for his tenants, and often served the whims of the Crown.

Lady Zoe was too young to do any of that. Kynthea, on the other hand, had the natural grace of a lady and the empathy that came from living on the lower echelons of polite society. All the rest of her duties could be taught, but grace and empathy were innate. Of all the ladies in the *ton*, Kynthea was the best suited to be his duchess.

But the final cap to his decision had come on the dance floor. Few ladies could handle such a spill with aplomb, but Kynthea had laughed with him. They'd both enjoyed the ridiculousness of the situation. That shared sense of humor meant more to him than he'd ever realized.

There was only one problem: Prinny.

The man had already said that Lady Zoe should be Ras's bride. There was no way he could convince the prince that Kynthea was a better choice.

"Miss Petrelli, I meant no insult. The question was an honest one, but not in the way you think."

She looked at her hands. Her fingers twisted in her lap, and he longed to soothe them. She was distressed and he hated that his bungling had created this tension between them.

"It is beneath you to toy with me like this," she said. "I am not a lightskirt."

"I do not see you as one. I never have."

She looked away, her gaze following the flow of houses along the street. "I did not come straight to Zoe's home once my parents passed," she said. "My brother was at sea, my parents were dead, and I had no money to pay off our creditors."

"I am sorry," he said.

She flicked her fingers at him as if his compassion meant nothing. "The vicar came to give me solace. I would have welcomed prayers. Instead, he tried…" Her words cut off as she took a deep breath. "I gave him a black eye. He damned me to everyone in the parish. He said that I was a wicked girl and God had taken my parents as punishment."

"Bastard." He spat the word out. "What is his name?"

She shook her head. "It doesn't matter."

It bloody well did. He would find out who it was and see him excommunicated and deported. And that was the kindest of possibilities. He might do something much, much worse.

"Not every man preys upon the weak," he said.

"The man in the mail coach did, as did a footman in my uncle's home."

"Bloody hell."

She lifted her chin to match him eye to eye. "My brother taught me how to defend myself. The man in the coach squealed like a stuck pig, and that footman is long gone."

"I am very pleased to hear that."

"I will fight you too, Your Grace. You are every girl's dream come true, and yet…" She swallowed and blinked away the sheen in her eyes. "It is so very cruel, Your Grace, to play games like this."

"I am not playing a game with you!" He spoke forcefully, shocked that she didn't understand he was in earnest. "At least not with you. Not like you think."

She dropped her gaze as she looked at her hands.

"I cannot marry you. The Crown must approve my bride, and Prinny wants Lady Zoe." Bitterness laced his tone. "But I don't have to marry you to make you fashionable."

She shook her head. "My place in society is doomed. And you need to leave Zoe alone if you will not have her."

He shook his head. "Nothing is set in stone. Certainly not in the *haut ton.* I can at least get you a Season. One where you might meet a man to marry." He risked touching her hands, startled by how cold they felt. "What other choice do you have?"

She released a laugh that held no humor in it. She had no faith in him. Indeed, he doubted she believed in any man's honor. "There are ways for a woman to survive."

"Many ways, but without a sterling reputation, where would you work?" He didn't have to enumerate them for her. She might find work as a laundress or a maid, but she'd never become a teacher or governess. Even a position as a lady's companion was doubtful. "You'd be miserable."

"And what would I get as your pretend infatuation?"

He winced at her wording. There was nothing imagined about his infatuation with her. "Time," he answered. "Time to redeem your reputation. Time to meet other men—"

"Time for you to seduce and discard me when your attention wanders. Or when you meet the lady whom you will wed."

He didn't think his attention would ever wander from her, but such was the illusion that came with infatuation. Instead, he addressed the latter issue.

"I will not wed this season. No one interests me." No one but her.

She looked at him, and in the darkness, it was hard to read her expression. Did he see hope there? Wariness? Then she sighed as she dropped back against the squabs. "It doesn't matter. I will be sacked in the morning."

The devil she would. "I will speak to your aunt and uncle."

"Again? You barely convinced them last time. They want you marrying Zoe, not courting me. Even if it is a ruse."

He ground his teeth. Damn it, why was this so complicated? "I will not marry Zoe." He sighed. "But I can introduce her to my friends. I can—"

"You will matchmake for me *and* her? You? A duke who hates the social rounds."

She was right. Nate would be a much better person for this. Nate knew everyone, including people on the fringes of high society. Surely there would be good men who were not in the social whirl. A wholesome husband who could give her the life she deserved.

"How can I convince you that I am in earnest?" In truth, he didn't need to convince her. He just needed to do it. But then her next words shot terror into his heart.

"I will find lodging near the docks. My brother is due to return in the next few months. I need only survive until he—"

"Months!" he gasped. Did she know what happened to women near the docks? "You cannot think that is safe."

"What choice do I have?" she whispered.

Me! he wanted to scream. He was her choice. But obviously she did not believe it.

It was panic that made him do it. Sheer terror at the idea of her disappearing somewhere near the docks, never to be seen again. He couldn't stomach the idea of what could happen to her there. Nor did he want her to just disappear from his life as if she had never been.

He couldn't allow that, so he reached for the one thing he knew would convince her of his determination. If he'd had time to think about it, he never would have done it. But emotions ruled him now.

He took off the ruby that held his cravat in place. It wasn't just a stone. The gold around it was fashioned in the shape of his family crest—a red swan symbolizing valor and purity. The gold alone was worth more than she'd probably ever had. Add in the ruby, and she could be set for years.

But that wasn't the real value of the jewelry. Any soul who saw it would know that it was his. It wasn't a promise as clear as a ring, but it was undeniably his. And it was a promise of a sort.

He prayed that it was enough. He pressed the heavy jewelry into her hand.

"What are you doing?" she gasped. "I can't take that!"

"You can and you will," he said, though the enormity of this action left him quaking.

"Your Grace! I cannot."

He wrapped her fingers around it and squeezed. "With my crest, I pledge that my actions are honorable. I will see that you are taken care of."

"You can't!" she squeaked.

"And yet I do."

Then he banged on the top of the carriage. He knew where they were. She could return safely to her home from here. The horses stopped and he quickly pulled the cloak over her head. She was still shocked by his action. Truth be told, he was as well. But he gave neither of them time for second thoughts.

The footman pulled open the door and he tugged her out of her seat. She had no choice but to get out. She pushed her hand forward, trying to drop the ring in his lap, but he encircled her hand with his fist. She would not drop it.

"That is my life and my honor you carry," he whispered. "Pray do not lose it."

"Your Grace—"

"Call me Ras," he said. He gestured to the footman who had a hand on her elbow. "See that she gets back safely." Then he shut the door on her shocked face.

Chapter Thirteen

KYNTHEA STARED AT the heavy jewelry in her hand. She was sitting upright on her bed after not sleeping the entire night through. What was he thinking, giving her this? Did he know what she could do with it? She could make any wild claims she wanted about him and use this as proof. Not everyone would believe her, but many would. Assuming she wasn't clapped in irons as a thief.

A single knock sounded on her door before it swung open. It was Zoe, of course, looking none the worse for wear after a night's dancing. Her cheeks were rosy, her eyes bright, and she had all the energy of a sixteen-year-old girl who was an early riser.

Kynthea closed her fingers quickly, then slipped the ruby into the folds of her gown. She smiled at her young companion and attempted to order her thoughts.

"Good morning, Zoe. You are looking very good. Did you enjoy last night?"

"I'm so glad you're dressed," Zoe said as she dropped unceremoniously onto Kynthea's bed. "And I had a wonderful time last night."

"Tell me about every moment," she said. "Were there any gentlemen who stood out? What caught your attention the most?"

Instead of bubbling over with delight, Zoe's expression turned sober. She adjusted herself to a demure position and regarded Kynthea with sober eyes. "You know what stood out."

Oh dear. "I didn't mean to trip."

"I know you didn't!" Zoe huffed. "But it doesn't matter. The biddies are saying you did it on purpose and Mother is beside herself. That's bad enough, but Papa's angry, too, and that's not good for him. He's still in bed and does not think he will be able to rise at all this day."

That had more to do with him exerting himself too much last night, but that didn't matter. Kynthea's spectacle had been a stress and society's reaction to it would weigh on both Zoe's parents.

"I tried to be circumspect," Kynthea said. "I sat with the chaperones for the rest of the set. I managed the servants during the supper buffet, then left the ballroom altogether. Last night was your night. I never meant to draw attention to myself."

Zoe looked around the room, her misery palpable. "I know you didn't," she said. "As if you could force the duke's spat to come undone. What they're saying is ridiculous, but that doesn't stop the gossip. And Papa hates gossip."

Kynthea touched Zoe's hands. The girl had a pure heart. She was clearly miserable that Kynthea was yet again the center of ugly gossip. So she took a page from the duke's book and offered up her sincerest apology.

"What can I do? How can I make this better?"

"I don't know that you can," the girl sighed. "Mama is beside herself."

Kynthea looked down at her pale yellow gown. It didn't suit her coloring, but had been given to her by Zoe's mother. Kynthea wore it when she wanted to please the lady, but it wouldn't do to be this bright in the drawing room. "I'll change into my gray gown and—"

"Don't go down."

"What?"

"Mama thinks it would be best if you stayed out of sight today."

Kynthea watched as Zoe looked everywhere but at her.

"If I am not in the drawing room for visitors, people will assume your mother blames me."

Zoe bit her lip. "I know."

"They'll get louder as they denounce me. Everyone will say I'm… I'm…"

"They already are," Zoe said. Then she stuck her hand into the pocket of her gown and pulled out a folded sheet of newspaper. It had been ripped out of the main paper, and she handed it over with a heavy sigh. "I tore this out of Papa's paper. I didn't want him to read it, but I couldn't stop Mama."

It was Mr. Pickleherring's column. He'd devoted himself lately to exposing gentlemen who were hiding a stark reversal in fortune. He'd also had a few dry comments about an audience that paid to attend the theater only to talk over the actors. Today's column followed the same pattern except for the last paragraph.

> *Miss Petrelli once again showed her desperation as she faked a stumble on the dance floor. The duke was gallant enough to pretend he was at fault, but since she'd bared herself for all to see, his gallantry fools no one. How long will the Earl of Satheath allow this Jezebel to poison his daughter? She should be hung for what she has done to poor Lady Zoe.*

Kynthea's hands shook as she read the words, which was an odd thing because she couldn't feel the tremble. She stared at the words wondering how this had happened. She was well and truly ruined now. Good God, she should be hung? For stepping on a duke's broken spat?

"I didn't," she murmured. "I wouldn't."

Zoe pulled the page out of her hand, crumpled it, and threw it into the grate. "I despise that Pickleherring."

"I should be hung for what I've done to you?" Kynthea echoed. Had she truly harmed the girl? And why did the *ton* need a villain anyway? Didn't they have enough to gossip about without picking on her?

"It's ridiculous," the girl said. "They think you've taught me lustful things, destroying my chances for a decent marriage."

"No," Kynthea whispered.

"If anything, I explained it to you. Remember how shocked I was that you'd never seen horses mate?"

Kynthea choked back a sob. What was she going to do? And what if it was true? Had she truly made things worse for Zoe? The girl wasn't truly tarnished by association. Right?

She wasn't being completely virtuous in her thoughts. If her aunt and uncle threw her out, her only hope was that Zoe married well and brought her along as nanny or companion or something.

"I admit that the situation is dire," Zoe said as she patted Kynthea's hands.

Dire? It was catastrophic. "How angry is your mother?" she whispered. The woman had only ever accepted Kynthea out of duty to her husband's family. Though she was kind enough, their bond had never been one of love. Her gaze went to Zoe. "She's going to sack me, isn't she?" she asked, doing her best to appear strong before her cousin. "I knew it last night."

Zoe jaw firmed. "Not yet, she isn't."

"What? Why not?"

"Because I put laudanum in her tea."

"What?"

The girl waved away Kynthea's shock. "Her joints are paining her after last night. She was going to take a little anyway, but I put in extra. Given how upset she was by that column, I was helping to settle her nerves."

"You lied to your mother," Kynthea said. "And dosed her!" She moaned. "I have been a terrible influence on you."

Zoe snorted. "As if this was the first time. I knew the uses of laudanum by the time I was eight."

That was not a comforting thought.

Meanwhile, the girl gripped Kynthea's hands. "Now listen. I have a plan."

It had better be one that got her a position well outside of society. Perhaps with an elderly woman who never left Yorkshire. Though the idea of moldering away in Yorkshire horrified her, it was better than being hung for whatever mysterious thing she'd done to Zoe.

The duke's ruby lay heavy in her pocket, but even so, she couldn't believe he'd keep so enormous a promise. And yet, she couldn't discard the possibility out of hand.

"Did the duke stop by?" She hadn't heard the knocker, and it was still early. Likely he wouldn't visit until later.

"He sent around a missive early."

"A missive?"

Zoe nodded, excitement sparking in her eyes. "An invitation! He's taking us to see Whirl tomorrow. I want to have a word with his stable master. He doesn't take care of the older mares. All his attention is on the promising fillies."

Kynthea felt her heart sink. He wasn't coming today. And she'd likely be tossed out by the time he arrived tomorrow.

"Don't you see?" Zoe pressed. "That's why Mama took to her bed. She doesn't know what to do."

"What?"

Zoe rolled her eyes. "The invitation was for both of us. He said that quite specifically. Me, with you as chaperone. That's what Mama was so upset about. She can't dismiss you if the duke doesn't want it. But with Mr. Pickleherring's column, everyone is telling her she must. She doesn't know what to do."

Neither did Kynthea.

"But don't worry," Zoe rushed to add. "I've got a plan."

Kynthea sighed. It was Zoe's love potion plan that had started this whole mess to begin with.

"You're coming with me tomorrow," Zoe said firmly, "and Mama and Papa are staying here because I told them they have to stay. I have a plan and they'd mess it up."

"Your mother won't do that."

"She will because I told her that together, you and I will bring him up to scratch."

Kynthea felt her heart sink. "Zoe, we can't—"

"Psst!" She cut off Kynthea's words with a hard slash of her hand. "I won't hear a word of disagreement. He'll propose and I'll insist that you stay as my companion. I'll even make you my maid of honor at the wedding!"

So many things were wrong with that statement, but her cousin clearly needed to believe it. "Zoe, the duke isn't going to propose. He thinks you're too young."

"Yes, he is because Prinny said so! Besides, no one else has my pedigree, beauty, or dowry."

"Prinny can't command—"

"Yes, he can! Mama heard it from the dowager duchess. And since Papa has already drafted my marriage contract, it's all but done."

Zoe was adamant, and Kynthea had enough experience with the girl to know she wasn't going to see reason. Still, she had to try. "It is not settled," she said as gently as possible. "Your father drafted the marriage contract before the season began. And there's been no direct negotiation with the duke."

Zoe shrugged. "We don't know that! Papa's been closeted with so many stuffy men. And the duke spoke to him for nearly an hour after the first Mr. Pickleherring article."

Damn that blasted writer.

"Anyway, it doesn't matter. When the regent says he approves of a match, it's as good as done." She folded her arms in front of her as if that was the final word on the subject. "I was willing to wait until the end of the season, you know. The Season isn't as much fun if you're spoken for in the first week. But catching a duke this fast is quite a coup. In fact, it's the match of the Season!"

"It is," Kynthea said weakly. It would be, if the duke were going to do it. "But Zoe—"

"No more buts." There was noise in the hallway as someone walked past. It could be any one of their many servants, but Zoe took it as a sign that her mother was rising.

"We're running out of time," she said hurriedly. "I need you to go to My Lady's Apothecary for me. Go now and stay away all day."

"What?"

"Mama can't fire you if she can't find you."

"I'll have to come back tonight." Not to mention what everyone would say if they knew she'd been out all day.

"I'm sending you on errands!" Zoe repeated forcefully. Then she pressed a purse and a list of purchases into Kynthea's hands. "Go buy things for me. Have the shopkeepers send them back to us throughout the day. I'll tell the servants that I want to hear when every package arrives. That way everyone will know that you are doing something wholesome."

Or it would keep her in the front of everyone's mind and on the tip of their tongues.

"Tell the messengers to relay how busy all the shops are and that you'll be gone a terribly long time."

"Zoe—"

"Don't worry. This will work. At the apothecary, you'll purchase the things I need to make more liniment for Whirl. I'll even tell anyone who asks that you'll be mixing the ingredients yourself. That's why you have to stay there forever."

Kynthea frowned. "You want me to mix it myself?"

"Don't be silly. I'll do it tonight. No one else gets the texture right."

"But—"

"And you'll need to get more love potion. I used all that I had on the duke yesterday."

Kynthea winced. "You didn't throw it in his face, did you?"

"I thought of something more clever! I put it in his finger bowl at dinner." Her expression fell. "But it wasn't strong enough. You have to tell Madame Ilie that." She blew out a breath. "I think he'll have to drink it."

"Zoe, this love potion nonsense has gone far enough. You

must know—"

"You aren't listening! I will not lose you, and this is the only way I know of to make everyone happy. The Crown has decided that I shall wed the duke. He will propose tomorrow because I can't keep Mama dosed forever. I can keep her from sacking you for a day, maybe two, but no longer. Not unless I'm going to be a duchess. The minute I'm engaged, I'll declare what I want. And I want you!"

Kynthea's heart warmed at Zoe's words. The girl was near tears as she dictated how things would go, even though she had little control over any of it. Certainly, she had no influence over the duke which was probably why she'd set her hopes in a love potion.

"And if none of it goes as you want?" she asked.

"It will!" She squeezed Kynthea's fingers. "You will help me. You'll see."

What could she do but embrace her young cousin? In Kynthea's experience, nothing ever went how it was meant to. At least not the way young girls thought it should. And yet, Zoe's desperation was real. Everything was changing for the poor girl. Her parents were ailing, she was being forced too young to marry, and now her friend and cousin was about to be ignominiously thrown away. As desperate as Kynthea felt about her own future, she still had compassion for the girl who clearly felt like her world was ending.

"I will do everything I can for you," Kynthea said.

"No, no!" Zoe said. "It's my turn to protect you. Now go. Go out the back and stay away all day!"

Chapter Fourteen

Ras pushed past the startled butler of Nate's gentlemen's home. The building housed four men of good rank but reduced funds. This allowed the men to share servants, but it did little to ensure excellent service, as evidenced by a butler who did nothing to challenge Ras as he stormed up to Nate's bedroom on the top floor.

He banged once on the door then pushed through to his former friend's sitting room. It was cluttered with books and papers of all kinds. Nate loved his scribblings and up until this day, Ras had supported the man's interests though it ran to literature rather than politics.

"Nate!" he bellowed. "Wake up!" He slammed the damned newspaper against the wall to vent his fury. Then he stomped into the bedroom intending to beat some sense into the man.

He should have noticed the scent earlier, but his blood was up, and he was moving fast. The room was too dark to see much of anything, and he fouled his footing on a stack of books. Cursing, he fumbled his way to the curtain and hauled the things open. At least it was a bright day so light flooded the room. He wasn't surprised by the groan coming from the bed. He was fully aware how light could pain a man with a sore head. But Nate deserved that and more, so he didn't moderate his voice as he bellowed again.

"Wake up, so I can curse you—"

He cut off his words with a choke of horror. Nate's bedsheets were stained with blood. Worse, the dark mass in the middle wasn't spoiled linens, but his friend with a swollen face and still seeping wounds. The man was in the clothing he'd worn last night, though now it was ripped from a thorough thrashing. No knife cuts that he could see, but his friend's feet—

Hell. The man's feet were cut nearly to shreds, looking as if he'd walked the whole of London without his shoes.

Then he noticed the smell. Old blood in a musty room. Not putrid, thank heaven, or sick, but the scent was not pleasant. And underneath it all, the fishy scent of the docks. What the hell had the man been doing?

"My God, Nate, what happened?"

He rushed to the bedside and saw that Nate had one eye open. "Ras? What are—ow."

Not dead then, nor insensate. That was something. No gushing wounds. Nothing large enough to indicate a stabbing. Footpads, most likely. Ones who liked a good pair of boots.

"Damn it, man," he muttered. "Why didn't you just give them what they wanted? No need to fight."

"You give 'em what they want," Nate grumbled. "I keep what's mine."

"You try to keep it," Ras said as he gently ran his hands down his friend's arms and legs. Though the man winced several times, there was no cry of pain from broken bones. "How bad are the ribs?"

"Leave me alone."

"The hell I will. Damn it, I came here to beat some sense in you. Leave it to you to get it done beforehand." Ras straightened up. "Stay here. I'll send for a doctor."

"No."

"If it's a matter of payment, I'll take care—"

"No!" Nate's breath wheezed into a whimper. When he spoke next, his words were slow and careful. "No doctor. He'll bleed me and charge you for the pleasure. I've lost enough blood." He waved absently at the window. "Close that and leave me to die."

He knew Nate was joking, but the possibility of death was all too real. Even without broken bones, the risk of infection was severe. And here? In a cluttered room with no manservant? This was not acceptable.

"What's the name of the butler here?"

"What?"

"Your butler's name. What is it?"

"Hopfer. Good man if you pay him extra."

That didn't sound like a good man to Ras, but then he had the luxury of retainers who had served the dukedom for generations. They often took his ducal status more seriously than he did and would never extort him for more money. Of course, it helped that he paid them well.

He walked swiftly to the top of the stairs. "Hopfer! I need clean water and linens. And you will send a footman to my home. I have a message for my housekeeper."

Mr. Hopfer peered up the stairs, his expression none too pleased. "And why—"

"I am the Duke of Harle, and I do not like being questioned." He rarely needed to throw his title in someone's face, but sometimes it expedited things.

He went back into Nate's sitting room and scrawled out a message for his staff. Nate would not lie here on bloodied sheets while he recuperated. Ras had few true friends among the sycophants and leeches who always surrounded a duke. He would not lose one now, no matter what Nate had written in his blasted gossip column.

He intended to wait until his friend was healthy and then thrash Mr. Pickleherring. Verbally.

Once his letter was done, he went into Nate's room. He quickly spotted clean clothes and the man's last pair of shoes. He packed what was needed in a satchel. Nate had fallen back into an uneasy sleep. Ras hated to disturb him, but it was necessary. Especially as a footman arrived with a basin of water.

"Wot happened to 'im?" the footman asked.

Ras raised a brow. He was not used to servants who asked cheeky questions. It was not the footman's business what had occurred, but again, that was a ducal privilege. Servants pried if they were allowed, and apparently Mr. Hopfer had a lax hand with his staff.

"Footpads," he snapped. "Tell my coachman I require Tillman's assistance." His coachman would have to stay with the horses, but Tillman, a groom, was young and strong. Together, they could get Nate into the carriage.

"You don't need anyone else. I can 'elp," the footman said. And indeed, the man was larger than Tillman, but his curiosity was palpable. His gaze kept running around the room, landing on papers and whatever it was Nate had strewn about. That was the attitude of a man looking to pinch something.

"You will help by showing Tillman up here. I will let you know if I require more."

The man sniffed as if he'd been insulted, but he did as he was bid. Meanwhile, Ras went to Nate's side and began to wipe away the worst of the damage.

"Stop," his friend moaned.

Ras ignored him. Normally, he'd strip Nate out of his clothing first, but that might as well wait until they got to his home. He was just mitigating the damage until he could get Nate transported.

"Where is your lock box? Your important papers?"

"What?"

"I'm taking you to my home, and I don't trust your butler as far as I can throw him. Tell me what you need to have with you because, by God, you are not staying here."

Nate blinked open one eye. "I don't need—"

"The hell you don't."

"I'll not be another Broderick."

Ras growled in frustration and fear. Nate had long since proven he wasn't a leeching sycophant. "You're a bloody idiot!" he fumed, startled when he realized his curse was literally true.

"Now let me make sure you don't die. If you must pay me back, you can scrub my floors afterwards."

"You scrub your floors," his friends muttered. "I need a nap."

He needed a doctor, clean sheets, and good food. And someone who took care of matters rather than argue with Nate's pride. So Ras didn't say more. He just took charge.

Looking down at Nate's feet, he decided that there wasn't a prayer in hell that Nate could get shoes on. Which meant he'd have to hobble barefoot down to the carriage. Or be carried, which would not go over well. But at least he could have on thick socks so that there wouldn't be any more damage.

He was just looking about the room when Tillman showed up. "Your Grace?" he said as he bowed.

"Find a pair of socks and put them on him. We're carrying him to the carriage."

The man didn't so much as blink. He nodded then began the search. The same could not be said of Nate who moaned as he pushed himself up onto his elbows.

"Have done, Ras. You're a good friend. A stand-up duke and all that, but I'm too tired to fight you. I'll be fine."

"Of course, you will be." Because he'd be at Ras's residence.

The water in the basin was now dark red, and the cloth would never be clean again. He carried the things out into the hall where Hopfer stood watching with undisguised curiosity.

"Excellent," he said as he shoved the basin at the man. Hopfer had to take it or let it drop on his feet. "Be aware that I will send my secretary and housekeeper to clean these rooms." His secretary would sort through whatever papers Nate had lying about and collect what was important. His housekeeper would see everything cleaned properly, and then the two would put a new lock on the door. If nothing else, it would keep what was left from being ransacked.

Predictably, Hopfer cut up stiff. "This house has no thieves. I run a proper household, but I cannot account for how the gentlemen spend their time."

Ras didn't bother answering. He'd known Nate since they were young boys at Eton. The man was casual about his papers, but he was neater than this. Or he had been when they were at school. Ras was startled to realize that he had no idea how Nate usually lived now because they'd always met elsewhere. This was the first time he'd been in the man's rooms since school.

Ignoring that unsettling realization, Ras sat down on the edge of the bed and regarded his friend. Though Nate was sitting upright, he looked pale and sweaty, which was not a good sign.

"Do you need a bucket?"

"No." The word came out as a bare whisper.

"I'm going to help you up. Tillman will be on the other side. Then the three of us are going downstairs to the carriage."

"God, Ras. Leave me alone." There should have been a bite to the words, but Nate was in too much pain to put force into his voice.

"I'm sorry," he said gently. "I can't."

Nate let his head drop. "Just leave me alone." There was a plaintive note in his voice, so different than his usual irrepressible humor. It suggested more than physical pain. There was despair.

Ras squatted down until he was eye to swollen eye with his friend. "What. Happened?"

The man wasn't going to answer. He set his jaw and looked away, but Ras wasn't going to let him hide so easily. He gestured Tillman to take Nate's things down to the carriage and he glared at Hopfer until the nosy butler shut the door. That left Ras and miserable Nate in the room.

"Tell me," Ras ordered.

Nate sighed. "Becky's here."

Becky? As in Lady Rebecca, the heiress? Nate's first kiss and the woman he'd pined for ever since?

"She can't be husband hunting. I haven't seen her, and I've been everywhere."

"She's hunting. Her father has decreed it."

Well, it was time. The girl was old enough to be on the shelf.

In fact, if she weren't so rich, people would have given her the label a long time ago. "Well, I'm sorry for that, Nate, but what has that got to do with—"

"I was gambling." The man straightened up as best he could. "I was *winning*. I thought if I had enough blunt, I could approach her father."

Oh hell. "Her father won't see you."

"He might. If I were rich enough."

"You could be a nabob, and it wouldn't be enough."

Nate shot him an angry glare. "My blood is just as blue as hers."

True, but he was a third son. And whereas that might be overcome, Nate had a much bigger problem. "Your grandfather swindled her grandfather."

"I know," Nate said with a sigh.

"And your father wasn't exactly honest with her father."

"I know."

"And Lady Rebecca thinks you are a fortune hunting scoundrel." She'd said it straight to Nate's face last Season.

"I know!"

Right. So he'd tried to win enough money to prove that he wasn't courting her for her dowry. "How much did you win?"

"Plenty."

"And it was stolen from you last night?"

Nate's head dropped in a miserable nod. "Every single penny," he moaned. "Gone."

Then, before Ras could ask more, Tillman tapped a discrete knock on the door.

"Right then," Ras said with a sigh. "Come on. Let's get you to my house."

It was hard work getting Nate into the carriage. The man had cracked ribs for sure, but it was his feet that were the biggest problem. Every step had him cringing in pain. They got him into the carriage and laid him down on the squabs. But even the best sprung carriage bounced when travelling through London. It would be a rough passage to the ducal home.

Ras was just about to climb into the carriage beside his friend when he noticed someone watching him intently. It was a man he recognized, leaning against the building. He wore his usual smirk, but this one was especially dark. And, he noted, the butler Hopfer was standing cozily close.

Ras straightened, closing the carriage door as he crossed to the now grinning man.

"Fletcher," Ras said slowly. "Fancy seeing you here."

"Is he dying?"

"What?"

Lord Fletcher, the arrogant, awful brother to Lady Rebecca, jerked his chin at the carriage. "Is he finally dying?"

"And what do you know about it?"

"Nothing. Just saw you carrying him out like a sack of meal." Fletcher snorted. "Seems you haven't learned the truth about him yet. Still falling for every 'poor me' lie from the bastard."

Ras stiffened, his thoughts whirling as he watched the butler greedily listening to every word. "Actually, Fletch, you're the only one I've ever caught in a lie—"

"He lies with every breath by not telling the whole truth! Printing shit about lecherous barons and spendthrift suitors. What about embezzlement? Murder? Does he ever print that?"

Ras shook his head. This was old ground between Nate's family and Fletcher's. He was not going to debate who stole what from whom and who died as a result. Especially since the so-called murder was a heart attack. "What do you mean he was printing things?"

Fletcher pushed off the wall, his disdain clear. "God, you don't know anything about your so-called friend, do you? When will you wake up? You're the only friend he has left, the only one keeping him from drowning like that rat he is." Then his expression turned gleeful. "But even you can't save him now, can you?"

"It is amazing to me that you and your sister could come

from the same family." Damn it, he wanted to punch the idiot in the face, but he needed information, not the satisfaction of beating Fletcher bloody. "Did you do that to him? Did you hire—"

"I did nothing but watch. Did you ask him what he was doing by the docks? Nothing good, that's for sure."

Fury burned in his gut. "You *watched?* And you didn't do a damned thing to stop it?" Or help Nate get home afterwards? "You bloody arse—"

"Just deserts, if you ask me. I wasn't going to stop it. Why would I risk my life for his?"

Rather than give into violence, Ras turned to Hopfer. "You and he together changed the columns, didn't you? Why? What did Miss Petrelli ever do to deserve that?"

Hopfer looked uncomfortable, but it was Fletcher who answered. "I did it," he said, pride in his tone. "The truth needs to get out and everyone knew the truth about her. Even you!"

"But why—"

"So you'd finally open your eyes! Damn it, don't you see how blind he's made you? You don't see his faults, you can't see hers. Wake up! Throw him aside. Leave him to die and let this damn feud end!"

There was too much to understand here, too much that was too crazy. And he needed to get Nate to a doctor. So rather than fight with Fletcher, he turned back to the carriage, but Fletcher jumped forward and grabbed his arm.

"Damn it, Ras, we were friends once!"

Distantly.

"You, me, my sister. We should all be together. This feud has poisoned everyone, and he's the cause of it!"

"Nate wasn't even born when your feud began. Neither were you! God, Fletch, have you gone mad?"

"No!" he said, jerking Ras's arm away from the carriage. "You have to see the truth! He's the problem!"

Never had he seen madness so clearly in a man's eyes. Madness coupled with the absolute certainty that only he saw the truth. It was frightening. And it was also not something he was going to indulge.

"Nothing you've said makes sense. Nate is not a villain," he said, firmly prying Fletcher's fingers off his arm. Then Fletch abruptly jerked his hand back.

"Blind. You're all so damned blind!" he screamed. Then he took a breath and moderated his tone. "Do you know what he does?" he pressed, jerking his hand at the carriage. "I've been watching him. It's nothing like you think."

And that was the first thing that rang true in everything Fletcher had said. He knew Nate did some strange things. He'd known it for a long time. But he had absolute faith in his friend. Whatever it was that Nate did, it wasn't nefarious.

"He lies," Fletcher said. "And like a blind fool, you believe him."

Ras didn't have an answer to that. Up until this moment, he would have said that Nate had never, ever lied to him. Except hadn't Nate said he'd been gambling? And yet Fletcher had claimed he'd been beaten up at the docks. If it weren't the fish smell he'd scented in Nate's room, he'd be inclined to dismiss it. But he had smelled it. He had wondered about it.

Which gave him enough pause to stop arguing.

"Get some rest, Fletcher. And some healthy food. You look awful."

The man wasn't completely stupid. His expression brightened. "You're waking up now, aren't you? You see it?"

Ras wanted to punch the idiot. Instead, he glared at the man. "Say one word against Miss Petrelli again, and I will put a bullet through your brain." He made sure there was no wavering in his tone.

"I don't care about her. I was trying to get you to see the truth about him!"

The illogic of that was clear. Worse, Fletcher didn't stop with that. There were more words, more angry curses, and a host of chaotic paranoid babble. But Ras didn't stay to listen to them. He swung himself into the carriage and banged the roof as soon as the door shut. A moment later, the carriage was moving.

He'd been right about the difficult, jostling ride. Nate moaned during the worst ruts. Ras hoped the man would lose consciousness, but halfway to the house, he spoke.

"How did you know?" Nate asked.

Ras jerked his gaze to Nate's one open eye. "What?"

"How did you know to come find me?"

"I didn't know. I wanted to discuss something else with you."

Nate groaned as the carriage jolted again. He closed his eyes and gritted his teeth, but a moment later, he spoke again.

"Well come on. What did you want?"

Ras shook his head, though Nate couldn't see it. He was not one to kick a man when he was down. "We'll discuss it later."

"Now. You came to my rooms. Never done that before."

"I didn't want to wait until our usual time at the club."

Silence reigned in the carriage for a bit. Nate's eyes were still closed, and his face was slick with sweat. A few minutes later, Nate kicked out with his foot, connecting hard with Ras' knee. It had been a common thing when they were children. They were boys kicking each other for one ridiculous reason or another. But this time, Nate had clearly forgotten that his feet were hurt.

"Ow! Bloody hell," he groaned.

"Why would you do that?" Ras demanded. His knee wasn't hurt, but he was sure the move made Nate's pain worse.

"Out with it!"

"I'm not—"

"I cannot abide a tease," Nate rasped. "What was so bloody important?"

No way to dissuade him now. Nate could be like a dog with a bone when his curiosity was piqued. "It was about your column."

"Mr. Pickleherring? Whatever did he say to upset you?"

Ras held onto his temper. "What exactly did you write about Miss Petrelli?"

The man groaned. "Everyone was talking about your dance. I

had to mention it."

"Did you call her a Jezebel who needs to be hung?" His voice was hard with fury.

"I did not!" Nate's head came off the squabs. His torso, too, as he gripped the handhold and pulled himself upright. It must have hurt dreadfully, but he was determined. "I said she was a good sport to forgive your valet for dressing you in a shoddy spat. I praised her."

Ras set his hand gently on his friend's shoulder, pushing him down. "Fletcher changed it. With the help, I think, of your butler."

"The devil you say." Nate held out his hand for the column, but another bump in the road had his arm flying wide. "Read it to me," he ordered. "Every damned word."

Ras obliged, though his voice shook when he came to the offending paragraph. The whole thing was not Miss Petrelli's fault, but thanks to this damned column, she would be drummed out of society for good. And that was something he could not allow.

He finished reading, his tone cold and hard.

Nate's voice was equally furious. "I did not write that."

"I know. Fletcher changed it." He leaned forward. "What has happened between you? He seems intent on destroying you." Ras frowned. That wasn't right. All he'd need to destroy Fletcher would be to expose him as Mr. Pickleherring. Instead, he was trying to poison the friendship between Ras and Nate. And perhaps take over the column.

"I don't know," Nate said, his voice quiet. "Nothing but that old feud between our families."

"And your affection for his sister."

Nate grimaced. "One and the same."

It wasn't one and the same. Especially since it was now affecting Miss Petrelli.

"Where were you last night? And before you answer, Fletcher said he watched your attackers try to kill you. At the docks."

Nate was quiet long enough for Ras to think he might have finally passed out. But in the end, he spoke. "Fletch is a bloody liar."

Yes, that was certainly true. But that didn't answer the question as to what exactly Nate had been doing last night.

"He's not the only one," Ras said. And when Nate's eyes opened, he met them with a hard stare of his own.

In the end, Nate sighed as he closed his eyes. "I can't tell you. I want to, but I can't."

And that was the end of it as they finally arrived at the ducal home—the end of that conversation, but not the end of the discussion. Because Ras would have the truth if he had to throttle his best friend to get it.

But first, the man had to be healthy enough to put up a good fight.

Chapter Fifteen

THE SUMMONS CAME in the early morning, well before most of the house was awake. But Zoe was an early riser as was her father, and so his valet passed the message to her maid who brought her chocolate in the morning.

Would Lady Zoe please visit her father as soon as she was dressed?

Zoe didn't need the message. She'd heard her father's hacking cough throughout the night. Their bedrooms were separated by a thin wall, and so she had started awake every time he'd wheezed.

"Good morning, Papa," she said as she breezed into his bedroom. It was as lovely a morning as could come in London, so she threw open the curtains to let the light in. Then she steeled herself to look at the figure on the bed while she forced her smile to its absolute brightest.

There was her father, looking as small and frail as it was possible to appear and yet still be alive. His chest was sunken, his thin whiskers poked through gray skin, but his eyes were bright. Or so it seemed through the sheen of her tears.

She was the youngest of his children, born when he was well past fifty. Everyone had thought Mama past childbearing age, and yet out Zoe came, a tiny, bawling girl too fierce to die. That was what her father had said. She'd been too fierce to pass on for all that she was small enough to fit in his one hand.

Her brothers were already at school and her mother remained frail after the birth. Zoe grew strong, thanks to a wetnurse, a loving governess, and her father's attention at the stable. He adored a morning ride, so she did, too. He loved horse racing, so she did, too. And because their stable was modest, she could learn the running of it when she was barely old enough to read.

Her father had never been one to study the science of horse breeding, but he praised her when she did. He also had never learned the details of doctoring the creatures, but he listened attentively when she explained it. He indulged her when she begged to learn about poultices from the local witch woman. He overruled her mother when it was thought that no girl should go to the horse market. And when he grew sick three winters ago, she'd sat by his bed and read him the racing news. They discussed it as passionately as Mama spoke about fashion.

At the time, she'd thought it merely a winter illness, and perhaps it was. But he'd had several of those sicknesses over the last three years, each attacking his lungs, each leaving him weaker than before. His hands shook now. He sat up to sleep to ease his breathing. And the smell that filled his bedroom grew a little worse every day.

It was why Mama slept in a bedroom down the hall.

"You're looking well this morning, Papa," she lied. "Do you come dancing with me tonight?"

Her father snorted, or he tried to. It ended as usual in a cough that left blood on his handkerchief. He folded it away so she wouldn't see it, but she knew it was there nonetheless. Even more so because when he collapsed backwards against the bed, his gaze was sad and a little afraid.

Strange to think that two days ago, they had opened up her ball together. She didn't know if he'd seen the tears in her eyes then. If so, he'd probably thought it was because she was finally out in society. The truth was, she knew it was likely the last time they would dance together. The last time she would feel her hand in his and his arm about her waist.

He had taken to his bed that night and not risen since. But

maybe he would rally again as he had all those other times. Maybe the potion for lung strength ordered from My Lady's Apothecary would help him soon. And maybe he wouldn't live through another winter.

He tapped the side of the bed, and she didn't want to see the spots on his hands or the thin, knobby shape of his knuckles. His riding gloves would be loose now.

She smiled even more brightly and settled on the side of his bed. She was careful not to jostle him, but a little movement was inevitable.

"Do you want more tea?" she asked as she reached for his teacup. It would be cold now, but maybe—

He shook his head. It took him a moment to pull in a breath, and when he spoke, it was with a semblance of his former strength. "Will the duke propose?"

She winced. "I don't know. I'm trying."

"Is there anyone else?"

She and Mama had gone over the list of eligible bachelors several times. "A few."

"Do you want them?"

No. None had decent stables. None could talk horses at a credible level, though the duke failed in that as well.

"You marry the man," he said. "Not their horses."

Clearly, he knew her very well. She shrugged. "Maybe not this Season—"

He gripped her hand. His was cold and skeletal, but she cherished it for the memory of all the times she'd been surrounded by his warmth. "I want you settled—" he rasped.

"I can be settled in a year or two. There's plenty of money to keep me and Mama. Even if Gregory gives me nothing—which you know won't happen—we can live happily off of Mama's money."

"Your dowry is set. And Gregory will do right by you."

"Exactly. And you're going to get better..."

She might as well not have spoken because a coughing fit

covered her words. She jumped to her feet and brought his cold tea forward. She looked for the medicine from the apothecary, but she didn't see it anywhere. Then she waited in agonizing silence as he continued to hack and hack. The handkerchief when he drew it away from his mouth was dark red with blood and his hand shook as he tried to take the tea from her.

She helped him drink. She helped him resettle on the bed. And inside, she cursed and screamed. Two days ago, he'd danced with her. Today, he couldn't get out of bed.

"You pressed too hard at my ball."

"I wanted to see my girl. The belle of the ball." His expression darkened. "Until your cousin."

"It wasn't Kynthea's fault. People trip. The duke's spat—"

He waved her comments away. "It was your night."

"And I loved every second of it." She smiled into his eyes. "I loved that you stayed up for me. And you loved the deviled kidneys." She'd made sure they were served at the midnight buffet just for him. He'd eaten them from the seat she'd had set for him at the head of the ballroom.

"A father watches over his daughter," he wheezed. Then his eyes grew moist. "I want to walk you down the aisle."

"Of course, you will!"

He shook his head. "It must be soon."

Her throat tightened. "You must take your medicine. You must rest more." She lifted his near hand and pressed a kiss to his knuckles. "Papa, I want you there, too. I want you to give me away."

With his free hand, he patted the top of her head. Then when she straightened, he cupped her cheek. It was a gesture he'd done since her earliest memory. He tapped her head, then cupped her cheek.

"My girl," he said.

"My papa," she returned.

They said the last part together. "Get the racing forms."

Then they laughed. The paper was on the table beside his

bed, and she grabbed them. She looked them over with him. She discussed the strength and lineage of each contender. And she kept talking even when he closed his eyes and drifted off into a light sleep.

He'd get better soon, she told herself. This was no different than any other time he'd over-exerted. He needed better air. London was no place for him with the coal ash everywhere. He needed to go back to the country, but he would never leave while she was husband hunting. He wanted to be here to negotiate the marriage contract. Which meant she had to get the duke to propose today.

A soft knock sounded on the bedroom door. She looked up to see her mother step quietly inside. Her nose wrinkled at the scent. Everyone's did. She pressed a lavender scented handkerchief to her nose as her expression turned exquisitely sad.

According to Zoe's governess, her parents' marriage hadn't been a love match, but affection had grown between them. And now Zoe could see her mother's heart breaking.

"We need to get him out of London," Zoe whispered.

Her mother shook her head. "Not until you're engaged." Then she gestured for Zoe to come out of the room. She did, nodding as a maid went in to sit beside the bed. Her father was never left alone anymore.

"The duke will be here in an hour to take you to his country estate."

Zoe glanced at the clock and mentally calculated what she needed to do before he arrived. "I'll be ready."

"Are you sure you want Kynthea to go? I can insist she stay here."

"No, no, I need her to help me."

"With the love potion? You have it, don't you? The newest mixture?"

"In my pocket," Zoe said as she touched the small bottle where it lay heavy against her thigh.

It had been her mother's suggestion months ago that as soon

as she picked a man, she should use a love potion to ensnare him. Zoe had thought it was a joke at first, but when they both decided the duke would be the best option, her mother had repeated the idea of a love potion. Her friend's daughter had gotten an earl that way, or so she said.

That was how the thing had begun, and now it was a touchstone in which they invested all their hopes and dreams. Zoe wasn't an idiot. She knew this was a ridiculous idea, but she couldn't stop herself from smoothing her fingers up and down the vial. Especially since it was her best hope for catching the duke.

Certainly, she knew how to dress pretty. She had a maid who was a great help at that. So long as she smiled and wasn't obnoxious, her dowry attracted all the gentlemen she could possibly want.

Except for the one she did want.

The duke didn't need her money, didn't seem to care about her looks, and was never more than polite to her. She'd tried everything she could think of to bring him up to scratch. She'd flirted, he'd seemed bored. She'd flashed her cleavage, he'd looked vaguely appalled. She'd asked about his interests and had listened as best she could to his fondness for a well-run society, by which he meant well-paid workers who were happy and not rebellious. He also enjoyed the engineering behind canals as it pertained to trade routes.

Why couldn't he just like horses? Or even dogs? Half of what she knew about horse breeding came from studying dog breeds.

Which was to say that the man was not interested in her. She knew it down to her bones. Fortunately, a duke's marriage had little to do with interest and everything to do with outside influences. The Crown had already approved their union. If that didn't sway the man, then she had to use alchemy—the love potion. And if that failed, well, her mother had one more plan.

"I've packed a bag for you," her mother said. "Clean underthings. Your first time can be…well, it can be bad, but clean clothes will help. And Kynthea will be there. She knows what to give you for pain."

Her mother wanted her to ruin herself with the duke. If that happened, then it would be easy to force his hand.

"We're not supposed to spend the night," Zoe began. "It'll look odd to have brought a bag."

"Say it's for the horses. You're always mixing things for them."

True.

"Are you sure you don't want me instead of Kynthea? If the *ton* has already labeled her a hussy, I'm not sure her word—"

"The duke is an honorable man. If we… If he…" She swallowed. She'd seen horses mate, and it was not a tender process. She was terrified of what it would be like for her. "He'll do the right thing."

"Of course, he will." Her mother bit her lip. "But maybe if I—"

"I won't be able to do it if you're there." The idea of seducing the duke while her mother paced in the next room horrified her. It would be hard enough with Kynthea nearby, but at least her cousin wouldn't make a huge dramatic scene after it was done. "Let me do this my way. Please."

Her mother nodded. "Just so it gets done."

"It will," she said as she looked back at her father's bedroom. "For Papa's sake, the duke and I will be married as soon as the banns can be read."

Chapter Sixteen

KYNTHEA LOOKED AT her travelling companions and wondered at their moods. Zoe looked determined, as if she were heading into a race with thousands of pounds riding on the outcome. The duke was thoroughly pleasant, but his expression turned grim when he thought no one was looking. The maid, of course, was completely placid. She was the oldest woman on their staff, kept on out of obligation. Mostly she oversaw the maids and took naps, which was what she was doing now.

As for Kynthea, she had made her decision last night. She'd even spoken with her aunt about leaving their home as soon as she could find a new solution. The lady had been gracious. She understood that none of this was Kynthea's fault, but she had to think of Zoe's reputation. She even promised to write a reference letter to help her get a position, on the condition that Kynthea went far away from London. "Spain, perhaps, or better yet, Russia," were the lady's exact words. There would be no reference if Kynthea wanted to stay in England. Or in any English-speaking country for that matter.

Clearly the association with her uncle's family was at an end, and so Kynthea's choices were to travel as a single woman to a country where she couldn't even speak the language, or find another path.

But what path was open to her? She had no marketable skills except her poise. And if she were to be damned as a jezebel, then perhaps she ought to become one in truth. A courtesan or a mistress. She knew the basics of copulation. She'd grown up in the country and had discussed horse breeding with Zoe. Plus, she'd learned that her maidenhead would be highly prized, which made her inexperience a natural expectation rather than a detriment. What she didn't have was the knowledge of who might be interested in her. She hoped that the duke would help her with that. It would be an awkward conversation to be sure, but she had no other male person whom she could ask.

So she dressed with care, then settled into the carriage and hoped for an opportunity to plead her case. This probably wasn't the usual way things were done, but she'd gotten an extensive education at My Lady's Apothecary yesterday.

The business of becoming a mistress was much more than understanding the physical mechanics. She needed lodging, a servant, and basic income. Many demi-reps were flashy, beautiful ladies who accompanied their patrons to all sorts of scandalous activities. Others were quiet, discreet women who served at the man's beck and call and never showed their faces in public. She guessed that the duke would prefer the latter as would many of his friends, but she had no way of knowing that for sure. And though he was likely an accomplished negotiator, she was completely untried in these waters.

She prayed that he would help her in these matters. And if a tiny part of her hoped that he would make her his, then that was only natural. After all, she was agonizingly attracted to him and believed that he returned her affection. Who better to start her on this path?

All these thoughts swirled in her head while the miles sped by. The conversation was general and therefore didn't require much attention. Especially since Zoe was making a determined effort to ferret out His Grace's interests. They learned that the duke enjoyed chess, though he was by no means a master. He had a fondness for tales about naval battles, but he was not a historian. And though he did like dogs, his favorite pet had passed away some years ago and he'd never had the heart to get another.

In short, they learned that His Grace was a humble man not at all interested in pushing his passions on anyone else or claiming that he was anything more than a hobbyist. Kynthea respected him all the more for it. Zoe appeared frustrated that she could not ooh and ahh over something, as if she, too, were fascinated by his amusements.

Having failed in that, Zoe tried a different tack.

"Did you know that our fathers were great friends, Your Grace?"

The duke frowned. "Truly? I had no idea." Indeed, from his tone, he appeared skeptical.

"Oh yes. My father has often said how his holiday at your Newbury estate was the happiest time of his life."

Now the duke's brows rose to fill his expression with doubt. "Truly? How so?"

Undaunted, Zoe continued, as if his posture weren't calling her a liar. "Well, it was your grandfather, of course, who had the true racing passion. Your father enjoyed it—"

The duke cut her off. "My father enjoyed riding, but it wasn't his happiest pastime."

"Quite right, Your Grace. Your father loved billiards. Apparently, my father spent his days talking horses with your grandfather, and his evenings playing billiards with your father. He was blissfully happy from dawn through dusk, and nothing has ever matched that joy for him. He called it, living a true gentleman's life."

Kynthea thought there was more to being a gentleman than riding and billiards. So, apparently, did His Grace, though his expression softened into wistful.

"It was the ideal boy's life, I suppose. I must confess I spent a great many days in exactly the same manner, at least until my father died and I had to learn the running of things."

"Did you know that my father and your grandfather created a plan for your stable? In fact, they corresponded regularly until his death a year later."

It was said that the duke's grandfather passed from grief after his son's death. Whether from grief or lung ailment, his death left Ras without a male guide before he turned twelve. That was much too young to assume the reins of a dukedom.

Meanwhile, Zoe pulled a stack of letters from her reticule. "I have some of them here. My father had them sent up from our country home. He'd kept them all these years."

"The devil, you say," Ras muttered as he leaned forward. His expression was eager as Zoe passed him the letters. "Have you read them?"

"Oh yes. I went over every one with my father yesterday. They're mostly about your breeding stock. Horses that are now, unfortunately, long gone. There is one letter of interest," she said as she pulled the top one off the pile. "I gather my father had proposed a daring expansion idea. He'd outlined it in great detail. As you can see..." She unfolded the missive. "Your grandfather thought it very interesting. I don't know if he was indulging a young man—"

"My grandfather did not indulge anyone," the duke said dryly. "If he praised the idea, then he meant it." He lifted the letter to the light and began reading. Zoe remained quiet as he did, but Kynthea knew the girl was bursting with excitement. Finally, she'd gotten the duke's attention on his horses. That was exactly the topic Zoe most desired.

After the duke finished reading, he dropped the hand holding the letter to his knee and looked straight at Zoe. "Do you have any idea what those plans were? The one that your father suggested?"

That appeared to be exactly the question Zoe had been waiting for. The girl brightened as if she were born to walk the boards. She blushed, smiled coyly, then pulled another folded sheet of foolscap from her reticule.

"I asked my father that exact same thing!" she said. "He didn't recall specifically. It was so long ago, you understand, but this is the base of it as he explained it to me."

She unfolded the paper, which Kynthea now saw was actually three pages plus the latest two racing sheets.

"If you would look here, Your Grace, I've taken the liberty of writing my father's idea down and inserting the name of current bloodlines. The horses have all changed from your grandfather's time, but Papa and I are both racing enthusiasts. You'll see here from the latest two racing sheets what we're thinking." She passed those over to the duke who did appear interested in what Zoe had to say.

So interested, in fact, that they passed the rest of the journey in discussion of Zoe's thoughts about his horses. The ideas for an expansion, how much money it would cost, and the signs of what would make her plans successful. Despite the way Zoe kept referring to her father and the duke's grandfather, Kynthea knew that this was Zoe's plan. Her father had likely helped, but the real brains behind this multi-year expansion came from Zoe herself.

The duke was fascinated. He listened attentively, looked at where she pointed, asked relevant questions, and even began to detail things his stablemaster had told him. Zoe agreed for the most part. Horse racing had some universally accepted thoughts. But when she disagreed, she didn't pull any punches.

"He's not wrong," Zoe said, referring to the duke's stablemaster. "He's just old. He thinks it should be done that way because it's always been done that way."

"You disagree."

"I think…"

If the duke resented having a female school him about his own horses, he didn't show it. Indeed, he challenged her straight on, forcing Zoe to defend her conclusions. By the time they arrived at his estate outside London, the two were having a lively discussion about breeding methods. It was not a proper topic, and yet, neither one flinched from the topic.

The discussion continued through their refreshment. The duke made pains to include Kynthea or to change the conversation to a more general topic, but she knew when she was beat.

She laughed as she waved them both away.

"Go on with the both of you. I know Zoe wants to show you what she means. She's always happiest when she has a horse nearby."

"Miss Petrelli," the duke rushed to say, "I'm afraid we've been terribly rude."

"You have been nothing of the sort. Now go. I shall enjoy this lovely lemonade and then stroll down to join you in a moment."

Zoe dimpled as she smiled at Kynthea. "My cousin understands me very well. She's been a loyal friend to me."

The duke agreed. "She has been very patient this day."

Kynthea laughed. "Go away! I want to listen to the birdsong. We never hear it so clearly in London."

The duke bowed to her and then escorted Zoe to the stables. Kynthea watched them go, her heart sinking at their obvious connection. She understood exactly what was happening here. Zoe was making her play for the duke's hand in marriage, and from the looks of things, she was succeeding beautifully. Given that the Crown had already approved of their union, a shared interest would overcome most scruples. Indeed, it was a godsend for the typical aristocratic marriage.

Which meant that His Grace and Zoe would likely be engaged by the evening meal. And what a shock that was! The duke had been clear that he had no intention of marrying Zoe. And yet, the two had found a common interest. And with the pressure from the Crown, a marriage was the most likely outcome.

Which meant Zoe would indeed ask Kynthea to be her companion. But that would be a big problem for Kynthea.

It was a stupid thing, really. Indeed, she couldn't possibly believe it had happened. She knew better, but it was too late. Her heart was engaged. She had no idea when she'd tumbled into love. Perhaps it was when he had sat beside her for a week defending her reputation. Or maybe it had happened when he threw off his spat and instructed the orchestra to begin the waltz again. She knew her body had thrilled to his kiss and then heated nigh until boiling at night. She couldn't close her eyes without reliving every single touch between them, from their most formal greeting to the intimate thrust of his tongue.

She'd relived that latter thing many times. And when Madame Ilie had explained more lustful activities, her heart had pounded with excitement, and she'd lost herself several times in her imagination.

She was glad that Zoe had carried the conversation in the carriage because Kynthea's mind had been almost wholly absorbed in wondering about the duke's hands and where he might put them. About how it would feel to have him kiss her breasts or spread her thighs. Far from being frightened at the idea of him in her bed, she had imagined his thrust as he filled her. Her nipples had grown tight and her nether regions moist. It was not something a proper companion would admit, but she couldn't lie to herself.

She lusted after the man, and it had been near torture to sit across him in the carriage and not feel his touch again.

She gave up the mental pretense of searching for a different protector. She wanted to become the duke's mistress. It was the best option for her, and indeed, a dream come true if one examined what she'd been thinking last night. But now His Grace was set to marry Zoe. And though many men had a wife and a mistress, could she betray her cousin like that? Could she lie with Zoe's husband?

The idea was repulsive. Which meant she couldn't be the duke's mistress. And she couldn't be Zoe's proper companion either. Not if this morning's carriage ride was an example of what was to come. While Zoe and the duke had discussed horses, Kynthea had nearly melted from lust.

She'd hid it the best she could. Thankfully, once horses became the topic, Zoe wouldn't notice a lightning bolt two feet away. But Kynthea knew how far she'd gone into lust, from the sweat on her brow and the uncomfortable way she'd shifted and moved on the squabs.

She wanted the man her cousin would marry, and if she remained Zoe's companion, she'd spend night and day in the duke's house. She'd likely have a bedroom down the hall from him. How could she possibly survive living in proximity to His Grace without completely disgracing herself? And humiliating her cousin in the process?

It was insupportable. And yet, what other option did she have?

Chapter Seventeen

RAS SMILED AS he watched his stablemaster take Lady Zoe to task for working in his stable without telling him who she was. When Ras had first told Mr. Barnes that "Miss Daisy Duncan" was a well-bred lady, his stablemaster had all but called him an idiot. But now, with the two of them face to face, he was able to sit back and watch the sparks fly. To her credit, Lady Zoe held her ground. She'd worked for free and done a good job of it. She didn't cower or apologize, and Mr. Barnes seemed completely flummoxed. At least until she started challenging his neglect of his older mares. Mr. Barnes had never neglected a horse in his entire life, but it was true that his attention centered more on the racing stock.

And so the two began a lively debate that would look to others like a full-fledged argument. But what he saw was two people who loved horses and who also enjoyed an energetic debate.

"Why don't you show Mr. Barnes your father's ideas for the stable?" Ras asked from a healthy distance. "See what he makes of them." Ras knew quite well that Lady Zoe was the author of what she'd presented. Certainly, her father had given his opinions, but she was the one with the true vision. And if she could get his stablemaster on board, then Ras would come along as well. But first he had to see what Barnes thought. And he also had to get out of earshot before the two deafened him with their discussion. "I'll go see if Miss Petrelli has gotten lost."

Mr. Barnes acknowledged the statement with a tug at his cap. Lady Zoe on the other hand waved with a distracted kind of focus. Her eyes were trained on Whirl who was just being led out for her inspection. Not Whirl, he corrected himself. The horse's name was… was… Oh hell. Now he'd forgotten.

He turned and went in search of Kynthea. He found her wandering down toward them. He took a moment to appreciate the sunlight as it turned her brown hair gold. Her gown was a muted blue, probably a cast-off from her aunt who preferred that hue. He would see her dressed in copper or gold. Or undressed and in his arms such that he could see the golden tones in her skin and the flush of rose as her breath increased. He would spread her thighs and…

Oh hell. He shut down his erotic thoughts and tried to focus on the woman as she approached. But that was a losing game. She was beautiful. She was refined in dress and composure. And he wanted her with a madness that was becoming uncomfortable.

She smiled when she saw him, and his body heated to flame. He smiled back and quickly made his plan. There was a tack room nearby. Perhaps it was empty…

"Have you abandoned Zoe already?" she asked, her voice light enough to tease. "Or did she ride off without you?"

"She and Mr. Barnes are coming to terms. I judged it best to back away until a truce has been called."

"Then you will be away from your stable for a very long time. Zoe never backs down when it comes to horses, and I gather Mr. Barnes is of the same ilk."

"He is," Ras confirmed as he made it to her side. He wished the ground was uneven enough that he could take her arm. It wasn't, so he contented himself with adjusting her direction toward the hopefully empty tack room. "It's a pity she wasn't born a man. If she were, she could have made a name for herself in racing circles. Why hasn't she improved her father's stables?"

"Oh, she has. Significantly. Enough that her best two mares are part of her dowry." She arched a brow at him. "I'm surprised you didn't know."

About Lady Zoe's dowry? He wasn't interested.

"You'd do well to listen to her ideas," Kynthea continued. "All the smart men in Cornwall do." She looked over at the yard where Zoe and Mr. Barnes were kneeling down in front of Whirl. "You should talk to Baron Borlaise about her. He's done very well with his horses thanks to her advice."

"And what of you?"

"I never argue with Zoe about horses."

He smiled. "Actually, I was asking what are your interests? What would you have done if born a man?"

She looked at him for a moment, then turned away, her gaze dropping to the ground. "I am a woman, Your Grace. Thoughts of "what if" only depress me."

And now he had an excuse to touch her. He took a large enough step that he could slide around her to block her path. And when she stopped walking, he caught her hand. "I can understand how frustrating it is to be an impoverished relation, especially when your path in society has been so unfair of late. But there are a great many things you could do—even as a woman—if you had the resources to pursue them. What were your childhood dreams, Miss Petrelli? What might you have studied?"

"The law," she said. Her words didn't come quickly, but they were clear when finally voiced. "I had a passing interest as a child, but it wasn't until my parents passed that I saw how easily the law could be used for ill. It's not how it was intended, to be sure, but some people use it like a cudgel to beat people."

"Who hurt you?"

She smiled. "No one. My parents had debts that were legally owed, but there was little kindness in the administration of it. Nevertheless, an impoverished woman hears tales that the wealthy might not. Contracts written such that they help only one party while the other is an unwitting dupe. Laws do the same sometimes." She took a deep breath. "My brother thought to become a barrister when he was younger. We discussed it several times, but sailing claimed him and, truthfully, I was the one who had the interest more than he."

"I should like to meet your brother."

"I think he will like you, Your Grace."

"I hope so. When does he return home?"

Her gaze grew sad. "Not for months. Last time we spoke, he said that he might have enough money upon his return. If his latest venture works out."

"Money for what?"

"To set up an establishment. He talked of how there might be enough for me to live with him modestly. That we might…" Her voice trailed away. "It doesn't matter now. There isn't time."

His attention sharpened. "There isn't time for what, Miss Petrelli?"

He watched as she steeled herself. Then she lifted her gaze to his and her lips curved in a wry kind of smile. "I should like to speak with you, Your Grace, about an arrangement between us. But this is hardly the moment." Her gaze skipped past him to where another horse was being brought out for Zoe's attention.

"On the contrary," he said, "this is the perfect moment." The tack room was right here, and if he didn't miss his count, all the stable hands were out listening to the loud discussion between Lady Zoe and Mr. Barnes. He cupped her elbow and quickly escorted her inside the barn. As he thought, the place was empty except for horses. When he pushed open the door to the tack room, it was filled with the pleasant scents of leather and linseed oil, and it was blissfully empty of people. "In here," he said as he pulled her inside and quickly shut the door behind them.

"Do you know," he said, "that I have done little in the last twenty-four hours but think of you?"

"Me? But why?"

So many ways to answer that. "Mr. Pickleherring was incredibly unfair to you, and I hold myself partially responsible for that."

"You? But you had nothing to do with it!"

It was his fault because she'd been targeted by Fletcher because of him. Even he didn't understand the logic there. Worse, he could not attempt to explain it without revealing Nate's role in all of this. Nate, who was recovering nicely at the ducal home in London, but who was still stubbornly silent about his other activities.

Which was a long way of saying that she was the most pleasant thing to think about in his life. And so he did think of her. Obsessively. And how he could help her weather this storm.

"It was my spat that came loose. You would not have stumbled otherwise."

"Your Grace—" she began, but he pressed a finger to her lips.

"Please, in private, call me Ras. All my friends do."

Even in the shadows of the tack room, he could see the pink of her cheeks. Or perhaps he felt the heat of her increase. The moist feel of her breath against his hand. And…

"I have promised to find you a husband," he rushed to say. It was an attempt to divert the direction of his thoughts. Sadly, it didn't work. He pulled his hand away from her mouth and yet the feel of her was burned into his consciousness. "But that is vastly more difficult now."

She nodded. "Any place for me in London is now gone. No one who has even the slightest association with polite society will have me." Her head lifted as she no doubt fought tears. "My aunt has offered to write me a reference, but only if I go to Spain or Russia."

"Spain or—" he choked off his word. "Do you have relations there?"

"No one. Nor do I speak the languages."

The cruelty of some people. "You'd be better off in a workhouse." Then at her wince, he quickly touched her arm. "You shall not be doomed to that. I swear it."

She flashed him a brave smile. "There is another option for me. One that I had hoped you would help me with."

"Anything."

"Understand that I have seen what happens to impoverished girls. If my aunt and uncle had not taken me in, I would have ended up on this path. I would rather have some control over it than…" She visibly shuddered. "I would like to choose."

He nodded, not understanding the direction of her thoughts.

"I know of no school who will take me as a teacher, nor a family who will have me as governess or companion. Not now that I have been so publicly reviled."

"Not everyone reads the paper." Just everyone in London and much of the outlying counties.

"Every respectable family does," she returned. "So my only options are an odious marriage to a man who—"

"No. You cannot marry someone vile. That's a fate worse than death." They both knew that any man who would have her with a tarnished reputation wanted her for the most despicable reasons. "You do not know what those men want."

"I do know, at least in part. I helped give comfort to some of my father's parishioners. I was sheltered, Your Grace, not blind."

She had a point. "So what is it that I can—"

"If I must sell myself," she pressed on, her words quick as she interrupted him. "I should like to choose my buyer. And get the best price I can for it." She took a shuddering breath, but it did not stop her from finishing her thought. "I need you to help me with that."

His breath froze in his lungs. His thoughts whited out as he stared at her. She wanted him to… She planned to…

"You know everyone, Your Grace, or at least more people than I do. You know who would be my best option and…" Finally, she faltered, her gaze dropping to the floor as she spoke.

"To be clear," he said, his voice icy cold. "You are asking me to find you a protector." He nearly choked on the word. "Not a husband."

Her gaze raised to his. "Do you know of a husband who would take me?"

Not a good one. Not one who was worthy of her. And he had

spent a great deal of time thinking about it. Thinking and rejecting every man who crossed his mind.

Protectors were an even worse lot.

"Do you even know what it is like? Do you know what to do?" He had already kissed her. He knew exactly how inexperienced she was. "You are not cut out for that kind of life!"

He watched her jaw firm and her eyes turn cold. "You know nothing of what a woman will do when she has no other option."

He took a step forward. "You will be at the beck and call of any man with coin."

She swallowed.

"Whatever he wants, whenever he wants."

"That is no different than a husband."

He couldn't deny that. But with marriage, she had some protection. As a mistress, she had none. "You must please him in every way. And when he tires of you anyway, he will discard you."

She nodded. "I know. But then I shall be free to find a new one."

If her looks were still good. If she were still young. If she knew the slightest bit about seduction. "Do you even know how to please a man? What he wants? What he needs?"

He'd come close as he spoke, towering over her as he tried to impress his words on her. Good God, she had no idea what she was asking, and yet he could see the determination in her eyes. And he knew, damn it, that if she could learn, it might be the best option for her.

"You cannot," he rasped.

"Not without help," she said. "I know other people to ask—"

"No!" He did not want to think of who might help her or how they might teach her. He did not want to imagine her married to an old widower or mistress to a depraved wealthy son. The idea that anyone but him could touch her made him insane. He cupped her cheek, the movement abrupt but he made sure his touch was gentle. "No one else," he said.

She touched his wrist, her eyes wide but still steady. "I must make the best choice I can. My life depends upon it."

She was right, and yet she was so very wrong. He had no space in his mind to weigh her choices, only a desperate need to see that she was not destroyed by the wrong choice. By the wrong man. By anyone but him.

He kissed her. He pressed his mouth to hers and plundered her in the most possessive way. He thrust into her mouth. He touched every part of her mouth. And then, because he could not be brutal with her, he softened against her. He let her duel sweetly with him.

She raised her hands to his arms, gripping them as she arched into him. His left hand was on her waist, then slid upward to cup her breast. He felt her breath catch at that, and he eased back enough to let her feel what he was doing. Indeed, with her eyes wide and her mouth wet, he gloried in showing her how it should be with a man.

He thumbed her nipple. It was tight as it pressed against her dress, but it was nothing compared to what he could make her feel.

"No one has ever done this to you before, have they?"

She swallowed then shook her head.

"Do you like it?" He already knew the answer, but he knew that her pleasure would be enhanced the more she admitted to the sensations he gave her.

"Yes," she whispered.

"This is how it feels when you want it," he said. He leaned forward, nuzzling her skin. "Say you want this."

"I do."

He pulled back. "Say you want me."

"You," she whispered.

He grinned. "Your gown is simple. I can show you more. Do you want—"

"Yes. Please."

It was a simple matter to open the buttons on the back of her dress and ease the shoulders of her dress down. Unlike Lady Zoe, she did not wear a riding habit. She hadn't intended to ride, so she wore a light spring gown. When the fabric was lax across her bodice, he untied the ribbon of her shift, and he slipped his hand inside.

Her breast had a nice shape and weight. It was rosy with her heat, and she gasped when he squeezed her nipple. He pinched it again, then rolled it. She grabbed onto the edge of a table as she swayed slightly. Fortunately, she couldn't raise her arms without ripping her dress. And so he pulled her other breast free.

Then he played, exploring her breasts. He kneaded them, squeezed them, then tugged at her nipples. Her eyes fluttered shut and she dropped her head back. Her breath was unsteady, and he wondered at her balance, but there was a rack behind her that would support her. Then he leaned down and captured a nipple in his mouth.

"Oooo," she moaned. It was a breathy sound of delight, and he loved it.

Her other breast was just as sensitive. Soon she was leaning back against the rack while he did what he willed with her chest. She set a hand on his shoulder and gripped him. He knew the steady rise of her passion by her breath, by her moans, and how tightly she squeezed his shoulder.

Then he kissed his way from her breasts, up her neck, to whisper into her ear. "Have you ever had a quickening?"

She shook her head.

"Do you want one?"

"Here?"

It wasn't respectable, but he didn't want to stop. And she was so ripe that he used a foot to pull a stool close.

"Put your foot there," he said, guiding her. She complied, though the movement was awkward. He eased her fears as much as he could, kissing her while he wrapped her left hand around a vertical part of the rack. Finally, he guided her right hand to his shoulder.

She was braced and open to him. Indeed, he would remember this sight for the rest of his life. Kynthea, so innocent and yet so open with her eyes dazed and her breasts free. He'd never seen anyone so beautiful.

"When it gets overwhelming," he said, "press your mouth to my neck. It will muffle the sound." And let him feel the intensity of her breath. He waited until she nodded, and then he set both his hands around her raised calf before sliding upwards. Over her knee and up her thigh, her skirt rising with him. Then he found the top of her stocking and kept going.

"Your Grace!" she exclaimed, but it wasn't a protest. Nevertheless, he paused.

"Do you want me to kiss you again? As a distraction? Or would you rather experience it just as you are?" Then his expression softened. "Or I will stop. If you want."

"No!" Then she swallowed. "I want to know. Truly!"

"Very well then." He winked at her. "A quick kiss first."

It wasn't a quick kiss. It was slow and deliberate. She melted into it. And when he pulled back, his fingers slipped between her thighs.

She was wet and, he thought, trembling. Her hand was tight on his shoulder, but her expression was interested. Eager even.

"Will you…will you put…" She didn't have the words, and her cheeks were crimson.

"Not this time," he said. Then his fingers began to explore her in earnest. God, if the scent of her arousal made him dazed with hunger, the feel of her so wet made his blood pound with need. But he knew better than to rush this.

He spread her wetness around, he stroked her petals open, and he rolled his thumb up over her pearl while she shivered in reaction. As if she were throwing off a lifetime of restraint, she dropped her head back, further exposing her throat and breasts. They moved with her breath while he stroked in and up. Inside her heat, then up across her pearl.

Her back arched, her breath came in hot gasps. And then he

increased his tempo.

He could feel inside her as she clenched, then mewed with her need. The rack behind her began to shake and he worried for its stability. He didn't want it tumbling down and he didn't want to interrupt her experience, but he had no choice.

"Come here," he rasped.

She blinked at him. "What?"

He pulled her toward him, quickly flipping her around. Her bottom pressed against his erection, and what he wouldn't give to plow into her from behind right here and now. He didn't. Instead, he bent her over the table. Her breasts dangled unrestrained, and he indulged himself as he squeezed them. Her nipples were so sensitive!

Then when he was sure she was ready, he pulled up her skirt again. Her legs were set wide, and he slid his hand down between her folds.

Inside and up. Inside and up.

She liked it when he drew the callouses of his finger across her pearl. She arched into it, and he…God help him, he felt as if he might explode in his clothing like a boy. Instead, he pressed his lips to her neck. He tasted the salt on her skin and whispered into her ear.

"Can you hold back your cry?"

She nodded.

"Good."

He pulled his finger over her pearl again.

Faster. Harder.

Sweeter.

Her body arched.

She pressed down against him.

She cried out.

It wasn't loud. Nothing more than a stifled mew. But what she lacked in volume, her body more than made up for. Every part of her reacted. Wave after wave with him riding her from behind. He wasn't inside her, but he might as well have been for the pleasure it gave him. She was wild, and he held her tight through it all.

Every muffled cry. Every gasping breath. Every wave of her hips pulsing back against him.

Until it eased. Until her breath slowed, and she lay nearly limp in his arms.

"That was a quickening?" she gasped.

"Yes."

"No wonder they don't tell girls. We'd never stop trying for it."

He smiled against her back. Lord, it was going to be impossible for him to stand up. Truthfully, he had no desire to leave this position, but she began to move. She pushed upright. He let her go and stepped back.

Oh my. He couldn't be seen like this. He couldn't even fully straighten up.

She turned with her breasts still out and her body still flush. "Thank you," she whispered.

"My pleasure," he returned.

Then she frowned. "Was it? I mean… I was told…" She bit her lip in embarrassment as she looked down at the thickness in his pants.

This was insane, but he wanted it so desperately. "Would you like to see it? Would you like to touch me?"

"Yes!" she whispered. "Can I do for you what…" She glanced sideways at the table.

"Yes. I would like that very much."

And so he did what he had never done. At least not in the tack room like a stable hand. But she was here, and the scent of her perfume was thick in the air. Indeed, his hand was covered with it, and her breasts were still free.

He opened his clothing, undid his falls, and let his organ spring free. It was so hard and desperate.

"Do I touch it?" she asked. "Do I suck it?"

What images flooded his mind. "How do you know about

that?" he asked.

"I went to My Lady's Apothecary yesterday. They told me about it."

She had asked in anticipation? Because she'd known he wouldn't be able to resist her here? Not where there were so many private corners where they could play.

"Do you want to?"

In answer, she reached out for him. He let her explore him for a bit, then he taught her how to wrap his organ in her hand. He showed her the stroke he enjoyed and began to thrust in a steady rhythm. But this was difficult positioning. And there was so much he wanted to do with her. So before he exploded, he disentangled her.

"Did I do it wrong?" she asked.

"No. But there's something else I'd like."

"Yes?"

He arranged her then. Just as he had imagined her. He set her against the rack. He played with her breasts and saw the flush deepen in her skin. "You're so voluptuous," he said. "I want to look and look forever."

"Voluptuous?" she said.

"Oh yes. Demure gown. Modest demeanor. But here with me..." He brushed her hair back. Then he kissed her deep. She melted just like before. And when he stepped back, she was a sight he'd never forget. "A vixen."

With one hand, he kept fondling her breasts. With the other, he worked himself. It didn't take long, but it held it back just to prolong his view. And while he tugged at her nipples, she began to undulate again. So ready, so soon!

It shot him over the edge. He had a handkerchief ready, but it still was a scramble to get it in place. He was overcome by her. And when he caught his breath again, she was looking at him with wonder.

He had no restraint to stop himself. She was still open and ready. He grabbed her skirt and hiked it up. Then he dropped to his knees and drank her. Lips, tongue, every part of his mouth on her. Until he thrust his fingers inside her and felt her glory again.

Such wonder.

Such bliss.

And when she shuddered again beneath his tongue, he felt such powerful emotions fill him that he could not contain them. He gripped her thighs, he straightened up from where he was, and he held her as he would the most precious treasure in the world.

In time, she recovered. In time, she turned her face to his. Which is when he spoke his truth.

"This thing—sex and all that can happen between a man and a woman—it should be between two people who love each other. It should never be sold to the highest bidder."

Her gaze focused, her expression tightened, but not so much that she withdrew from him. "And do you love me?" she asked.

Part of him screamed, *Yes, yes, a thousand times, yes*. But a century of ducal breeding held his tongue. He could not promise that and not promise all the other things that went with it. Respect, status, her place at his side. A duke could not be devoted to a woman so socially compromised. And he certainly couldn't choose her against Prinny's command.

And yet, how could he not? How could he do what they had done without giving himself to her? Without loving her as he had just declared was the only reason to be with one another this way?

And as he fought with himself, with his responsibilities to his title and the Crown, she slowly withdrew from him. Her expression fell, her eyes slid away, and she steadily set her clothing back in order.

He helped her, and she did not fight his aid. But she certainly didn't welcome it either. And in the end, when they were both attired as they ought to be, she looked at him one last time.

"If the man I want above all else cannot claim me, then I shall make what future I can without him."

He wanted to argue with her, but what could he say? She was right. But he couldn't promise to help her. Not into another man's arms. And apparently not into his own. Because the idea of making her his mistress was abhorrent. She was worth so much more.

He didn't know what the solution was. And in his silence, she left him. Then, once the door shut behind her, shame brought him to his knees.

Chapter Eighteen

KYNTHEA WALKED SLOWLY out of the tack room. Her body was steady, but inside every part of her was shaking. In the space of five minutes, she'd gone from the heights of delight to the cruelest pain she'd ever felt.

And what a ridiculous statement that was, she admonished herself. She had felt aching grief—still did—whenever she thought about her parents. A man could not compare to the loss of her parents. Especially a man she'd known only a very short time.

It was the depth and speed of the fall that so shocked her. She'd had a few days to prepare for her parents' deaths. This swing had happened in minutes. And it had shattered everything inside her.

She found a bench to sit upon. It was a lovely place amid the flowers. Even the sun shone on her face if she tilted her head just right.

These feelings inside her were her own fault. She'd known from the beginning that a duke could not love her. She'd known that anything they did together was just a dalliance. And yet she'd allowed it. She'd wanted it. Whenever he was near, her body overcame her reason. And when he touched her... Well, there was no space for clear thinking. She doubted she would have stopped him if he'd tried to take her maidenhead.

And that made her ten thousand times a fool.

It was time for her to grow up. Only silly girls dreamed at

night about a duke. Romantics spoke of love. She could not afford to be either. She had days at most before she would be out on the street. It was time for her to think of a solution other than the perfidious duke.

She wiped her tears away and stared hard at a sunlit weed. That was her, she decided. Somewhere else, she might be a prized plant. But here, she was an outcast, soon to be uprooted and tossed aside to die. But she was hardy, and she refused to go quietly. She'd heard of weeds that came back year after year, growing in the sunlight despite everything a gardener did to keep them out.

She was not going to Spain or Russia. That was a death sentence. She could not go back to Cornwall. Too many people knew of her, and it would be a miserable life. Excited by fantasies of the duke, she'd imagined being his mistress. No matter what she'd said to him—or herself—she now knew that her heart had always been planning to be his. Why else would she have gone so blithely into the tack room?

Because she loved him. And that was a stupid, ridiculous, idiotic thing to do.

She couldn't be his mistress now. Even if he wanted her—which he clearly did not—her stupid heart couldn't take it. She wanted more with him, and since he could not give it...well, she would have to look elsewhere.

But could she do that with someone else? She'd thought so, but now that she'd tasted physical intimacy, the thought of doing that with anyone else made her physically ill. Damn it, she hadn't known what it felt like. If she'd never experienced what they'd done, then maybe...

But she had and she did and now...

What was she going to do?

She heard voices coming up the walk. Women's voices, laughing as they carried food toward the kitchen. The housekeeper and the cook, perhaps, back from shopping. She smiled at them, trying to be friendly and because she desperately needed a friend right then.

They saw her, of course. They had to walk right by her. But once they realized who it was, they gave her their back. One whispered comment between the two of them, and they turned in unison, walking steadily to the servant's entrance.

That was a shock. She'd never been given the cut direct by the haut ton. At least not yet. She knew that servants had their own, even stricter codes of acceptance. It was no surprise that the staff at a ducal residence would be stiffly correct. But to be cut by a servant when she was a guest in the duke's home?

Good God, she'd fallen far. And she feared that she hadn't hit bottom yet.

She swallowed, her gaze falling back on the sunlit weed. She wondered how many servants had trampled it, and yet it still grew. How many souls cast it ugly looks, and yet it still absorbed sunlight and proudly displayed its leaves.

If she were in charge of this household, she would end such uncharitable attitudes. She would, of course, teach Zoe how to handle such things, but the girl was sixteen. She was in no way prepared to handle a ducal household.

Oh, the things she could do if only she were given the chance. But that was not to be. And yet somehow, some way, she would survive.

First things first, she needed money. After all, she hadn't forgotten that her brother was due back in a few months. She had learned from Madame Ille that virginity was highly prized. So highly, in fact, that it might cover her expenses for as much as a year.

She could do that, right? She could sell her virginity. Indeed, what other choice did she have? The question was...to whom?

Only one man came to mind. It was, of course, the one man she'd been thinking of since this whole debacle had begun. He wasn't opposed to the idea, she was sure of that. She just needed to make him pay for it.

And she needed to be sure her heart did not get broken in the process. Or more broken.

Chapter Nineteen

Zoe looked up in shock as the duke declared from the fence that it was time for tea. Tea? That wasn't until…oh my. The sun was already waning in the sky, the stable hands looked like they'd worked a hard day, and Mr. Barnes… Well, he'd been scowling at her all day. But since the duke himself had told the man to hear her out, he'd had no choice but to listen as she demonstrated her skills.

Of course, there had been many arguments, but she had prevailed in most cases, and she was well satisfied with her day's work. Except, of course, her work was supposed to be getting the duke to propose to her. Instead, she'd spent the day working his horses.

Oops.

He joined her in the center of the paddock and smiled warmly into her face. "I can see you've lost your sense of time."

She wiped her forehead, appalled by the amount of sweat that accumulated there. "You and Mr. Barnes were most kind in indulging me."

"It was my genuine pleasure," he said as he looked back at his stablemaster. "Well, Mr. Barnes? What do you think of her ideas?"

The man grunted and pulled off his cap. Then he looked away as he shuffled his feet. "I don't like ladies pretending to be stable lads."

The duke chuckled. "Duly noted. What else?"

"Well, the girl has some ideas."

"Good ones?"

"Some."

"Interesting ones?"

"Mebbe. If that's where you want to take your stable."

"Do you know the horses that are in her dowry?"

Excitement tightened Zoe's belly. He knew details about her dowry. Surely, he wouldn't know that if he weren't considering her hand in marriage. Meanwhile, Mr. Barnes nodded slowly.

"I know them," he said. "She mentioned them."

Yes, she'd made sure to let Mr. Barnes know what she'd be bringing to this marriage. That she wasn't just a title or a pretty face. She came with equine assets that could greatly benefit His Grace's consequence in the racing community. Not to mention what breeding mares of their quality could do for the future of the stable.

"Well? What do you think?"

"I think they're right fine females." He glanced sideways at Zoe. "All of them."

Unlike most women, Zoe didn't take offense at being lumped in with her mares. She was of equally fine breeding and training as her horses, among humans, of course. And if the duke didn't see that, then he was a fool.

"Excellent," exclaimed the duke as he held out his hand. "Shall we head up for tea and then we can discuss your thoughts in more detail?"

She nodded, pleased with the outcome. "I'm afraid I smell of horse, Your Grace. I thought that might happen, and so..." She frowned as she looked around. "Where is Kynthea?"

"Over here," came her cousin's response. "I have your bag," she said, holding it up.

"And there is a bath waiting for you. We will wait on tea," the duke said.

"You've thought of everything," she said with a grin.

The duke shook his head. "Actually, it was your cousin's

idea."

Of course, it was. Kynthea always thought three steps ahead in every social situation. It was a quality Zoe greatly admired. "I'll be very fast."

"Take your time," he said as he escorted her up to the house.

Kynthea joined them, taking a moment to pass her bag to their maid. Zoe smiled her thanks then rushed ahead. At home in Cornwall, she was always late, but it wouldn't do to be tardy here. Duchesses weren't supposed to be late ever.

She stripped out of her clothes as fast as possible. A few minutes later, she was washing away her sweat and wondering what it would be like to be mistress here. She would have to learn how to handle the servants, of course. Her mother and Kynthea did that at home, but they could teach her. Or, if she brought Kynthea here as her companion, that could be one of her cousin's duties.

She thought of the duke's different properties and horse stables. They needed to be reorganized with specific locations designed for the different types of training required. She could visit each location on a rotating basis. At least she knew how to hire stable hands. It was household servants that bedeviled her.

She had other thoughts, of course. Plans, hopes, and even one inspiration. But they were all ways to avoid looking at the bed. After she married, she would have to produce an heir. It was a duchess's first responsibility. But how would she do the work she'd done today—work she loved—when heavy with child?

As for the first part, the part about creating that child in the first place... Well, she steadfastly refused to think about that.

She didn't have time to dry her hair in front of the fire but tied it back with a ribbon. The ends would curl sweetly about her face, but it did make her look younger. Unfortunately, there was no hope for it. It was well past teatime.

She put on some earbobs because she liked the feel of them when they tapped against her neck, then rushed downstairs to where Kynthea and the duke were conversing about the corn laws, of all things. Zoe had heard of them, of course. It was all the men discussed outside of dogs and horses. But far from being bored, Kynthea appeared to enjoy the discussion. Indeed, she and the duke were involved in a lively debate, and all Zoe could think was, thank God. After Zoe and the duke were married, Kynthea could handle the boring discussions. She was much more of an age with the duke. Her conversation would make the time bearable while they waited for the nursery to fill.

"Don't you look lovely?" said the duke as Zoe entered the room. He stood up as was polite and guided her to a chair.

She went where he led because that was her duty as his future wife. It was only after she sat down that she realized that Kynthea was already placed behind the low table where the tea service would be set. That wasn't appropriate. That was the duty of the lady of the house, but she supposed it happened because Zoe had been late.

"My mother should be here any minute," the duke continued. "But she hates to delay teatime for any reason, so she won't mind if we drink something now."

"Your mother?" Zoe asked.

"Yes. She's coming tonight to dine en famille. Indeed, she wondered if you might consider staying for the meal rather than rushing back to the city."

"Yes, of course. That sounds lovely." A lie, but a necessary one. No doubt that the dowager duchess wanted to see if she could act appropriately. She would be judged every second on how she spoke, moved, and ate. It would be a difficult meal, to be sure, but she had been trained from the cradle in how to go on as an elite member of society. She would manage. Meanwhile, she turned to Kynthea. "You don't mind, do you?"

It was another step in the negotiation. Since Kynthea was her companion, she must naturally stay or not as Zoe decided. But Zoe wanted to make it clear that her cousin was a person, not a servile attachment. She would be respected as she so often had not been during the past two weeks.

"Of course not!" Kynthea said.

Meanwhile at the duke's nod, a footman stepped out to inform the butler that tea could now be served. A moment later, the butler appeared carrying the tea tray, but he hesitated when he should have set it down. Naturally, the man knew that it should go in front of Zoe, but the duke was quick to solve that problem.

"You don't mind, do you, Miss Petrelli? Lady Zoe has been working so hard this day, I thought she would enjoy a rest."

"Of course not," Kynthea answered, but Zoe perked up at the implied insult.

"I am very hale, Your Grace. I think I can manage pouring a spot of tea."

"I'm sure you can," the man returned gently. "Nevertheless, Miss Petrelli? Would you do the honors?"

Kynthea had no choice now. Fortunately, she too had been trained since birth to perform the basic tasks of an aristocratic lady. She served the duke his tea (cream, no sugar), then Zoe (sugar, no cream), then was about to pour her own when the door knocker sounded.

It was the dowager duchess, and a more intimidating woman did not live in England. The woman swept in, frowned as everyone scrambled to their feet to greet her, then settled like a queen in the chair nearest her son.

"Late tea?" the woman asked.

"I prefer a casual schedule," the duke responded.

"Hmmmm," retorted his mother as her gaze hopped between Kynthea and Zoe. Oh hell. The woman wanted to know why Zoe wasn't serving. She was about to explain when Kynthea solved the problem.

"You prefer lemon alone with your tea, correct, Your Grace?" she asked.

"Correct."

And where Kynthea had learned that, she had no idea. Oh wait, of course she did. Zoe's mother had told her that while

Kynthea was in the room. Fortunately, her cousin had remembered. She poured and passed the drink, spilling not a single drop. Well done. Zoe always rushed the serving and spilled a little, but her cousin was deliberate in her actions. Personally, Zoe found such care exhausting, but Kynthea seemed to take to it naturally.

"Why is your hair wet?" the dowager demanded as she peered at Zoe.

"Mother, please. Lady Zoe is not here for an inquisition."

"Ras—"

Zoe knew how to smooth this one over. "I was working with your son's horses and begged the indulgence of a bath."

"I offered it," the duke corrected.

"And we were just talking about her ideas," Kynthea interposed. "About the horses. Indeed, she learned about your father's plans and would like to help His Grace implement them."

The duke nodded. "I am most intrigued."

Everyone, it seemed, fully supported the idea except for the most important one. The duchess pursed her lips and scowled. "That is not a proper activity for a lady."

"Are you sure?" the duke countered. "Lady Zoe is quite accomplished at it. Even Barnes complimented her."

The woman's brows rose up to her hairline. "Indeed?" That did not sound like the woman approved. But then, she didn't have to. Once Zoe married her son, Zoe would be able to say what a duchess did and did not do.

In fact, it was best to begin as she meant to go on. Or so her mother had always said. And she meant to be a duchess who managed a racing stable.

"Indeed," she stated flatly. "My dowry will bring to the dukedom a pair of prized mares of impeccable bloodline. They will breed the next generation of racing stars, and I mean to be the one who sees it through. That involves daily work that is neither glamorous nor sweet smelling, but it does produce results." She shrugged. "I'm afraid I will often arrive late to tea and with wet hair. But if His Grace doesn't mind, I believe we shall get along quite well."

She looked at the duke as she spoke and was pleased to see his lips curve in amusement. Indeed, her father had that exact look whenever she'd told one of his friends something clever about his horses. Zoe took it as a good sign.

Kynthea, of course, kept steady, neither blushing nor looking away. It would fall to her to smooth over any unpleasantries today and in the future. She likely had a half dozen new topics at the ready but knew better than the push them forward too soon. Especially as everyone waited for the duchess's response.

"Well, that's putting it bluntly." To her credit, her tone was more thoughtful than critical.

Zoe smiled. "I find it best to speak my mind on matters that pertain to me."

"And what of matters that pertain to my son?"

"Then he may choose to speak bluntly or not."

It was a gamble to speak so tartly, especially to her future mother-in-law, but she had never been one to guard her tongue. Her cheeky response worked on the duke as it startled a laugh out of him. He didn't even bother to change it to a cough. Kynthea smiled because she was always kind. But the duchess was a different matter altogether.

The woman turned to her son. "She's too young for you."

Damn it. She should have taken the time to pin up her hair. But then she would have a soggy mass on her head and that always gave her a headache. She opened her mouth to object, but it was Kynthea who saved the day.

"She need not marry tomorrow, you know," Kynthea offered, her voice cool. "An engagement could be announced soon, say at her presentation at court in a few weeks. But the actual nuptials could be delayed a year or more."

A year or more would put a crimp in her plans for the horses, but she could adjust. Especially if it soothed her future mother-in-law and delayed her time in the marriage bed. Besides, couldn't an engaged woman take control of the stable? If the duke allowed it?

But the duchess was not assuaged. "My son needs an heir now."

"I'm hardly about to expire, Mother."

No. It was her father whose days were numbered. "I am young and healthy," she inserted forcefully. "I will do my duty with regards to the ducal nursery." She arched her brow as if she weren't shaking inside. "As soon as you like."

This time, the duke did cough. Clearly, he was uncomfortable discussing that aspect of married life with his mother. Well, his mother had brought up an heir, so he couldn't blame her. Instead, he offered his mother some cut bread with a wry expression.

"These are quite delicious, today. Would you like to try one?"

His mother sniffed. "What are they?"

"I have no—"

"Grated carrot and raisin bread," Zoe said. "It was originally Kynthea's recipe, but I improved on it."

The lady frowned at the neatly cut triangle. "You brought food to a duke's home?"

"I, uh, brought it to see if His Grace might enjoy it." Because she'd wanted to show the duke that she had skills other than with horses. She could see now that it might be interpreted as rude. "I enjoy baking," she said, realizing how silly that would sound, coming from a future duchess.

The lady waved Zoe to silence. "We have an excellent cook." Then she took a careful bite. "Hmph," she commented, as if that meant anything. Then she added, "But I cannot understand why our chef allowed strange food into the house."

"I hardly think she was trying to poison me," the duke said. "And I do find them quite tasty." He took another slice for himself.

Excellent.

And while Zoe was enjoying his praise, the duke offered the plate to Kynthea. She took a slice in one hand, then bit down, her eyes closing in appreciation. "It tastes like home," she murmured.

"Only better."

"I can barely fathom all that you have lost," he said. He spoke the words softly, his attention riveted to Kynthea's face. She looked away, her shoulders stiff.

Zoe watched, her brows tightening. Even Zoe could see that the duke had a great deal of affection for Kynthea. So, too, could the duchess as her eyes widened with surprise.

He couldn't possibly be developing a tendre for Kynthea, could he? She bit her lip as she thought of all the time he and her cousin had spent together. And that most people adored Kynthea once they got to know her.

Which meant that, of course, the duke's affection had been engaged. And how stupid was she to have not seen it before? Damn, damn, damn! She wasn't averse to the idea. Given Kynthea's social disasters, becoming a demirep was one of her cousin's best options. And being a duke's mistress would keep her in society.

But why, why, why did she have to try for the one man Zoe needed to attach?

"Miss Petrelli, is it?" the duchess barked. And it was a bark, sharp and loud akin to the sound small yapping dogs made.

"Your Grace?" Kynthea responded.

"Can you tell me why Mr. Pickleherring has made you his target?"

Kynthea didn't show offense at the harsh demand. It was never good for a lady in her position to openly flout a duchess. The duke, on the other hand, was clearly angered on her behalf.

"No," he said. And he punctuated the word by pushing to his feet.

"What?" cried his mother, insult reverberating in the word.

He smiled genially as he held out his hand to Kynthea. "I said no, Mother. I wanted you to meet these ladies, and now you have. But it's a lovely day. I thought we could all go for a stroll. I am sure Lady Zoe wants to check on the horses again. She gave Barnes quite a few instructions."

Actually, that was true.

"And Miss Petrelli hasn't seen the gardens in back."

"But what about tea?" his mother asked.

"Hmm? Well, you're welcome to have more. As for me, I'm itching to go outside."

And what were any of them to do but follow the man as he directed? They all abandoned their tea and bread to stroll out in the gardens which were small compared to some estates, but stunning nonetheless.

The conversation remained genial. With the duke's prompting, Kynthea offered several ideas for medicinal plants. She'd learned of them because she'd had the care of her parents during their illnesses, but swore that they would grow nicely here. Zoe made her suggestions for beautiful plants. She'd memorized them in case of exactly this kind of discussion. But flowers were not her forte, and the duchess was quick to dismiss her.

"Everyone likes roses," the woman drawled.

"Just because they're popular, doesn't make them any less beautiful," Kynthea said.

"Well put," enthused the duke. Indeed, he had been enthusiastic about everything Kynthea did and said. And now Zoe had no choice but to recognize the truth.

Kynthea was her favorite person outside of her parents. She was her friend, her confidante, and the kindest soul on the planet. She was also, Zoe suddenly realized, her rival.

Chapter Twenty

RAS DID NOT have a great deal of experience with shame. It was not an emotion he experienced often. Certainly not since achieving adulthood. He treated his servants with respect and paid them a good wage. He was thoughtful with his responsibilities to his title, his estate, and his position in the House of Lords. He loved his sister and even maintained a generous attitude toward his mother, which he felt was quite virtuous of him.

So shame was a rare and difficult experience. So difficult, in fact, that all afternoon, he had shoved it down and away. He had maintained an amiable persona throughout tea and supper. He had done everything he could—within reason—to show that he valued Kynthea. He'd gone out of his way to be kind to her today, all while reminding himself that no duke would feel shame for sharing physical pleasure with a woman who asked for it.

Better yet, he had not taken her virginity. Indeed, he had made sure that what they shared had no consequences.

And yet, he felt such burning shame that now—alone in his bedroom—he was choking on it.

He was wealthy, educated, and titled. In fact, he was the most eligible bachelor in all of England right then. If he could not find a way to marry the woman of his choice, then he was not worthy of his privileges.

Kynthea was his choice.

His shame came from the fact that it had taken him this long to realize it.

Step by step, he reviewed his day. Most importantly, he thought about her and how she had come through everything with grace.

He spun through the experience in his tack room slowly, lingering on the best moments. His favorite was Kynthea's face as she discovered her own sexuality. The memory of her breasts still brought his cock to attention. Indeed, he doubted that particular pleasure would ever fade. How odd that the sight of her serving his mother tea was equally delightful. Her poise despite the duchess' scrutiny filled him with pride. So different from Zoe's fire. Kynthea didn't flash like the girl did, but her strength shone brighter. A steady hand was always better than a sudden fist.

He listened as the house grew quiet around him. His mother had left soon after the meal. She wanted to sleep in her own bed tonight, and so had departed. He hadn't needed her approval to wed Kynthea, but he'd seen her grudging respect grow as Miss Petrelli balanced her cousin's interests, his mother's probing questions, and—oddly enough—his servants' casual neglect.

Everyone, his mother included, assumed he intended to wed Zoe. And though his staff was well trained, they immediately gave deference to the child and set the lady last. They served Zoe first, his mother second, and Kynthea third. That wasn't the correct order of precedent since his mother should be first. It wasn't the nature of proximity because they often went around Kynthea to get to Zoe. It was simply his staff acting as they thought he wanted, and that was inappropriate. They should act as was proper.

Normally, he would have a stern word with his butler about it. Indeed, he had spoken sharply to the man before heading to bed. But it was a pleasure to see Kynthea subtly correct his staff without ruffling a single feather. Every time they headed toward Zoe first, she commented sweetly, "Oh look, Duchess, the wine is here. Do you favor the cabernet?" Or some such comment.

His servants had had no choice but to serve his mother first because Kynthea had made a point of it. Zoe hadn't noticed. Indeed, he was fairly certain the girl was overwhelmed by the situation. She'd held her own at first, but as the conversation wore on, she proved to be sadly out of step with anything that wasn't about horses. He was sure that single vision would expand as she matured, but at the moment, she was too young to show well against her cousin.

Kynthea, on the other hand, had proved that she was intelligent, could handle the servants, and even gain his mother's grudging respect. All of these things were important to him, but they weren't what decided him upon her. That was something much more elusive. So elusive that he didn't know what it was and had sat down to contemplate the matter while he waited for the rest of the house to go to sleep.

That, of course, was the best part of the day. He had convinced Miss Petrelli and Lady Zoe to spend the night. It had been easy to take Zoe back to the stables where she burned away the evening checking his horses. By the time she was done, it was too late to travel back to the city. And suddenly, his guests had to spend the night.

Kynthea was one door down the hallway from him. And he hoped that she would give him the chance to apologize. He wanted to tell her he was an idiot. And he wanted to talk about the future—*their* future together. But he would wait a few moments longer just to be sure everyone slept—

A scratch sounded at his door. His brows rose. He hadn't thought her bold enough to seek him out but was grateful for the surprise. He stood up, not even bothering to adjust his evening robe. He didn't plan to wear it for long.

He was just reaching the door when the knob turned on its own and a figure stepped inside, rapidly shutting the door behind her.

"Lady Zoe?" he gasped, quickly pulling his robe closed. "Is something wrong?"

She was wearing her hair loose about her shoulders and her

blue eyes were impossibly wide. She wore his mother's borrowed dressing gown which was a thoroughly disconcerting sight given her diminutive stature and China doll looks. His mother had never been that small, so it gave Zoe the appearance of a little girl playing dress up.

"Y-yes, Your Grace," she rasped, her voice very high and small. "I, um, I cannot stay away."

"What?"

She spoke right over him. "You overwhelm me. I—I am overcome!"

Wasn't that the dialogue from the very bad comedy playing at the London theater? And—oh no!

Lady Zoe launched herself at him. It wasn't done from impulse. It looked like she steeled herself to do it and then jumped like she might leap over a very large puddle. Either way, he was obliged to catch her. Or rather deflect her as he quickly leaped to the side. He made sure she didn't fall, but he was not going to let her pursed lips land anywhere near his face.

She stumbled as she landed but remained true to her athletic nature. She pivoted quickly, then cried out.

"Your Grace! I need you!"

"No!" he snapped. "You most certainly do not!" And in case she didn't understand, he held his hand straight out in front of her. She would have to bodily overcome him to approach. Unless she used his hands to her advantage, which she did to horrifying effect.

She grabbed his wrist and slammed his hand against her breast, what there was of it. She was mostly muscle and surprising strength.

"Oh, Your Grace!"

"Absolutely not!" He leaped back, bodily jerking his hand away. And when she stepped closer, he let out an undignified squeak of alarm. He could overpower this child in a heartbeat, but he didn't want to touch her. He didn't want her to touch him!

He scrambled to his bedroom door and hauled it open fast

enough to roar, "Kynthea! Come out here immediately!"

If he'd been thinking properly, he wouldn't have used her formal name. He had no right to call her Kynthea yet. And damn it, Lady Zoe was quick enough to catch the slip.

She frowned, stumbled to a halt, and whispered, "Kynthea?"

The lady in question came rushing out of her bedroom, hastily buttoning up her dress as she bolted from her room. Her hair was down, and he was man enough to see how beautiful it looked. But he was more interested in the way Zoe's gaze hopped between the two of them.

"You called her Kynthea," she accused. "You have… You are…" She sniffed. Was she crying? Surely not! She wasn't a girl who cried, but clearly something was overcoming her emotions.

"What is happening?" Kynthea said, her eyes widening as she took in the sight of the two of them. "Zoe?"

Oh hell. It looked just like…well, just like Zoe had probably intended. "She came to my room," he said. "She… I did not!" He backed away from the girl like she was the destruction of all his hopes. And damnation, if any of his staff discovered them like this, then it might just happen. Even the most loyal servants whispered. "Damn it!" he cursed. Then he jerked his fingers at Kynthea. "Get in here. Please!"

His gaze must have been wild enough to convince her. She crossed the hallway quickly and he shut the door solidly behind her. Then, keeping himself as far away as possible from Zoe, he gestured to the girl.

"She is confused. Nothing happened." He looked desperately at her. "Can you help?"

She'd already understood and was crossing to her cousin. But Zoe skittered backwards as she wrapped her arms tightly about herself. "How could you?" she asked as her eyes shimmered with tears. Her gaze was all on her cousin and there was true pain in her voice. "You knew he was to be my husband. You *knew!*"

"Zoe, please try to understand—"

"I even put the potion in his wine. He drank all of it!"

Ras jolted. "What? You dosed my drink?"

Kynthea shot him a frustrated look. "It did not harm you."

"You knew?"

She shrugged. "Not that she'd done it. And I did warn you."

He threw up his hands as he looked at the girl. "Why would you do this? I have been clear with you from the beginning." He frowned. "Even Mother said you were too young, and she said it to your face!"

"I am sixteen!"

"Exactly!"

Kynthea held up her hands. "Hush! Both of you! Or we'll end up with an outcome no one wants!"

To which Zoe rounded on her cousin with a harsh expression. "But I do want it!" she all but screamed. "That's why I'm here. Do you really think I want to… to…" She glanced at the bed and shuddered. A real live shudder that shook her whole body. He would have been insulted if he weren't so relieved.

"Think, Zoe," Kynthea pressed. "You would have to do *that* every night until you conceived."

"I know!" she sniffed. "I am prepared to make the sacrifice."

You'd think he was hideous or something.

"No man wants to be married for his stable," Kynthea said gently.

"No!" Zoe said, her shoulders raised up to nearly her ears. "It was for Father." She swallowed. "You know he wants me to make a brilliant match. He wants to walk me down the aisle."

Ras huffed. "You would make us both miserable for the rest of our lives just so your father can have one day of joy?"

Zoe lifted her chin. "I wouldn't be miserable. I would have the running of—"

"Of the stables," everyone finished for her.

The girl jutted out her chin. "I will be very happy," she said firmly.

"I would not," he retorted.

Kynthea sighed as she stepped between them. "This is getting us nowhere. Zoe, even you must see that it isn't possible."

"Of course, not now," the girl sulked. "Not with you here."

How anyone could appear so tragically betrayed when she'd created this disaster was beyond him. He would have said she had a future on the boards except that he remembered her badly done words when she'd first walked into his room.

"Do not blame your cousin," he said firmly. "You dosed me, you burst into my room, and you…" He looked at his hand and surreptitiously wiped it on his pants. He did not want to know the feel of her breast.

"But what am I going to do?" she cried. It wasn't a wail like he expected. Indeed, if she had continued making that noise, he would have thrown her out of his room and the gossips be damned. He would not have a wailing child in his bedroom. But the words were whispered with a choking kind of sob. She really was overcome and desperate, by the looks of her, as only a spoiled girl could be.

"You are going to go back to bed," Kynthea said sternly. "It is wrong to trick a man into marriage. You know that."

"It was Mama's idea."

Oh heaven. Not that he was surprised. She wasn't the first girl to try to trap him into marriage. Only the youngest.

Kynthea managed to get the girl to take a step, but then Zoe dug in her heels and looked first at her cousin and then him. "But what about you two? What are you… When did it…" She was struggling with her words and no wonder. Just those aborted questions had everyone's face blushing.

He held up his hand. "First, Lady Zoe, my affection for your cousin has nothing to do with you."

"Affection—"

"Second!" he interrupted. "You had no right to dose me and then burst in here without my leave. That is beneath you, no matter who pushed you to do it."

The girl pressed her lips together and tried to look defiant. It didn't work. Eventually, her head dipped in shame. "I was thinking of my father."

"Poppycock." He wanted to say something much stronger, but he tried not to curse in front of children. "You were thinking of my horses and very little else."

She had no response to that which was very wise of her.

"And finally, I should like to discuss something with you in the morning. An arrangement that I think will benefit us both."

Her head snapped up. "What arrangement?"

"In the morning!" he repeated, now all but shouting. "When we are both properly attired." He pulled his bedroom door open then stepped to the opposite wall. "You may go back to your room and think upon your crimes." He winced at the stuffy phrasing. And damn her for making him sound like his old nanny. Think on her crimes, indeed. But she'd tried to trap him into marriage. For his horses!

Thankfully, Kynthea was gentler. She wrapped her arm around the girl's shoulders and urged her forward.

Undaunted, Zoe tried one last time. "But what about—"

"Hush," Kynthea said firmly. "We're going back to your room now. His Grace has had enough for one night."

"But—"

"Zoe!" The word was sharp, and Ras was relieved to see that there was an end to Kynthea's well of sympathy for the spoiled girl. "We will talk in your room." Then she steered the girl firmly out of his bedroom.

Kynthea closed his door behind her which left him to stare at it with an angry glower. So much for his hopes of a conversation tonight. Not to mention anything else. It was childish of him, but he needed to talk to Kynthea, and now he'd have to find another way to get her alone. That wouldn't be easy in the middle of the Season with prying eyes and plotting mamas everywhere. But he would find a way because, damn it, he was determined to make Miss Petrelli his bride.

Chapter Twenty-One

KYNTHEA WAS NOT one to shy away from hard talks. That didn't mean she relished them. But it was past time to explain things to her cousin.

Zoe shuffled into her bedroom and plopped down on her bed with a dispirited grunt. "I thought it would work. I really thought it would."

"Did you?" Kynthea challenged. "Or did you close your eyes, cross your fingers, and hope."

The girl's head jerked up. "Mama's friend's daughter says—"

"Nothing you can trust."

Zoe pushed out her lower lip in a sulk. "You helped me, you know. You helped me get the potion."

"I did," she said softly. "And I hoped it would work out for you."

"Then why did you..." Her words trailed away but the meaning was clear. Especially when her gaze slid to the door and the duke's bedroom beyond it. "You're doing something with him!"

How to answer that? She sat down on the bed beside her cousin. "Let's talk about you first. Are you truly heartbroken? Or just embarrassed? And maybe a little bit relieved."

Zoe crossed her arms across her chest. "You know the answer to that. I'm mortified."

"And relieved."

"Yes! Yes, I'm relieved. I don't really want to get married. I wouldn't mind the dress and the party and all. Everyone likes being a bride. But—"

"Yes," Kynthea interrupted. "I know it's all about the stable for you."

"And having everyone say 'Your Grace' to me would be nice."

"You're already Lady Zoe. 'Your Grace' carries a lot more responsibilities than you realize."

Zoe sighed. "The Crown approved. I didn't think he'd say no."

Kynthea winced. He might still be forced to say yes. When royalty decided upon a thing, even a duke had to comply. "It doesn't matter what the Crown says. It's a terrible idea to start a marriage with a lie."

Zoe rolled her eyes. "It wasn't supposed to be a lie. He was supposed to be enamored of me. Head over heels in love. Instead, he fancies you." She tilted her head and gave Kynthea a sidelong glance. "Do you think it was because you were the one to spill the potion on him the first time?" She gave a slight nod. "That must be it. The potion worked, just on you, not me."

Kynthea had no response to that. Whatever the cause, the duke was not enamored of Zoe. But then the girl finally got around to thinking of someone other than herself. Truthfully, given the magnitude of her embarrassment, she'd made good time. Many sixteen-year-olds never thought beyond their own embarrassment. Instead, Zoe's eyes held sympathy as she looked at Kynthea. And her words were gentle though they cut deeply.

"You don't think he's going to marry you, do you? I mean, I wouldn't be bothered, but the rules of society are very clear. You aren't even Lady Kynthea. You're just Miss Petrelli, and he's a duke. And the things that Mr. Pickleherring has printed about you make it worse. He might look past it if you were rich, but—"

Kynthea squeezed Zoe's hands to make her stop. If things were different, if she had been born to Zoe's parents instead of her own, if a thousand things were changed, then this next stage of her life could be very different.

But things weren't as she'd like. So she shook her head. "I know he won't marry me."

"Well," Zoe said slowly, clearly trying to be gentle. "He might *want* to. He might say nice things to you—"

"But he won't marry me. I know."

Her words hung heavy between them both. There was no fighting the truth of it, and it took them both a while to absorb that. Zoe recovered first.

"What are you going to do?"

Might as well say it. She'd made the decision, but it was still so hard to speak it aloud. "I have two choices. I could become a governess or more likely a housekeeper somewhere that doesn't get London gossip."

"You'd have to go to Scotland for that. You don't want that."

"Your mother said Russia."

"You can't!"

"No," she agreed. "I won't." She swallowed, forcing herself to say it aloud. "Or I could become the duke's mistress."

Zoe's eyes widened. "You *want* that? I mean, to do the job of the marriage bed without benefit of a ring?"

"Do you see any other options?"

Zoe threw up her hands in disgust. "That's why I was trying to seduce him. If I became the duchess, you could be my companion and—"

"And there would still be gossip. As long as I'm in London, the tales will follow me."

Zoe shrugged. "They will get a lot worse if you become a demirep."

Very true. But she'd have rooms of her own, perhaps even a servant.

"You want to do it!" Zoe gasped in surprise. "You're not frightened of it!"

Kynthea shrugged, fighting the ache in her whole body. "I've learned a lot recently—"

"What!"

"From Madame Ilie at My Lady's Apothecary." And from His Grace. "It's not as awful as you think."

Zoe grimaced. "That's not what it looks like when horses do it."

"No. But I understand among men and women it can be very pleasurable."

Zoe squirmed. "You're staking a lot on the possibility that it will be fun. You might be better off in Russia."

Kynthea smiled. "But then I'd never see you again." Her heart squeezed a little bit. "You'd miss me, wouldn't you? If I were all the way in Russia?"

"I'll miss you when you're right here!" she cried. "I'm not allowed to see a demirep. You know that."

All too true. And that thought depressed her more than she could say. "But there are places we could meet. Maybe I could come riding with you sometime."

"Mama will never forgive you if you become exactly what everyone has said."

Kynthea nodded. The irony of it was not lost on her. The *ton* had decried her as a harlot and thereby forced her into that very path. She squeezed Zoe's hand. "It's my decision, Zoe. Do you think you can forgive me for making it?"

Zoe's expression grew sad, but there was a maturity in her tone that was surprising. "I'm not completely blind," she said. "I know that you faced hard choices before you came to live with us. And that your life won't be easy after you leave us." She shrugged. "I dosed a duke with a love potion. I cannot blame you for making the best choice you can." She gripped Kynthea's hand tight. "And I will find a way to see you. I don't care what Mama says. I will not abandon you!"

That made her heart light. Such fierceness in her cousin. In a few years, Zoe would be a formidable woman indeed. "Thank you," she whispered as they embraced. And when they separated, there were tears in both their eyes.

"What will you do now?" Zoe asked.

Kynthea pressed her palms down on her dress. "Well," she said slowly. "I doubt there will be a better time to put my proposal to the test."

"Are you going to seduce him now?" Zoe looked around. "Now?"

"I doubt it will be a seduction. These things are a matter of business, not love." Oh, how it hurt to say those words. She didn't examine why. She would break if she focused on her true feelings. Instead, she put on her bravest face. "If he is amenable, I will have my future set on the morrow."

"And if he is not?"

"Then I suppose I am off to Russia."

"Ireland might be nicer. Not as cold."

"Ireland it is."

Then she kissed her cousin on the cheek, squared her shoulders, and headed off to not-seduce the duke.

Chapter Twenty-Two

RAS SIPPED HIS brandy and felt his body mellow with the drink. He needed it after that scene with Lady Zoe. How else was going to erase the sight of that girl in his mother's dressing gown? He'd much rather remember Kynthea with her hair coming out of its plait. It was a honey brown color that made him think of summer days. He wasn't sure why that was, but looking at her reminded him of the sweetest days of his childhood. Of course, his imagination put them both by a stream engaged in a very adult activity. But thanks to the brandy, he could revel in the thought without throbbing with uncomfortable needs.

He jerked out of his reverie at a scratch at his door. If that girl was back, he was going to lock her in her bedroom and have a footman guard the door. He tied his robe tight and opened the door a small crack. Then he jerked back in shock.

Kynthea's pale face gazed up at him.

He swung the door wide, glanced down the hall to make sure no one else was there, then quickly pulled her inside, closing the door behind her.

"Is everything all right? Is..." Damn it, he didn't even want to say the girl's name. "Is she all right?"

"She's embarrassed."

So was he.

"But she'll recover. Isn't that what being sixteen is all about? Doing stupid things for glorious reasons?"

"She'd said she'd sacrifice herself to me like a virgin on some hideous god's altar," he grumbled. Then he gestured her to the other chair set near the fire. It was too warm to have started one, but the location was cozy, especially with the moonlight streaming in through the window.

She took his suggestion, sitting down with casual grace. Looking at her bathed in moonlight soothed his heart even as his blood began to heat at the sight. She didn't have that restless energy of so many. Neither did she fake a bored disdain. She was composed and elegant. And she was twisting her hands together in anxiety.

"Would you like some brandy?" he asked.

She looked at first like she would refuse, then she smiled and nodded. "Yes, please."

He poured, then watched as she took a large swig. She was definitely nervous. He wanted to ease her strain but wasn't sure how. So he waited, knowing that she would come to it eventually. And in the meantime, he enjoyed simply watching her.

"Thank you," she said, indicating the brandy.

"Have more if you like."

"That was plenty, thank you."

She'd consumed half the glass rather quickly. Her cheeks were starting to color, but he didn't know if that was from embarrassment or nerves.

"Would you like some food? I could find us something without waking the—"

"No, no. I'm not hungry, but I would like to discuss something with you."

"And I would like very much to apologize to you. I bungled things so very badly."

She blinked at him. "You bungled things?"

"You caught me off guard. I wasn't thinking—"

"*I* caught *you* off guard?" Her sarcasm couldn't be more plain.

He rubbed a hand over his face. "I'm not doing this well. Miss Petrelli—Kynthea—I wish—"

"Stop!" She held up her hand, her expression fierce. "You do not need to apologize for this afternoon. In fact, that is what I wish to speak with you about."

He closed his mouth, damning himself for drinking the brandy. He was not normally this tongue-tied, but he'd never proposed to a woman before.

"Please," she pressed. "Just let me say this."

He leaned back, grateful for the reprieve. "Of course," he said.

"I should like to…um…I should like to sell you my virginity."

Thank heaven he'd finished his drink. He might have choked on it otherwise. "I see," he said slowly. "Exactly what would be the price?"

"The, um, usual arrangement would suffice," she said. Her hands tangled now in her skirt. "I assume…er…after this morning, that you are interested?"

No, he wasn't. Well, he was absolutely interested as his cock was already thickening at the idea. But this was not what he'd expected at all. "You have my attention," he said. And at her widened eyes, he hastened to explain. "And I most definitely want you in my bed."

Her gaze skipped sideways to the furniture in question, then rapidly returned to him. "Um, the usual is a room somewhere. I don't require much, though I would appreciate a maid of all work." She swallowed. "I shall need it for a year."

"Where did you learn this?" His voice was growing tight as his anger stirred. She wanted to sell herself to him!

"The L—" She cut off her words. "It doesn't matter. I spoke to people who know, and they were most helpful."

"Really?" he drawled. "And what else did they tell you?"

"That as a lady of quality, I am worth a premium."

He winced at her blunt phrasing. "It seems you are very well informed. How much do you think that should cost?"

She named a figure that had him gripping his empty brandy glass in fury. Not because it was an outrageous amount, but because it was so damned low. She was worth ten times that amount! She must have noticed his reaction because her chin firmed as she steeled herself to continue. This was hard for her, as it should be. And he was angry enough to force her to continue.

"Anything else?" he asked.

"Yes. I do not want to bear children out of wedlock. I have gotten these..." She pulled an envelope that no doubt contained French letters. "I'm told that they are effective, but most men don't like them."

"That is correct—"

"I insist." She looked down at her hands. "This is my choice, you understand. To become risqué. But I will not impose that choice upon a child. Bastards are not treated well, and I won't—"

"You will have no bastard by me." His voice was harsher than he intended. He wanted children with her. Bright boys and sweet girls. Or sweet boys and bright girls. It didn't matter so long as he saw her in them, and he could love them as his father had loved him. But rather than focus on that, he noted that she had come here prepared not only with information, but also with condoms.

"You seem to have thought this through," he said.

"I always try to be prepared," she acknowledged.

"Then what happened this morning?"

Her head came up. "What?"

"I could have had you this morning in the tack room," he said. "You never mentioned French letters then, nor the price of your virginity." He sounded like the worst kind of libertine, but he couldn't control the hard tone in his voice. He was furious.

"I...no, I guess I didn't," she said. "I suppose I am lucky then."

"Lucky?" he rasped. "My dear, you are playing with fire."

If he thought to cow her, he was sorely mistaken. Her head came up and her eyes flashed. It was likely the moonlight, but it seemed like she had a fire kindling within her. One that strengthened her voice and straightened her spine. "If you do not wish this...this...relationship, then we need speak no further."

"Oh, I am definitely considering it. But I have a few questions to match your requirements."

She nodded. "Very well. Ask them."

"After our evening is done, do we continue our situation? I would be paying for a year, you see. And are your terms for me alone or are you available for other protectors?"

She blinked twice before she answered. Clearly, she hadn't even considered the idea. "I don't understand."

"I know a baron who is searching for a new paramour. Would you consider—"

"No!"

She spoke with pleasing vehemence, but he was not done. "Perhaps you object to his low title. I am a duke, after all. But I could bring you to Prinny's attention. Becoming a royal consort would keep you in society. And I understand he sometimes pays very well." *Sometimes* being the important word. With royalty, one never knew what bills they might forget. Not to mention the fact that the idea of her with Prinny made him want to vomit.

She appeared to feel the same way. "Absolutely not! How could you think I'd want that?"

He arched his brows. "These are the questions I'd ask any potential mistress." He leaned forward. "I need to know why you picked me to gift with your virginity."

"It's not a gift. It's a… a…" Her words failed her.

"A transaction?"

"Yes." Her hands gripped her skirt, but she didn't flinch from the truth. Indeed, she met his gaze with a challenge of her own. "If you will have me."

He moved so fast, she released a squeak of surprise. One second, he was in a chair across from her, the next he was on one knee in front of her. He wasn't immune to the irony. He would propose marriage this way, but tonight's discussion was very different.

"If I'll have you?" he scoffed as he reached up to cup her face. "Kynthea, why are you selling yourself so cheaply?"

She looked at him, her eyes wide and earnest. Damnation, she was so innocent, and yet their discussion was anything but. "I should ask for more? You mean…like, jewelry?"

She made him want to scream. "I mean, why aren't you asking me to marry you? Why don't you want to be my duchess?"

She recoiled from the question. And he saw her blink away tears. "Don't mock me, Your Grace. It's beneath you."

"I'm not mocking!"

She turned back and there was bitterness in her gaze, poison in her words. "Do you think me stupid? I know you won't marry me. Compared to you, I am nothing. *Miss* Petrelli, impoverished and uninteresting to anyone except as an object of pity. Or scorn." She added that last word with clear rancor. Then again, the *ton* had not treated her well.

"You interest me," he said. And when she did not respond, he tried again. "Why don't you want to marry me? Why don't you dream of standing by my side, of bearing my children, of holding my hand as our grandchildren play at our feet?" That was what he saw when he looked at her. He saw a future. He saw a woman who could stand with him before royalty and not be cowed. He saw a mother to smart children who could make a difference in this troubled world. And he saw a woman who set his blood on fire.

"You know nothing of my dreams," she whispered.

And perhaps that was the problem. He didn't know what she wanted. Circumstances had forced her hand, otherwise she would not be here. But ignorance could be remedied. He cupped her cheek and pulled her face closer to his even as he stretched up for her. He could not be this close without wanting to kiss her.

"What do you dream of?" he asked. "Tell me. Maybe I can make it come true."

Her expression shifted, twisting in ways that hurt to see. She was in pain, and he was making it worse. But he had to know why she couldn't even imagine more for herself.

"You must know," she whispered.

"I swear I do not."

She touched his hand where it cupped her face. "I dream of

you, you idiot. Why else would I have gone into the tack room with you?"

The urge to kiss her nearly overwhelmed him, but he had dreams as well. And she was too perfect a woman for him to *not* question it. "Why me? Is it because I gave you your first quickening? Is it because I am a duke? Why me, Kynthea? Why would you offer me something so precious as yourself?"

"You can ask that? You sat by my side for a week defending me against every snide, crude remark. You who sit with royalty, defended me."

"You were innocent of their charges."

"You discussed literature and Corn Laws with me without condescension."

He shrugged. "You had read the books, and you asked the questions."

She shook her head. "You say I am precious, and yet you have no idea how rare a man you are. A duke without arrogance, one who is kind to someone as unimportant as me. If you said you could grab a star from the sky, I would believe you."

He chuckled. "You are not that foolish. You know I am flesh and blood like everyone else."

She touched his mouth, traced the curve of his jaw, and stroked fire along his neck. "If you want me, Your Grace, I am yours." She quirked a brow at him. "Or do I go to Ireland?"

Ireland? What did that have to do with anything?

"You come to me," he said.

He kissed her. Not a gentle kiss as before or even a teasing one. This time, he took her mouth with the fierceness of a man staking his claim. He thrust inside her. He dominated her tongue and teeth as if he were a warrior born to possess her. And when she made a sound of hunger, when she grabbed his arms and held on with strength, he broke their kiss and scooped her up in his arms.

"Your Grace!" she cried.

"Ras!" he commanded. "Say my name."

"Ras," she whispered. Then she arched her brows at him. "Erasmus Oliver Arthur Stace, Duke of Harle."

He groaned. "Ras is plenty." Then he carried her to his bed, setting her down gently before diving in for another kiss. He wanted to say more to her. He wanted to declare himself. He could command her to be his wife, not his mistress. But she entwined her fingers in his hair, and she smelled like vanilla honey against his lips. And part of him knew that she wouldn't believe him anyway. She was as swept away as he.

So he enjoyed the rush, and he vowed to make this her first of many awakenings in his bed.

The priest would have to wait until tomorrow.

Chapter Twenty-Three

He called her precious. He looked at her like she was the most beautiful star in the sky. What woman could resist that? Not her. And so she let herself experience it. She felt his hands on her dress, pulling open the buttons. She let him kiss her with such need that her own heart responded. So fast. So hungry. Both of them, and yet he seemed to know what he was doing while she fell into the storm he created in her.

He unbuttoned her dress completely, and she helped him pull it off. She hadn't bothered with stays and so all that remained was her shift as he peeled her gown down. He cupped her breast through the thin fabric, thumbing her nipple while she felt her excitement surge and recede. She rushed for his mouth in a frenzy of desire. Then when the passion became too much, she pulled back to take in great gulps of air. The excitement simmered instead of boiled, and she had the awareness to push off his evening jacket and stroke the solid planes of his chest.

She rubbed her nail across the nub of his nipple and was pleased to hear a rumble deep inside his chest.

"You like that?" she asked.

"Yes."

A simple answer was all he offered because he was busy trailing his teeth along her jaw. And when she lifted up her chin, he nibbled down the side of her neck. Such feelings he stirred in her! She didn't think her shoulder could be that sensitive, but she felt his breath upon her skin and wondered how she had ever lived without experiencing this before.

"I'll buy you a new one," he said.

"What?"

He ripped her shift in half. She jolted in surprise at the sound, but when the cool air hit her skin, she arched in delight at the feeling. And then he caught her nipple in his mouth, and she was lost to the stroke of his tongue and the scrape of his teeth. Perhaps that was what she loved the most. She never knew what he would do next. There was no rhythm to his strokes, no pattern to anticipate. If she settled into one, he changed it. That kept her attention, increased her passion, and let her experience so much more.

She tried to touch him, but the storm was too much for her. She could only grip his shoulders, and then, as he kissed down her belly, she ran her fingers through his hair. The brush of his curls felt sensual against her skin. And then he kissed into *her* curls.

She tensed, remembering what he had done in the tack room. That had been wonderful, but surely he meant for something else tonight.

"Your Grace?" she gasped.

He held her hips down with his hands, spread large across her belly.

"Ras," he corrected.

"What are you doing, Ras?" she asked.

He flashed her a wicked grin. "Do you trust me?"

"You know I do."

He scrambled up to his knees, grinning at her like a boy with a treat. His evening jacket was gone, and she saw the breadth of his chest illuminated by the moonlight as he settled between her thighs. It was an undignified position for her, but he appeared to love it. She was spread out naked before him, and he stretched forward to rub his palms across her ribs and breasts.

"I didn't get to enjoy this as much as I wanted to earlier. Believe me, Kynthea, I'm going to enjoy this as much as you do."

She didn't think that was possible, and so she would have said except that she had no breath. He was fondling her breasts and she couldn't stop her eyes from rolling back in pleasure. Then he gave them one last pinch before sliding his hands down to her hips. Looping his arms beneath her legs, he raised her up.

Her eyes flew open. Lord, he was stronger than she'd thought. And while his eyes danced with delight, he set his mouth to her most private parts.

His tongue was clever, surprising her with the very randomness of his exploration. Long strokes, penetrating thrusts, teasing flutters—he did them all, and she wanted to laugh at the playfulness of it. Instead, she was overcome by the sensations.

Her body was tightening, each tease of his tongue making her belly quiver. Her legs tightened, and she couldn't keep herself quiet. She had the wherewithal to put a pillow over her face, but the sounds she made were only a distant echo of the turbulence within her.

He was unrelenting as he kept her body on the edge of the cliff without pushing her over. And she was in heaven. She'd never acted with such abandon, never felt more wonder in her body. She'd… never…

Never ever.

She never wanted it to end.

He increased his pace, and there was nothing to do but ride the dance of his tongue. Her belly rolled, all unbearably tight. Like a spring coiling to the very edge of possibility and then…

Flight. She didn't so much leap off the cliff into her quickening as let him throw her into the air. How glorious it was! So much more now that she understood what this was. She didn't know if each one would be like this, and she didn't care.

She soared.

And when she came back, he was stroking her belly, kissing the underside of her breast, petting her arms and her shoulders. He seemed to need to touch her, and she loved the way he caressed her.

Until he left her side. She felt the bed react to his movements and hated the suddenly cool air around her. She turned to see where he went and was warmed to see what he did.

First, he stripped out of the last of his clothes. She saw the corded thickness of his thighs and calves. He was a man who exercised, that was for sure. His buttocks were trim, his torso broad and strong. And his organ thrust thick and proud to her hungry sight. She remembered touching it earlier in the day, and her hands coiled with the desire to do so again. But it didn't look like she would get the chance.

He grabbed the envelope with the French letter in it. He happened to be in profile as he slid it on, and she watched with fascination at the movement of his body. His hands looked big and sure. His back curved as he worked, but that only emphasized his height since even bent over, he appeared tall. His legs were spread, but from the side she saw the ripple of his muscles as he balanced. And then—tease that he was—he turned to grin at her. He'd known she was looking and now straightened to his full height and faced her.

He looked magnificent.

"Don't be afraid," he said as he stepped forward. "I swear we will fit together like a hand in a glove."

"I'm not afraid," she said as she pushed up onto her elbow. "I'm just wondering how a man shaped like a Greek God has come to want me."

His expression fell and his eyes grew sad. "You underestimate yourself," he said gently.

No, she didn't. She knew her value by society's standards. But perhaps that was the point. He judged her by his own standard, and because of that, her heart swelled.

He came close, settling onto the bed as he touched her face. "You're beautiful, intelligent, and everything I value in a woman. Why don't you see that?"

He was sincere. She could see it in his expression and feel it in his caress, and yet part of her refused to believe. "You have heard what people say about me. And now…" She gestured to the bed.

"Now, I am a fallen woman."

"Fallen to me."

"Either way. There are poor women everywhere who are lovely and intelligent. They are abused constantly."

"Who abused you?"

"No one."

"Someone had to. Someone taught you long before we met that you have little value." He frowned. "Was it the vicar after your parents died?"

"Him? No. The depths of his depravity surprised me, but not his lack of character."

"Then who?"

She had no answer except perhaps the worst possible one. "My mother taught me to be aware of such things. She pointed to poorer children and expressed dismay that such bright children would have a hard life. She stopped me from playing with children of modest means, afraid of the diseases they might carry. She looked at the aristocracy with awe, never criticized their actions and always found something to praise."

"She taught you society's values. When did you learn differently?"

She shrugged. "My father never much agreed with her. He judged people solely on their ability to discuss anything logically." She pitched her voice to match her father's. "A discerning mind is the only hope for England. Logic! Reason! Anything else is just frippery." She smiled. "And he hated frippery." Then her smile faded. "If only he'd hated gambling as much."

Damned idiot man. "So why do you judge yourself by your mother's standards and not your father's?"

He asked such difficult questions! "I suppose because no one saw reason. They only saw that I was orphaned without a penny to my name."

He touched her face. "I see you differently."

He did. And at that moment, she saw herself. It was there, in the way he touched her with reverence, slowly and carefully, but in a way designed to maximize her delight. He continued in that vein when he kissed her. His lips, his tongue, even his breath seemed to impress his esteem into her body.

And she drank it in like a woman lost in a desert. He nourished her soul, and she loved him for it.

She still wasn't comfortable with that word. *Love.* But she couldn't deny it. Her feelings for him had deepened every moment they were together. Even when she'd been angry with him, he had returned with a sincere apology. What man—let alone a duke—did that?

Only him.

And only he pressed kisses into her skin as if he was worshipping the body of a goddess. It was so easy for her to open to him. So easy to adore him for the way he treated her. So easy to love him.

When he tongued her breasts to their peak, she rose to meet him again.

When he spread her legs and set his cock between her folds, she gripped his shoulders and begged him, "Please. Please yes."

He worked himself into her slowly. She felt the thickness of him, so very present, so very large. But she was wet and empty. He would fill her there as he filled her heart with love.

She arched into his gentle thrust, then gasped when he withdrew.

Tempo. Rhythm.

"Yes?" he asked.

"Yes," she answered.

He thrust.

Her maidenhead must have broken. No other had ever been so deep within her. If so, she barely felt it. It was uncomfortable, to be sure. He was so very large. But when he lay embedded within her, she could think of nothing more than that she had him now. A tiny piece of Erasmus Oliver Arthur Stace, Duke of Harle, would always be with her.

"Are you all right?"

"I am wonderful. You?"

"You are more than wonderful. And I…I cannot hold back much longer."

He was holding back? Why? "Give me everything, Ras."

He grinned. "As you wish." His hips began to move, and his cock slid in and out. Her knees rose as she gripped him, and the impact of his thrusts increased the beat of her heart. He pushed up off her without breaking the steady rhythm of his thrust. And his expression remained fierce as he looked at her.

Her body moved with each impact. She coiled her hands around his arms, gripping him tight. She arched her back so she could feel him go deeper, harder. Her belly coiled, a familiar feeling now. But it was magnified by the way he moved inside her. He felt part of her climb. And as his tempo increased, she timed herself to him.

Faster. Deeper.

She would have cried out if she had breath. Instead, she squeezed everything tight. Her hands, her legs, and deep within her.

He groaned as she did and went faster still.

More.

Yes.

Now.

Bliss.

Chapter Twenty-Four

RAS STRETCHED OUT beside her, gathering her close. Sleep tugged at the edge of his awareness, but he fought against it. He did not want to miss a second of his time with this glorious woman.

He could hardly believe his luck. He was going to have pleasure in his marriage bed. So many of his peers did not, but her responsiveness filled him with joy. And desire as well, given how quickly his cock was already responding to having her pressed tight against him.

Her eyes were drifting closed, and he watched her face as she relaxed into sleep. He couldn't join her, of course. It would be too easy for him to drift off and then they would face unwanted consequences in the morning. So he let her rest while he enjoyed the feel of her body against him, the rhythm of her breath matching with his own, and the wonder of a future he planned now with meticulous attention to detail.

She didn't believe he could love her. In truth, he was a little startled by how quickly he had tumbled into it. As a duke, he'd had the opportunity for lovers galore and in his younger days, he had indulged as much as a randy teenager could. But he quickly learned the emptiness of such liaisons. And the two times he was foolish enough to think he was in love, his mother had made things crystal clear. She hadn't forbidden him to marry. Instead, she had told him to spend all his time with the woman for a full month. Every second of every day and night. If he still believed he was in love, she would give him her blessing.

It was a feasible arrangement because the ladies had climbed into his bed first, then convinced him they were in love second. And so he had thrown himself into their presence, demanding their company non-stop, certain that his love for them would grow.

The first woman had lasted two weeks before he was heartily sick of her. The second made it almost a month before he began to question her. There were little things remembered differently between them. Stories she told that did not make logical sense. Bit by bit, his rationality asserted itself and he quit the woman the next day.

That was ten years ago. He'd never believed in love again.

Until now.

Looking back, he didn't know how he could have thought that was love. What he felt for Kynthea in a few weeks was so much richer, deeper, and truer than anything he'd ever experienced before. This was love. It had to be. Because he was about to defy a royal command in a rather spectacular fashion in order to bind her to him permanently. And he wanted to do it in such a way that she would never question her worth to him again.

It took nearly an hour for him to decide on a path, one he would have to implement with care. He didn't relish the deception that it required, nor did he want to be apart from Kynthea for the next two weeks, but there was no choice in the matter.

But first he had to wake her.

"Kynthea," he whispered as he kissed her. "Kynthea."

She came awake with a start, her eyes wide. "Is something the matter?"

"Nothing," he soothed. "But we can't sleep here. We'll be discovered."

"Oh." She started to get up, but he held her back.

"We need to speak about a few things first," he said. "Then I'll escort you back to your room."

"Escort me?" Her lips curved in a sleepy smile. "I'm a demirep now. I don't think such women get courtesies."

His expression hardened. He didn't like her saying that word much less putting herself in that class. "If you are my mistress now, then I get to establish a few rules of my own."

Some of the dreamy happiness in her eyes faded, and he cursed himself for what he was about to say. Especially when her gaze dropped as if she were surrendering to him.

"Of course, Your Grace. What do you require?"

He groaned at her formality. "First off, you'll call me Ras when we're in private."

She nodded and bit her lip. Very impish of her. "Very well," she said. "Ras."

"Good." He kissed her lips to show he wasn't annoyed, and he indulged until he felt her relax against him. "I have the housing of you now, correct? And you'll wear what I ask, yes?"

She swallowed. "Yes."

"Then I'll tell you now that I want you to stay at your aunt's house through Zoe's presentation at court. That's in three weeks, yes?" Both the Regent and Zoe's father had suggested he attend.

"I believe so, but I don't think my aunt—"

"Leave that to me. I'll speak with Zoe's father as soon as I can. They'll treat you with respect or I'll know the reason why."

She winced. "Even a duke can't declare such a thing about another man's house."

"You'd be surprised what a duke can accomplish when he puts his mind to it." She opened her mouth to argue, but he continued. "I'll pay for your court gown, of course. Make sure it is worthy of your association with a duke."

"A gown!" she gasped. She was so startled that she pulled out of his arms to look at him more directly. "You cannot think that I'll be allowed to go."

"On the contrary, you will go with Zoe as her cousin. You will be introduced to the Regent—"

"No!"

"Yes." There was no leniency in his voice. "You will do as I say in this."

She gaped at him. "I can't. My aunt will refuse."

He touched her face with a long, gentle stroke. "She will not. Leave that to me."

"Because I am your mistress now?"

He shrugged. "If that's what it takes to get you there."

She shook her head. "You cannot manage it," she stated flatly. "But if by some miracle you do, I will go." Her lips curled. "And I will wear a dress fit for a princess."

"I expect you to hold to your word."

"I expect you will apologize for your failure in a most gracious manner."

She had no idea what he could do. "You must learn to not be afraid of good things happening to you."

Her expression softened. "And you will learn that sometimes a guarded heart is necessary and reasonable."

He pulled himself upright and imitated his stuffiest relative. "I am not a reasonable man. I am a duke."

She laughed and kissed his upturned chin. "You are both, Your Grace." And when he shot her a hard look, she quickly amended her words. "Ras. And I couldn't be more pleased to be your paramour."

She was going to be a great deal more than that, but at the moment, he let the word pass. "I'm going to order the servants to set up a bath for you in the morning. It'll be in here."

"Here!"

"I do not want them to wake you before time. Filling a bath can be a lengthy process."

"There's no need—"

"There's every need. You may feel good now…" He let himself caress her hip to emphasize how good she felt to him. "But in the morning, there may be soreness."

"I will be fine."

"You will listen to what I say. I will have them set up a bath for you. Take your time in it. I have some things to discuss with my steward. And Mr. Barnes. And…" He groaned as he dropped his head onto her shoulder. "Damnation, if I allowed myself to think of all the people in line to speak with me, I shall go mad."

"I can help you with that, you know," she offered quietly. "I often helped organize things for my father. And when he grew ill, he left many things to me."

He didn't think she could be more perfect, and yet here she was proving him wrong. "I should like that very much."

She grinned, kissed him deeply, then when he was about to press her into the sheets again, she scrambled backwards and grabbed her dress. "If I am to leave this chamber before dawn, it should be now."

She was right. And yet, he was man enough to regret the necessity. Indeed, his cock was becoming increasingly manly by the second.

"We are agreed then?" he pressed. "You will stay with your aunt and uncle. And for now, no more talk of being my paramour." He pushed up from the bedsheets. "It would embarrass them and do no good for me either."

"A secret then," she said, and he thought there was a note of relief in her voice.

"For now, yes. Eventually, everyone will know the truth." Including her.

She finished pulling on her dress. He kept her ripped shift to dispose of properly later. Then she looked at the empty envelope that had once contained the French letter. "I'll need to get some more."

Good that she wanted to do that again. It reinforced that the experience had been good for her. "I'll manage that."

"You won't forget?"

As if he could forget anything about her. "I swear it."

She nodded, accepting his word. He pulled on his dressing gown before crossing to his bedroom door. Pulling it open, he saw the hallway was empty. Nodding he reached for her, but when she went to go through his door, he pulled her tight.

"Soon we will not worry about such things," he whispered. Then he kissed her with all the desire building inside him again. And when they separated, he was gratified to see she was as flushed as he felt. "You dazzle me."

"You overwhelm me," she returned. "And I have never been so happy to drown."

He didn't like the image, but this was not the time to argue. Instead, he held out his arm as if he were escorting the queen. She set her fingers upon him in an equally formal manner, and together they walked as proper as royalty. Well, royalty who wore nothing more than the flimsiest of coverings.

"My mother has clothing here. I'll get you one of her shifts," he said as they made it to her bedroom door.

"Won't she realize—"

"Hush," he said pressing his lips to hers. "Trust me."

"I do."

Two very beautiful words. He intended to make her say them again very soon.

He was stepping away when she gasped. He looked up sharply only to find her holding something out to him—his ruby crest. How his heart stopped to see it in her hand. Damn it, he wanted his crest *on* her.

"Ras," she said. "You need to take this back."

"You should keep it," he said. "So you know I am serious."

She laughed, but the sound held a note of sadness. "I have made my choice, and I don't regret it." She took his hand and pressed it back into his palm. "I do not need this to have faith in you. Indeed, I have set all my hopes upon you."

He curled his fingers around the jewelry. When it was time, she would wear his ring for all to see. But it wasn't time yet.

"I will not fail you, Kynthea."

"I believe you," she said, and he knew she lied.

Kynthea believed only to a certain point and no further. It was up to him to show her that more was possible.

Chapter Twenty-Five

THE DUKE WAS as good as his word, which shouldn't have surprised Kynthea, but it did. He managed things exactly as he'd promised. While she had a luxurious bath the morning after she became his paramour, he had a private discussion with Zoe. Kynthea had no idea what they discussed, but by the time they were travelling back to London, the girl was back to acting like her happy, horse-mad self. And though the girl occasionally sent knowing looks at Kynthea, she never spoke of or even seemed to remember the night's antics.

Not so for Kynthea, who relived every second as often as possible.

When they arrived at Zoe's home, His Grace requested and was granted a private audience with Zoe's father. It lasted a very long time and ended with a cordial invitation to join them at Zoe's court presentation. After the duke accepted, the earl casually mentioned that Kynthea would attend as well. And when Zoe's mother objected, the earl stopped her cold.

Kynthea would attend. Indeed, he expected that she would go to every ball, musicale, or theater evening with her cousin, and he would hear no more about it. When Kynthea pointed out that her invitations would likely be rescinded, Zoe blithely quipped that if Kynthea was barred from the door, Zoe would not attend either.

"I think I've had plenty of the social round this Season anyway," she said. Then she waved a hand and disappeared to grab the racing forms.

Kynthea's aunt was dumbfounded. As was Kynthea. But when she tried to ask His Grace for more details, he kissed her hand and apologized for having to leave quickly as he had urgent matters to attend.

Then he was gone.

If Kynthea thought to get more information from Zoe, she was sorely mistaken. Since the earl was visibly tired from the discussion, Zoe assisted him in returning to bed. They could be heard discussing horse breeding for hours after that. And no one—not even Kynthea—could discover the reason for the girl's unabated jubilance thereafter.

Zoe was happy when she dressed for the evening's party. She even giggled the next day when her father announced that he would retire to the country, returning only for Zoe's presentation at court. And she was blissfully irreverent when Kynthea asked if something momentous had occurred to keep her in such a fine mood.

Her answer? "I'm a mature woman now. And if my father finally sees that I'm old enough to make my own choices, then why shouldn't I be happy?"

That explained absolutely nothing, but Zoe could not be persuaded to say more. Truthfully, Kynthea had not thought the girl capable of such secrecy, but apparently Zoe had found a solution to the challenges in her life. And the only solution that fit, as far as Kynthea could see, was that Zoe and the duke had come to an arrangement.

As much as she didn't want to think that the duke was arranging for a wife in the same twenty-four hours that he had taken her as a paramour, the evidence was mounting. He spent a great deal of time with both Zoe and her father. He found time for her, of course. They always danced at whatever ball Zoe attended.

They were walking together in Hyde Park when she learned that Mr. Pickleherring had written an entire column about how Lord Nathaniel had been beaten up by unknown persons and was now recuperating in the duke's residence. It was an uncharacteristically vicious column, in that it included all sorts of salacious speculation as to why the man had been attacked. And it cast aspersions on a man who was supposed to be at death's door. It was a distinctly nasty turn for the column to take, and Kynthea was not at all prone to giving any credence to it.

Neither was the duke.

"It's almost as if it were written by an entirely different person," he said dryly.

"Exactly!" she said, glad that he had put voice to what she'd been struggling to understand.

"Since Pickleherring is obviously a pseudonym, the columnist could change from one writer to another, and we'd never know."

"Do you think that's what happened?"

"I do," he said firmly. "It's unfortunate that Nate became the target of this new writer, but I've spoken to the paper and to a wide variety of my friends about it."

She turned to him. "But how can you stop a gossip column?"

He shrugged. "Obviously, I can't. Especially since readership has increased thanks to his recent viciousness. But I've pushed Prinny to express his dismay at such cruelty. That will have some effect in moderating the situation."

He spoke as if talking to the Prince Regent were akin to stopping by a haberdashery to order a new set of buttons. "Do you often have conversations with Prinny?"

He cast her an amused glance. "Do not be star-struck by royalty. It is important to remember at the center of it all, they are human beings just like you and me."

Humans who had the power to create laws, steer the government, and make or break simple people like her. And yet, standing beside Ras, she felt as safe as it was possible to be. If Prinny had suddenly appeared and began to publicly damn her, she believed she could withstand it. Assuming, of course, that Ras stood by her side.

But rather than focus on whether that was good or foolhardy of her, she changed the topic.

"How is Lord Nathaniel? Will we see him in society again soon?"

"He is recovering. It was mostly his feet that were damaged, and so he is resting until they heal."

"But what happened?

"Footpads. Stole his money and his boots. He had to walk a very long distance to get to his home."

She glanced at him, feeling the stiffness in his body as he answered. There was more to the situation there, but she wasn't sure she should push to know more. He must have realized her hesitation and so flashed her an awkward smile.

"I think there's more to the situation, but Nate hasn't confided in me yet. All I can do is make sure he heals…and keep an eye on—" His brows narrowed. "Do you know Lord Fletcher?"

She frowned. "I think I danced with him at the beginning of the Season, but I haven't seen him since. I don't remember him as being anything unusual."

"You will let me know if he comes about again? And you will not be alone with him." That last was as much a command as it was a request.

"Is he dangerous?"

"I don't know. I believe he is the new Mr. Pickleherring, and he has a particular interest in hurting Nate."

"But why? And why did he write such awful things about me?"

He sighed. "That I do not know. I have been trying to find him to ask just those questions, but he has gone to ground." Then he squeezed her hand where it rested on his arm. "I believe the danger to you is past, but pray be on your guard just in case."

"I will," she said. But she hardly needed to since he attended every event that she and Zoe did. Indeed, he'd escorted them on more than one occasion.

And that was the last thing of consequence they shared. She tried in private moments to ask about the details of where she would live, but he deferred, saying he was setting matters in order. She asked when she could see him again, when they might be alone together again. He answered with this ball or that rout and never arranged a private meeting. If it weren't for a few lustful kisses in darkened corners, she would think he'd lost interest in her. But those few moments proved he was still very much interested. And the way he looked at her in public was equally explicit. He seemed to hang on her words, his gaze lingering on her face, and he continually asked about her welfare. Was she being treated well? Had she been snubbed by anyone?

And then came his casual comment the night before Zoe's presentation at court. They were standing in the back garden of a ball. Though others stood nearby, they were private enough for his words to be just for her.

"I thought you would be interested to know that Vicar Chapman has been relieved of his parish. Indeed, an investigation into his actions regarding several young women has caused him to be excommunicated."

Vicar Chapman? The one who had made such unseemly advances to her after her parents' death? "He's been... Been..." She couldn't even ask the question.

"Drummed from the church in disgrace." The duke's eyes seemed to burn as he squeezed her hand. "He will never prey on defenseless young women again."

She found that unlikely. Once a man had that inclination, he would likely always seek the vulnerable.

The duke must have read the doubt upon her face because he was quick to soften his statement. "He will never use an ecclesiastical position to find his victims. He is no longer a priest, no longer affiliated with the church—"

"Indeed, he will not be allowed into heaven," she said. That was what excommunication meant. His eternal soul was forever damned to hell.

"Do not feel sorry for him," the duke said. "He victimized several women in his parish, not just you. I am only grateful that you were strong enough to resist him."

Only because she had a place to go. And because her brother had taught her how to punch a man where it hurt. "You did this?" she whispered.

"I initiated the inquiry," he said. "The rest was up to the church."

She didn't know what to say. She hadn't thought that wretched man still had any hold upon her life. But knowing he could no longer use his position to hurt anyone else lifted a weight off her that she hadn't even known was there. And it was all thanks to Ras.

"You astound me," she whispered.

"It was the least I could do," he returned.

She would have given him anything at that moment. If he had wanted to whisk her away to his bedroom, she would have willingly thrown herself into his arms. Indeed, she tried, but he held her off. "We are not alone," he murmured.

"We are never alone," she groused. "I must confess that I thought becoming your paramour would mean—"

"Hsst! Lower your voice."

She huffed out a breath. How could she explain that she missed him? That though she had seen him nearly every day since their night together, they had always been surrounded by others and were forced to be circumspect. It wasn't just her physical desires, which were plenty strong, but they couldn't speak of anything meaningful. Not with people in earshot. She certainly could not demand to know what he planned with Zoe.

"I thought..." she tried, but she could not find the right words. "I wish..."

"I miss you," he said as he lifted her hands to his lips. "But all will be settled soon. I swear it."

They were suddenly interrupted by a gentleman who wanted to speak with him about politics. That was the interruption this time. The last time, another gentleman had wanted to speak to him about his horses. And yet another wanted his opinion on Ireland. He was a powerful man, and she must stand beside him and smile, knowing that everyone looked slyly at her and wondered at their relationship.

How desperate she was to have this charade over with! Couldn't she hide in her room until he had found a place for her to live? Then she could declare to one and all that she was his mistress, and everyone would stop whispering behind her back.

But that was not to be and, truthfully, she was beginning to despise the gossips so much that her thoughts turned to contempt. Let them whisper! So long as Ras looked at her the way he did, she would be content.

At least, she tried to be content.

Just as she tried not to scream into her pillow at night while wondering what was in store for her.

Chapter Twenty-Six

"I CAN'T WEAR that," Kynthea gasped as the maid set a gown out before her.

She'd known that she was going to be presented at court beside Zoe. She'd known that there was a dress being prepared for her, but she'd never seen it before this moment, mere hours before they were due to leave for the palace.

"Of course, you must wear it!" Zoe exclaimed. She'd wanted to see the unveiling of the gown as well. "It's stunning! You'll look like a goddess."

She'd look better than Zoe. She'd look richer than Zoe. Damnation, she'd look as if she were the one being presented instead of her cousin.

The gown was designed with the family colors of blue and white, as was appropriate. Indeed, Zoe's gown was resplendent with those hues as well. She would look like an ice princess, especially with the family pearls that would adorn her ears and neck.

Kynthea's gown was dark blue in a rich velvet. That choice was bold, given that Zoe's gown was made of silk. Kynthea felt that it emphasized the difference in their ages, making Zoe look more like a doll and Kynthea as the stately woman. Even worse, the accents on Kynthea's gown were red and gold, both of which were the duke's colors. To her mind, anyone with eyes would know that she was claiming an association with the duke, which she absolutely could not do. Only the most outrageous mistresses would do such a thing, and Kynthea wasn't outrageous. Even if she were, she wouldn't do it at Zoe's presentation!

"It's wrong," she said as she looked at Zoe. "This is your day."

"It's our day," Zoe said as she came forward to kiss Kynthea's cheek. "You're being presented as well."

"Only as your cousin—"

"As yourself." She smiled in a tender way that was wholly new to the girl. As if she had somehow grown up in the last few weeks without anyone the wiser. "This is as it should be," she said firmly.

Kynthea grabbed her cousin's arm and held her in place when the girl would have left. She stood there a moment, looking her over. And though she'd vowed not to ask, she couldn't stop herself. "What arrangement have you made with the duke? Please, you must tell me."

Zoe's brows rose in challenge. "Like you told me about your arrangement with him?"

Now there was the sixteen-year-old she remembered. One who had an edge when she felt left out. "You already knew," she said softly. "Besides, he swore me not to tell."

Then Zoe displayed her new maturity by softening instead of growing more jealous. "He swore me not to tell as well. And the consequences if I betray him are severe."

"Severe! How—"

Zoe held up her hand to quiet her. "The duke was persuasive, and I am happy. Even Papa agrees! Can't you trust me that everything's going to be perfect?"

She had no choice but to trust. Zoe was brimming with happiness. Even better, she'd spent hours writing letters to her father about something. Kynthea had seen the missives as they went out. Fat letters about horses, no doubt, with equally large things coming back. And once the earl had returned to London for tonight's presentation, he and Zoe had holed up in this library for more than an hour. It was all so mysterious, and Kynthea was not used to being ignorant about what was happening with her normally talkative cousin.

"I wish I understood what you've done," she said, hating the plaintive note in her voice.

Zoe dropped a quick kiss on her cheek. "Put on the dress, get your hair set, and then we shall have the most glorious evening."

That wasn't an answer, but it was all the information she was going to get. Zoe had to dress as well, and so Kynthea surrendered to the inevitable. She wore the gown as if she were a princess. She rode in the carriage to the palace. And she prayed, prayed, *prayed* that she didn't make a fool of herself in front of the Regent. Because never, even in her imagination, did she think she would be presented to royalty.

And yet here she was, all thanks to the duke.

He joined them soon after they arrived. She knew what all his regalia meant. She'd helped Zoe memorize it before the Season began. But she'd never seen it on him in such a resplendent way. He was so handsome that he took her breath away. He also looked at her as if she was the goddess Zoe had talked about. She wasn't, but as he brought her gloved hand to his lips, his eyes seemed to burn into hers.

"You look exquisite," he said.

"I was about to say the same to you," she said.

He greeted Zoe and her parents. Then his mother joined their party. She looked as regal as a duchess ought. Her gaze cut critically over her and Zoe, but her words were neutral enough. Something about holding their heads up and to make sure to smile.

That was really all Kynthea could process. She was about to meet the prince! They were at the royal palace! And right when she was about to lose her nerve, she realized something shocking. She was too intimidated by the grandeur of the entire place to be cowed by any one thing. It was as if the whole event numbed her enough that she could relax. She was fine so long as she stood up straight, smiled when spoken to, and kept the duke near enough to strengthen her when she felt her spirit waver.

So long as he stood right beside her. Which, thankfully, he did.

Zoe was nearly jumping with excitement. There were several other girls being presented at the same time and they clustered together to whisper and giggle like the teenagers they were. The duchess frowned at them, but Kynthea couldn't help but smile. Why stifle natural enthusiasm in the name of propriety? They were teenagers. Let them enjoy being such.

"You seem unusually composed for a woman in the royal palace for the first time," the duchess said to her. "One about to be presented to the Prince Regent."

"I am extraordinarily lucky to be here at all," she returned. "I suppose I am trying to drink it all in. I know I shall spend many evenings reliving tonight." She took a slow circle, seeing the people in their finery, the opulence of the palace, even the royal servants where they stood in uniforms finer than most of her clothing. But as usual, her gaze inevitably landed back on the duke. She tried to memorize how he looked standing nearby, speaking with Zoe's father. She liked the way a few locks of his hair always escaped placement to land dashingly across his forehead. She saw how others responded to him with respect or hunger. And she knew deep inside that he had held her tight and whispered how much he adored her. She'd seen admiration in his eyes, and that steadied her now.

She was worthy of a duke's esteem and that made her believe she was worthy of standing here among the peerage of England. At least for now. Once her true status as his mistress came out, she wouldn't be allowed in here. Neither would his mother deign to speak to her. But for now, she had this glorious evening of respectability, and she was going to savor every moment.

"Hopefully," the duchess said not-so-tartly, "you will have more glorious things to remember than tonight."

"I don't think so," she returned. Certainly, she had a lovely future ahead as the duke's mistress. But eventually he would marry someone else. Eventually he would tire of her. When that happened, she hoped that she would have enough money stored up to live quietly with her brother. Perhaps near enough to Zoe to know her cousin's children.

"That's because you are young yet," the lady said. "In truth, you have no idea what is to happen to you."

Well, that was enigmatic. But there was no time to question it as a royal footman lined them up for their presentation to the prince. The girls were placed in some kind of order, but Kynthea could not make sense of the reason for it. It should be by order of precedence, but that wasn't quite right.

"Are you noticing that the girls aren't in proper order?" The duchess' voice cut through her thoughts.

"Yes. It should be—"

"Royal whim. Some families are in favor, some are out. Not out enough to be blocked, but enough to be set back in the line."

That didn't bode well for Zoe. She was the very last with her family, Kynthea, and the duke standing behind her. "But what could have happened to put Zoe last?" she whispered. "And is that good or bad? Do the favored ones come last or—"

The duke's voice interrupted. "It was by special request," he said into her ear. "I'll explain later."

He took her hand, and his mother slipped behind them. That wasn't right. He should escort his mother.

"I don't understand," she whispered.

"I swear I'll explain. But I can't right now."

That had been his constant refrain for the last two weeks.

"You know, even a mistress gets impatient sometimes."

Far from being upset, he grinned down at her. She thought for a moment that he would say something. There was clearly a lot on his mind. But rather than speak, he seemed to get lost in staring at her. Or maybe it was she who lost herself in him. Either way, by the time she got her wits back, Zoe was next in line to be presented.

The girl stood proudly on her father's arm. Her mother remained a step back. As the cousin without a title, Kynthea was behind her aunt. And she was shocked that the duke remained on her arm, but he would not dislodge. Which meant the Dowager Duchess took up the rear of their little party.

When indicated, they all walked in formation through a grand hall between rows of courtiers. If the waiting room was overwhelming, this room was staggering, breathtaking, and probably paralyzing if it weren't for the duke beside her. She squeezed his arm and prayed she didn't make a cake of herself.

"Lady Zoe Elizabeth," the major domo announced. "Earl and Countess of Satheath."

Zoe curtsied deeply to the prince who was lounging in a seat at the top of the raised dais. The earl bowed, the countess curtsied. Everything was exactly as it ought to be.

"Miss Kynthea Petrelli." Was there a sneer in his voice? Or did she imagine it? It didn't matter. Kynthea dropped into a deep curtsey.

"Duke of Harle. Duchess of Harle."

Ras had pulled her into a space beside Zoe. He and his mother took their place even with Zoe's parents, behind Kynthea. And everyone remained in their lowered position while the general murmuring quieted. Silence reigned for a heartbeat, then two, then several more of rapidly-pounding panic.

What was happening?

Kynthea peaked as she saw Prinny rise out of his chair and step forward, a clear frown on his face. What was he doing? What had they done wrong?

"Get up, get up. Let me get a look at you."

Everyone straightened and thank heaven for that. Kynthea's knees had started to strain. She kept her gaze lowered, of course. One didn't look boldly into a prince's eyes. Except she had no choice when she abruptly felt his finger beneath her chin, tilting her head to look straight at him.

"Your Highness?" she gasped.

He frowned at her, looking her over left and right. Then he

turned to Ras. "Are you sure?"

"Absolutely, Your Highness."

Prinny grunted, then turned to Zoe. "And what about you? Didn't you want to be a duchess?"

"No, Your Majesty," Zoe said with a grin. "I've got bigger plans than that."

The prince recoiled. "Bigger plans than being a duchess! Do you look to wed a king somewhere?"

"Oh no!" Zoe said, her skin flushing pink. "I have wagered my dowry that I can make the duke's stable into the finest one in England."

Prinny tilted his head. "Wagered how?"

"Two mares," Zoe said. "The most valuable part of my dowry. They will live under my care at the duke's stable. With my training regimen and breeding plans, I will produce a horse that will win the derby in five years. I have sworn it."

"You?" the prince gasped. "You're naught but a girl."

"But I'm a smart girl, Your Highness."

The prince frowned. "And what about a husband? Wouldn't he want these horses of yours?"

Zoe dimpled as she grinned. "I can wait five years to wed. And when I succeed, I get my pick of the duke's stable to add to my dowry."

The prince looked to Zoe's father. "You have agreed to this?"

The earl nodded. "The girl's got a knack for horses and a mind to make it stick. She'll impress you, and the duke likes her chances."

"Of course, he does," the prince scoffed. "If she succeeds, he'll have the finest stable in England. If she fails, he'll have her breeding mares and five years of her work."

Zoe lifted her chin. "I'll be paid for my time, Your Highness. And my father will live with me. He loves the horses as much as I do, and the air will do him good."

The prince looked at the duke. "So you're betting on the father."

"No, Your Highness. It is Lady Zoe who impressed me. And if she succeeds, it will be worth every penny."

"Huh." The prince's grunt was appreciative. The man loved a good wager. "I believe I shall take that bet as well," he said. He waved a finger at a footman. "In five years, Lady Zoe, I think you will fail. What shall be my forfeit then when you do?"

Zoe frowned, clearly insulted and tongue-tied. She didn't have anything else to offer but the horses in her dowry. Thankfully, Ras was quick to help her out.

"You may have any one of my horses as recompense. But if she wins, then you must allow her to have her pick from your own stable."

"My horses are a great deal better than hers."

"No, they are not!" Zoe said. Then when the assembled courtiers gasped, she quickly added, "I mean, I respectfully disagree, Your Highness."

"So do I," drawled Ras.

The prince frowned. Zoe dropped her head in embarrassment, but Ras only flashed a cheeky grin. Clearly, he'd wagered with Prinny before. And in the end, the prince agreed.

"Record it!" he bellowed. Then he smiled at Zoe. "And so we shall see if a girl is worth her weight in horseflesh."

"Much more, Your Highness," Zoe said, her eyes flashing. "I am worth a great deal more."

Far from being offended, the prince guffawed at her audacity. And now Kynthea knew what arrangement Ras had made with her young cousin. She only hoped the girl lived up to her bravado. Meanwhile, Ras whispered in her ear.

"We couldn't tell anyone before it was done. The prince had to approve it."

Ah, now she understood. Better to bring Prinny into the wager than have him find out after the fact and voice his displeasure at a girl running a stable. Though they could have told her. She wouldn't have mentioned it to a soul.

"And what about you, Miss Petrelli?"

Kynthea jolted at the prince's booming voice right in front of her. "Your Majesty?"

Ras stepped forward coming even with her before the prince. "She doesn't know."

"What?"

"She doesn't know," Ras repeated, his voice firm. Then he smiled at the prince. "I thought you might enjoy being a witness."

The royal grinned even as he folded his arms. "Are you sure about this? Seems like the cheeky horse girl would make more sense."

"My heart chose this, Your Highness, not my pocketbook."

"That is obvious." The prince stepped back, waving his arm in front of him. "Very well then. Go on."

Kynthea was getting a little annoyed at all this attention when she had no idea what was going on. This was her life, damn it, and she didn't like people knowing more about it than she did. Especially when one of those people was the Prince Regent.

"Your Grace," she said softly to Ras. "This is unseemly and embarrassing. I cannot…" Her voice choked off when she watched Ras drop to one knee before her. She wanted to scream at him. What the hell was he doing? But no words came through her constricted throat.

"Miss Petrelli. Kynthea. You are everything I want in my life. You call me to account when I stray, you make me smile when we are together. You fill my loins with fire and my heart with joy. Say you will make me the happiest man on earth and be my bride."

She stared at him in shock. He didn't need to propose. She was his mistress! And he certainly didn't need to do this in front of everyone! Not just his royal highness, but the entire royal court.

"You didn't think I could see it, did you?" the duke continued.

She had no idea what he was talking about.

"What?" asked the prince.

"Her worth, Your Highness. She said she was just a Miss and

that I couldn't possibly want her. As if a title made one worthy. As if there weren't a million young misses who are smart and capable beyond measure." He winked at the prince. "The English raise fine daughters."

"That we do," agreed the prince.

"Kynthea," Ras continued. "I see your strength, your goodness, and Your Grace. I love you." He pulled out a ring from his pocket—a very large ring set with his family crest and designed to slide over a gloved hand. It was a signet ring, but one designed for his duchess. "Say you love me as well."

Love him? She'd loved him from the moment he'd sat in her aunt's drawing room defending her. She'd loved him even when she'd been angry at him. She loved him despite every whisper and rational thought that he couldn't ever want her. "You know I do," she said. "You know, I love you."

Prinny chuckled. "Then say yes, girl. Let him off his knee."

He wanted her to be his duchess? Not just his mistress, but his wife and companion for life? "Yes!" she cried. "Of course, yes!"

He grinned as he slid his signet over her gloved finger. And then he straightened up like a god before her, drawing her steadily into his arms. "I love you," he murmured just before he kissed her. He claimed her mouth as a man did his bride's, and she returned it a thousand fold.

He loved her! He wanted her as his wife! She could hardly believe it. And he had declared so in front of the most powerful people in England.

She clung to him then. She felt his arms surround her and was swept away by his kiss, filled with so many emotions that she could hardly breathe.

"I love you," she said when he finally released her mouth.

"My love, I am never letting you go."

She smiled. "Where would I go but back to you?"

THEY WERE MARRIED by royal command at St. James three very short weeks later. The day was fine, Zoe was radiant as maid of honor, and Kynthea was so in love that even the disaster created by best man Lord Nathaniel didn't dim her happiness.

And what a glorious disaster it was.

Don't miss *The Truth Serum*, coming soon, to find out what difficulties have befallen poor Nate and Lady Rebecca, the woman he's always adored.

About the Author

Flirty, dirty and fun! That's how Katherine Lyons likes her love stories. One would think that would lead her to contemporary romance, but she's always loved the witty dialogue and hot, sexy humor of regency romance. She's a big fan of *The Bridgertons, Big Bang Theory* (even though it's over), and her favorite movie is *The Avengers* because she loves the MCU. Stop by her website to sign up for her newsletter, special contests, and geeky giveaways!

www.katherine-lyons.com

www.ingramcontent.com/pod-product-compliance
Ingram Content Group UK Ltd.
Pitfield, Milton Keynes, MK11 3LW, UK
UKHW020723180525
458644UK00001B/1